Waterworks

a novel

Lara and Uri
Book 5

Jack Winnick

ISBN: 9798637542901

Table of Contents

Chapter 41

Acknowledgments

Author's Note

Waterworks is a novel; it is fiction, pure and simple. The persons described in this book, except for some well-known political figures, are creations solely from the author's imagination. Furthermore, the events depicted have not occurred; let's hope they never do. But the science here is real, not science fiction.

The technology is also real—and available. Additionally, the desires, resources, and abilities of the current Iranian regime are known to us all; there is no mistake about that. The leaders of Iran have been totally transparent as to what they can and will do, given the opportunity, to annihilate the lawful nation of Israel and its citizens.

The murder by poisoning of Russian dissident Alexander Litvinenko is well documented. The element polonium is not found in nature; it can be produced only in a nuclear reactor as described in this book. It is as lethal as portrayed.

The factual elements in this book have been obtained from a variety of reliable technical sources. None originated from entries in Wikipedia or any other unsubstantiated forums.

The author wants to make these realities, chilling as they are, totally clear.

—Jack Winnick
Los Angeles
March 2020

Chapter 1

Eddie sat back in his chair and stared out the window. It was a bright, sunny day in the San Fernando Valley, or just "the Valley," as they called it in the Los Angeles area. Nothing new about that; almost every day was like that out here. Eddie Moskowitz had moved out here from Chicago, like many thousands of others, looking for just that: unlimited sunshine, no problems with cold, snow, or rain; and lots of girls in bikinis.

His old pal from high school, Steve Finley, had planted the seed a couple of years ago in the midst of a typical Chicago winter. Steve called him one day, as Steve was prone to do, and as Eddie complained about the grim weather and lack of action, Steve yelled at him over the phone: "Schmuck! When are you going to listen to me and get out of that crappy Midwest?"

It was not the first time he had heard this from Steve, who had moved to the Coast five years earlier. It seemed like every time a particularly brutal winter storm hit Chicago, he would call Eddie and tell him to "get your ass out here where there's abundant sunshine and available young women." But this year, it finally hit home. Eddie quit his lousy job with the city, packed his bags, and drove to Los Angeles. He shared a place with Steve out in Van Nuys, where the rent was at least reasonable, and scouted for a job.

He'd searched around for a couple of weeks, looking for a "starter" job, one that he could use as a base while he looked for something better. He didn't have a whole lot going for him: a diploma from a Chicago public high school and a couple of years working in a testing lab at a mortuary. Not a brilliant resume, but he was a steady worker with an excellent recommendation from his boss. He'd gotten lucky with this Los Angeles

Aqueduct Filtration Plant, part of the Los Angeles Department of Water and Power (LADWP). The plant was in Sylmar, in the northern reaches of the Valley. Someone had quit the position unexpectedly, leaving the Waterworks, as they jokingly called it, with an urgent need for a lab assistant. It turned out that the simple testing he had learned at the mortuary fit well with the requirements at the plant.

The drive from Van Nuys to Sylmar and back turned out to be lucky as well. It was counter to the bulk of the traffic; most commuters headed into LA in the morning and back to the Valley in the evening. His drive was short and painless. He fit into the job well, too. The requirements were simple: routine testing of the water coming in and out of the filtration plant. Most of the time Eddie just had to check the readings on the computer and note them on a scoreboard, a holdover from the old days when everything had been done by hand.

There was rarely a problem; the system practically ran itself. He had lots of time to sit around, read, and daydream about his evenings at the clubs and weekends at the beach. His pasty-white body would soon match those of the young men who frequented the beach volleyball courts. Well, once he tuned up with weightlifting and running, he promised himself.

As he looked lazily around the room, checking the readouts on the computer screens, his eyes happened on the fishbowl. They kept a few goldfish in a standard bowl on the cabinet next to the sink. Someone refreshed the water every day, using water from the filtration system. It was their "canary in the coal mine." Hank, Eddie's helper in the lab, had to make sure the goldfish got their daily ration of fish food. Hank was the only employee beneath Eddie at the plant; he didn't even have a high-school diploma.

Eddie's eyes froze as he stared at the fish. They were floating belly-up, dead. He knew he had checked them only a half hour ago. They had been fine. "Hey, Hank," he yelled to his helper in the lab, "what the hell you been feeding the fish?"

Hank walked over to the fishbowl and looked at the corpses. They had occasionally lost fish, usually because the aerator quit working or one died from old age. But to lose all three in such a short time was rare. "We better call Burt," Hank said unnecessarily. Eddie was already dialing the head of the laboratory.

"Don't get all in an uproar," Burt said over the line moments later, calming Eddie down. "Happens once in a while. One gets sick, then the others get it. Been feeding them on schedule?"

"Sure, boss," Eddie replied. He glanced at Hank, who was listening on the speakerphone. Hank nodded meekly.

"Aerator running OK?" Burt inquired with no sense of panic.

"Yes," the employees replied simultaneously.

"When's the last time you changed their water?"

"I did it early this morning, as usual," Hank replied at once.

"Dechlorinate?"

Hank nodded.

"OK, well, then, check the oxygen levels, OK?"

Hank scrambled over to the oxygen meters, reporting that the levels were well within the required limits. There was an alarm that buzzed if any of the water-chemistry limits were breached, or even close. Eddie scanned all of them; the whole bank of gas and chemical-element analyzers were well within their normal values. Lead, arsenic, chlorine, bromine, ozone, and many other chemicals were continuously monitored. Chemists tested the instruments every morning using accepted analytical techniques. Nothing had been out of order during Eddie's tenure at the plant; in fact, he had never heard of a disruption.

When he heard that news, Burt told them he was on his way from his office and they should stay calm. It was then that Eddie looked out at the holding tanks and saw the birds. Gulls and other birds often stopped for a drink of the only fresh water in the vicinity. The water would get a final cleaning downstream. Eddie's stomach turned as he saw no fewer than five gulls and a couple of smaller birds lying dead in the grass around the tanks. This was bad—real bad.

Burt came in and took one look at the fish and the birds; he was immediately on the phone to city hall. Eddie couldn't hear the conversation, but Burt's face told everything.

"We're in emergency conditions as of right now," Burt announced, his voice cracking. "We've got to figure out what's going on before this water hits the city!" He raced around the control room, looking out at the tanks and ponds every few seconds, pulling at his face and hair, clearly in panic mode. "Get the chemists out there right now! We got to figure out what's in that water."

The word had apparently gone to the top within minutes. The mayor, Christian "Chris" Atkins, ordered his senior staff to hustle out to the Sylmar Plant immediately. By 10:00 a.m. Atkins and his entourage arrived. There, they were shown the sudden and unexplained deluge of dead animals around the holding tanks. The chemists and other technical staff were at a loss to explain it.

The mayor's staff advised him to put out an immediate alert to the city and environs to stop using city water for food preparation at once. "There is no need to panic," he assured everyone in a hastily called televised news conference in a meeting room at the plant. "It appears that some foreign substance has found its way into the storage tanks. That could be the result of our heavy winter rains; we just don't know yet. But just to be safe . . . use bottled water for all drinking and food preparation. The city water is perfectly safe for other purposes, such as washing and watering." Everyone in the conference room noticed his knees were shaking; Atkins hoped the home audience didn't.

Two hours had elapsed since Eddie had noticed the problem. The chemists had found nothing out of order in their check for contaminants. There was nothing unusual in the water; they were sure. No physical or chemical contaminant. No color or odor. No measurable radioactivity. The water was crystal clear and sparkling clean. They found no heavy metals: lead, mercury, strontium, chromium, even uranium, and plutonium were absent to the parts per billion!

Maybe it was a fluke, the administrative head of the LADWP suggested. Maybe those birds and goldfish were already sick . . .

"You really want to wait until a couple of people drop like those birds?!" The mayor's hands were white with rage and fright as he squeezed the podium, totally frustrated. The other officials in the meeting room at the Plant had nothing to offer. The local and national news stations had repeated the warning about the water for more than an hour.

The LADWP, meanwhile, was in a holding pattern. As the public demanded an update, Atkins agreed to another news conference. "The matter is receiving the utmost attention from local, state, and federal scientists and other authorities . . . ," he said. This wasn't completely true, although water chemists in other cities had been consulted—without success. They had nothing to suggest beyond the comprehensive chemical tests that the LADWP's scientific staff had already performed. But they all agreed with the water advisory.

Suddenly, in the midst of the news conference, Regis Trombley, the LADWP's chief scientist in residence, strode majestically into the room and pronounced, "There is absolutely nothing wrong with this water!" Trombley had a PhD from Cambridge University. He drew a glass of water from the drinking fountain behind him and held it out for everyone, including the television audience, to see. Trombley had the final word on anything and everything to do with the city's air and water chemistry.

There was dead silence from the officials as the distinguished, silver-haired Englishman displayed his glass of tap water. "Our team of chemists has thoroughly tested this water and found nothing whatsoever wrong with it," he declared with authority. Before anyone could stop him, he drained the glass.

There was absolute silence in the room as the professorial Briton placed the glass on the shelf by the sink, glared at everyone in the room, and sat down jauntily. Nothing happened. The Englishman sat there, straight as an arrow, for a full fifteen minutes while the mayor reassured everyone watching before finally rising and saying, "Now, if you don't mind, I have work to do." Then he strode out of the room to a sprinkle of applause.

The mayor stared at Burt, the head of the LADWP, who declared, "Don't try that at home, not yet."

There was brief, nervous laughter from the assemblage. Then the mayor declared that this did not mean that the emergency situation was over. The ban on drinking and cooking with the city's water was still in place until further notice.

Chapter 2

In the next few hours, word started to come in to the newsrooms of birds and pets falling over sick after drinking tap water left for them in the last few hours. Television stations broadcast emergency warnings to use only bottled water for feeding all animals as well as people. In the meantime, stores met with an unimaginable panic as people raced in an effort to hoard as much bottled water as humanly possible.

In the midst of all this, Dr. Trombley made an appearance in a news conference. He was dressed, as usual, as if he were about to give a lecture at the Royal Society of London. "As you can see," he declared emphatically, brandishing his ebony walking stick like an implement to ward off the demons of hell, "I'm still around." He gave the cameras a wan smile and waved as he left the room.

"Son of a bitch," the mayor whispered to his staff. "What the hell is he thinking?" He quickly called the LADWP chief. "Any more word on the water?"

"Don't drink it, and tell everyone in the city the same thing. I think we have something. And it isn't good."

"What is it?"

"You remember what happened to that Ukrainian guy in London a few years ago?"

"You mean the politician who suddenly got sick and then died from that Russian poison . . . ?" There was a ghastly pause on the line as he waited for the chief to respond.

"It could be . . . polonium, I'm afraid."

"What do you mean, you're afraid? Do you know, or don't you?!"

"We're not completely certain, but a lot of things point that way. We've examined the gulls who died at the ponds. Their organs show the kind of damage you might expect—"

"Might expect!" the mayor exploded. "We've got the whole city in a panic and you don't really know?"

"Polonium is a very rare type of radioactive material, extremely poisonous. Trombley is sick," the chief continued soberly. "Just the early signs, but it's scary. I told him not to show his face or say anything. We're getting him the only stuff that may be able to help. It's a chelating agent that—"

"Oh my God! Don't let any of this get out. People are frightened enough already . . . "

"You've got to get the word to the emergency rooms. They're going to see some people with the symptoms. People who didn't follow the warnings, or just didn't know . . ."

"What do we tell them?"

"To prepare for a rush of patients with urgent digestive or urinary problems; possibly facial ulcers. They should know how to handle it. As long as it's not too widespread."

The terror on everyone's face was obvious.

Chapter 3

Four weeks prior to the water poisoning in Los Angeles, a clandestine meeting occurred in Tehran. Afternoon sunlight gracefully lit the tall, beautiful dining room in the extravagant palace that held two of the most powerful men in the Middle East. It filtered through luxurious draperies giving an almost heavenly atmosphere to the elegant mountainside structure. Sheikh Hassan Nasrallah, the general secretary of Hezbollah, a portly, bearded man, sat calmly beside the table he shared with his host, the current president of the Islamic Republic of Iran. The two had enjoyed a pleasant meal of roasted chicken flavored with herbs in keeping with Nasrallah's known preferences.

These men shared many qualities: both were firmly committed to the destruction of the State of Israel. They had similar, totally anti-Semitic views of that entity, vocalized loudly and often. Nasrallah was quoted as calling the Jews "sons of apes and pigs," while the Iranian vowed to "wipe Israel off the map." They had comparable views of their Sunni-Arab neighbors but kept their comments away from the world press. The envy and hatred were there nevertheless.

Nasrallah was physically similar to his Iranian benefactor as well; both were in their mid-sixties, short in stature and sported equally heavy facial hair. But the hold on his people, the militant Lebanese group known as Hezbollah, was even more precarious than that of his host. The president of Iran owed his office entirely to the whims of Iran's Supreme Leader, the religious demigod of the Shia nation of Iran. Nasrallah's hold on Hezbollah depended on his ability to convince the people of Lebanon that he was acting in their best interest. His was a tenuous grip, to which the numerous attempts on his life attested. But he survived, mainly due to his support of the notoriously vicious Syrian president in the massacre of his own people. Indeed, the unholy alliance of Syria, Iran, and Russia had a willing ally in Nasrallah and his Hezbollah.

"Well, then," the Iranian said as he wordlessly gestured for two young women to clear the table, "let us get down to business." He made sure that the servants were out of the room before he proceeded. What he had to say was for no one else's ears, especially the delicate ears belonging to the lovely girls.

"Yes, indeed, my friend," Nasrallah said smiling, as he wiped his face, making certain that no trace of the meal lingered there. "I am very curious why you have summoned me here to your lovely palace." They spoke in Farsi, a language natural for both men.

"We have a singular opportunity to deal a telling blow against our enemy, the Jew." The Iranian paused to let his Lebanese guest get the full power of his next words. Seeing he had Nasrallah's complete attention, he continued. "You know that any strike we make against the United States in the name of Allah will strain their sympathy for Israel." He wiped his mouth after each word, as if he could remove that nation as easily as a lingering bit of grease. "For example, do you recall how our ally, Russia, was able to publicly remove one of its most vocal critics from the land of the living?" He said this last with a proud smirk; the Russians knew how to handle their enemies.

Nasrallah thought for only a moment: "Do you mean Alexander Litvinenko?"

"Very good, my friend! You knew instantly what I'm talking about."

"If I remember correctly, he was assassinated in England. By a dose of poison."

"Your memory is sound. But exactly what poison, do you recall?"

"Not completely. However, it seems like it was a tiny amount of poison the assassins deposited in his tea, while in some sort of public place . . ." Nasrallah was intrigued, totally captivated by this tale.

"You astonish me with your accurate recollection, my friend," the Iranian said with an earnest grin. "But it was not just any poison. It was a highly toxic bit of radioactive material—polonium."

"Do you mean plutonium, the nuclear fuel?"

"No," the Iranian said gently, "polonium is an element that does not have any value in that regard, but it *is* produced in a nuclear reactor. In fact, that is the *only* way it can be produced. It is sort of a side product in the operation of such reactors."

"What use does it have, then, if not for bombs or nuclear energy?"

"It has limited use in the laboratory, that's all. But it must be used with the utmost caution. You see, as I understand it, it releases a most vicious form of radiation called alpha rays. They are not very penetrating; they cannot even pierce a piece of paper or human skin."

Nasrallah was mesmerized. "What, then, is the danger?"

"None, if handled properly. But once *inside* the body, it causes irreparable damage to the vital organs. Death is nearly guaranteed."

His guest was about to interrupt, but the Iranian president stopped him with a quick wave of his hand. "What is even more amazing is the tiny amount necessary to bring about this death. You know, of course, the deadly nature of cyanide."

Nasrallah nodded slowly.

"Well, polonium is more than a *billion* times more lethal. In fact, a piece the size of this dot on the paper here"—he pointed at a note that lay on the table— "could kill nearly a thousand people!"

That was too much for the Hezbollah leader. "How is that even remotely possible? Why isn't the whole world dead by now?"

"That was my first reaction when hearing of this from our Russian friends. They told me it is because the lifetime of the material is so limited. It decays to a different, harmless element within days of its production. And as I said, it can be produced only in a nuclear reactor specially designed for it. It is nonexistent in nature. The Russians have the only known reactor, and its production is carefully monitored."

"I see. And they are willing to let us have some?" Nasrallah was practically salivating at the thought of using some of this magic on his enemies.

"Not quite. You notice I said 'known' reactor. But the Americans were kind enough to let us proceed, for a while at least, with our 'peaceful' nuclear program." His evil grin was contagious. Nasrallah could see where this was going. "Our brilliant scientists, schooled in the United States, were able, with the help of the Russians, to build such a reactor, hidden here in the mountains. It is relatively small and requires only a small amount of fuel."

"How small is 'small'?" Nasrallah was nothing if not curious.

"Those kinds of facts I cannot tell even you, my friend," the Iranian said, smiling. "But the shielding itself occupies most of a laboratory. It's located near here, where we can keep an eye on it." He winked conspiratorially.

"And you can supply my men with all they need of this astonishing material?" The terrorist's heart was beating wildly at the idea. He had not even heard the plans for the use of this terrible poison, and he was already fully invested.

Chapter 4

Sheikh Hassan Nasrallah had barely arrived home in Beirut before he assembled his chief lieutenants. These were the warriors who would lead the terrible raid they were about to execute against the ultimate Satan, the protector of the Israelis. And in one of the densest pockets of the American Jew, Los Angeles.

They gathered in the war room of the infamous sheikh, located in the basement of a large apartment building in the Haret Hreik neighborhood of South Beirut. Ten faithful acolytes of the most blessed sheikh sat mesmerized as Nasrallah projected on the large screen in front of them an aerial view of the famous Los Angeles Aqueduct. This enormous channel brought no less than three hundred million gallons of fresh water each day from the mountains in the north to the sun-dried desert called Los Angeles. Without it, the depraved denizens of that evil hellhole would die of thirst; there was no other adequate supply of the precious fluid.

The smell of nervous perspiration saturated the crowded room as the sheikh carefully unveiled the plan as set out for him by his Iranian benefactor. The select group of assassins drooled like a pack of hungry dogs at the start of a foxhunt as they learned the details. "There is this deadly material called polonium," he told them. "With it, our friends the Soviets; that is, the Russians, were able to eliminate one of their enemies from inside the apparent safety of London and never suffer the consequences." He beamed at the upturned faces in front of him as he went into the plan in more detail.

"The amount of this poison needed to kill a man is so small that a speck smaller than a pea could massacre a full stadium." He wasn't exactly certain of the magnitude of this slaughter, but it seemed within keeping of what he had heard from the Iranian president. In any case, it had the intended effect on his audience. They were captivated at the thought of such carnage within the bounds of the United States.

Now for the details, thought the chubby sheikh. "We will be supplied with a sufficient quantity of this deadly material by our Iranian friends. It is up to us to deliver it into the aqueduct so that it reaches all through the city of Los Angeles before the authorities know what hit them." He paused and waited for the anticipated flurry of questions.

"If this stuff is so poisonous, how can we carry it without dying ourselves?"

Luckily, he was ready for this one; it had occurred to him as well.

"It's only poisonous if you ingest or inhale it. The deadly rays won't pass through your skin." That seemed to mollify the gathering only slightly.

"How does it kill you, then?" came the next logical question.

"What I understand is that once inside the body, these deadly rays lay waste to the internal organs by generating intense localized heat, up to five hundred degrees! Have you seen pictures of that traitor Alexander Litvinenko?" He fiddled with his PowerPoint projector until he found the ghastly images of the man, slowly being torn apart from the inside. His skin had peeled away, mirroring the internal destruction. He died a horrible death within days.

The gravity of what they were about to do had an immediate quieting effect, even on these hardened gangsters. There was silence in the room as they visualized it. But before they could back down, Nasrallah quickly reminded them of the monsters they were about to terminate. "These are American Jews, remember. These are the people who fund the Israelis in their quest to destroy us! Without them, there would be no Israel. There would be only Palestine, our Muslim country! Islam would once again rule this entire subcontinent, as it did for a thousand years."

That did it. All doubt evaporated from the room. They were about to be heroes, venerated forever in all Islam!

Nasrallah then went into the details of their plan of terror and murder. These ten lieutenants and their men, perhaps more, would travel legally to the United States under the guise of student visas. There were fifteen or more universities in southern California eager for trained chemists and other scientists to help with their research programs. Each of the men, and only men, would be supplied with outstanding credentials from friendly faculty in Egypt, Jordan, and other Islamic countries, as well as the United States itself. The reservoirs of help for jihad were boundless.

Seeing that his troops were eager for even more information, he supplied them. "Once in Los Angeles, it will be a simple matter to find your way up the highway to a little town called Sylmar." He pointed to a location twenty or so miles north of downtown Los Angeles. "The water flows down the aqueduct from the north to a treatment station here, where the last testing is done. From there, it heads into a reservoir that delivers it to the rich, populated areas like Beverly Hills and Hollywood, full of Jews."

"How do we get the poison into the water? Isn't it guarded?" One of the most experienced of his men was already considering the details; that was a good sign.

"Not as guarded as you might think. You see, at that last treatment plant, they constantly check the water for contamination. If necessary, they can capture any foreign substance before it reaches the population."

"Then what happens when they see this—what did you call it?"

"Polonium," the sheikh answered promptly. *This man, Rashad, is quick and bright*, he thought; *he will be useful*. "But, you see, it is so rare, they are not equipped to test for it. In any case, the concentration will be so miniscule that by the time they figure out that something is amiss, the water will already be to the consumers. By then, it will be too late."

The potential attackers were spellbound. They could already imagine the Americans in their death throes.

Another jihadi had a question. Jamal was a chemistry student, Nasrallah knew. His parents had been killed during the last war with the Israelis as they exited a tunnel into the Galilee, on their way to murder a small farm family. It was their bad luck that an enemy patrol had happened upon them just as they'd emerged from underground. "Just how much polonium is needed to cause death?"

"Good question, Jamal." The boy beamed at this approval from his master. "The Iranian chemists have gone through all the details. I wish I could give you a more precise answer. But they tell me that if we can get even a hundred grams into that open ditch called the aqueduct, it will be sufficient to wipe out a sizeable fraction of the city."

An excited buzz ran through the attendees. "How is that possible, that small an amount in that huge stream of water?" Aram, another of the more experienced men, was skeptical; he knew all too well how difficult it could be to kill a man, or even a child. He had done just that a number of times already.

"I know it is hard to believe. But remember, the poison in the tea that killed Litvinenko could not even be found; it was nearly immeasurable. As I told you, a pea could kill tens of thousands."

"Then why hasn't it been used more often, if it's that easy?" Aram was not easily convinced. *Good for him*, the sheikh thought to himself.

"You must remember, this material is nearly nonexistent in nature. All of the world's supply comes from the Russian reactor and is closely monitored. It is only because of the hidden Iranian reactor that we have been able to get our hands on some."

A low murmur went through the assembly. There were still questions the sheikh must answer. They wanted details. "I have with me nearly two kilograms of this powerful poison! It is almost a full year's production from the Iranian reactor."

That statement set off a cry of astonishment through the gathering.

"Two kilograms!" Jamal clapped his hand to his head. "How . . . where . . ."

"Relax, everyone. You are all perfectly safe. The powder, in the chloride form—that is, polonium chloride—is safely stored in airtight bags. It looks like yellow sugar, if seen. Your job—our job—is to deliver these bags into the Los Angeles Aqueduct upstream of the Sylmar plant. The bags will dissolve slowly, just fast enough to completely poison the entire Los Angeles water supply!"

There was a moment of absolute silence; then a roar of excitement and anticipation flooded the small basement room. The men shouted and congratulated each other on their coming adventure and, no doubt, martyrdom and Paradise.

It took a few minutes for the room to resume some semblance of order. Then the sheikh got back to business: "We have to deliver the poison into the aqueduct before the water reaches Sylmar. That way, there is little to no chance of detection. There are a few bridges over the long aqueduct on its way down from the mountains; we have chosen one that crosses the waterway about twenty miles upstream from the plant. You will be safe from detection in the surrounding rural desert area.

"You will take the packages of poison, which are already in these dissolving bags, into the United States by hiding them in white athletic socks that will be in your carry-on luggage. Don't worry," he added, as he noted a few furrowed brows among the faithful. "The polonium will not set off any sensors. The radiation it emits will not even pass through the plastic bags.

"Each team will drive a rental car from Los Angeles International Airport to the spot marked on your maps. Memorize the directions and destroy the maps before you board the planes that will take you out of our country. That's right, I said 'planes.' Once we part here in Lebanon, we won't see each other until the task is concluded." There was a slight rustle of concern among the younger men. "We *must* succeed! Even if all of us do not complete the mission, there will be enough poison in the water to kill hundreds of thousands of infidels!"

After a few moments, the restlessness abated, and the sheikh once again had their attention. "You will drive to the bridge shown on your map and, between two and four a.m., stop on the bridge. There should be absolutely no traffic at that time of night. If there is, merely drive on and come back in fifteen minutes. The driver will stop at the ramp leading onto the bridge, and his partner will take the bag of poison and drop it from the bridge directly into the flowing water." He checked to make sure he had all their attention. There was no need; they were transfixed. "Then both get back into the car and continue on to your destination in Los Angeles. Your job is done.

"If anyone does see you stopped on the bridge, put on your emergency lights. If they stop, you tell them there is something wrong with the engine, but help is coming. Gently refuse any assistance. Hopefully, this won't happen at that time of night in this near-desert locale.

"The poisoned water will flow from there directly to the Sylmar filtration plant, where it will be examined and treated before going into a large reservoir. Our engineers tell me it will take some time, perhaps a day or two, to get the poison fully into the water supply. Even diluted by all the water in the reservoir, the concentration of the polonium will still be well above the lethal level. But there is no chance of detection. The staff at the plant have never even heard of polonium, let alone know how to take care of the problem."

There was a slight murmur of relief as the sheikh concluded this lecture. It sounded simple enough; and was certainly thought out well. The invigorated group headed for the dormitory. As they left, Nasrallah shouted to them, "Inshallah, we will succeed! And remember, don't drink the water." They all laughed merrily at this standard caution given to tourists and headed out with high spirits.

* * *

Aram looked out the window as the jumbo jet glided toward Los Angeles. He took a quick look over at his partner, Jamal, across the aisle. He, too, was enchanted by the huge urban landscape unfolding beneath them. Darkness was approaching, and long shadows passed under the plane. Several groups of tall buildings passed by as they hurtled toward the airport. He could imagine Jamal's amazement at the vastness of the city. He knew the young student had never before even been on an airplane.

Even Aram, who had traveled a bit, had never seen anything like the astonishing number of small blue patches of water, reflecting flashes of light into the evening sky. *Every home here must have its own swimming pool!*

he thought. *What grotesque decadence.* The ground grew steadily closer, with still no sign of the Pacific Ocean, when there was a sudden jolt as the plane touched the runway.

"Welcome to Los Angeles," the flight attendant greeted them. "Please keep your seatbelt . . . " As she continued with the absurd announcement while they taxied to their gate, Aram felt a surge of adrenaline that came with the realization that they were actually here, the center of Western debauchery. The infidels would soon learn a cataclysmic lesson. The woman in the middle seat, next to him, smiled knowingly at the excited foreigner. *She must see me as some sort of yokel, thrilled to be in the big city,* he thought. He returned her smile. "Remember," Nasrallah had told them, "Americans are terrified of anyone with a Middle Eastern appearance. So be friendly whenever possible."

In no time at all, the plane was at the gate, and the sleepy passengers were already eager to escape their confinement, searching for their belongings. The flight attendant continued with her script, completely ignored by the restless travelers. They had been on this crowded plane for more than twelve hours and were more than ready to leave it. Aram resisted the urge to look at Jamal. They had been told to look like strangers, not colleagues, for as long as possible. Americans were warned to report any "suspicious behavior."

When they finally filed into the airport and headed to the line for US Customs, Aram nodded briefly to his mate. This reassured the younger man, who was worried about the upcoming baggage check. However, it went easily, with the agents merely poking casually through their clothing and toiletries. When asked the purpose of their stay, both men answered as taught: to visit several college campuses in the area. They held their breath as they presented their visas and their bags went through the X-ray scanner. As they hoped, nothing metallic showed up. They headed to the rental car counter, very much relaxed.

Both travelers looked like they belonged in Los Angeles. It was a city of a multiracial population, so their relatively dark complexions were not in the least uncommon. In fact, to the casual observer, they could easily be mistaken for Hispanic. They were dressed like many of the young people here: worn denim jeans, college sweatshirts, and old tennis shoes. They each had two full days' growth of dark, black beard, making them absolutely indistinguishable from roughly 30 percent of the population.

They had a reservation for a compact sedan, which was ready for them. Aram, as the older of the two, had an internationally accepted driver's license; he would be the only driver. He purchased the minimal amount of insurance and, as instructed, accepted maps of the state and local roads. They had long since memorized and discarded the maps given to them back in Beirut. But it would have been unusual for foreign visitors to refuse maps.

They easily found their vehicle, put their bags in the trunk, and before heading out, turned off the power to the navigation unit that was standard in rental cars. They wanted to leave no trail; instead, they powered up the GPS they had brought with them. It had no preset destination; they were to use it only if necessary, once on their way.

It was already dark when the two jihadis drove out of the airport toward the interstate, leading north. They did not look for and did not see any of the other teams aiming for the same target that coming morning. As one of the first teams to reach the bridge at about 2:15 a.m., they would not see any of the others until reaching their lodgings in the small town of Chatsworth. A family of friendly Syrian refugees would house them until it was clear for them to return to Lebanon.

As they now had several hours to themselves, they searched for inviting places to eat. Along the highway through the San Fernando Valley, they saw many casual fast-food restaurants, many of them chains they had seen advertised on television. While in Beirut, they had been encouraged to watch American programs, even though most of them were well acquainted with the brutal action shows so popular around the world.

They spotted a restaurant they recognized with a large number of cars in the parking lot and pulled in. Televisions were blaring in every section of the large diner, and they had to wait in line for half an hour to get served. Aram paid for both of them with cash—American money, of course. They then found a small table, sat down, and casually ate the calorie-rich fried food. The usual Islamic rules for food had been waived for this junket, and they actually enjoyed the unfamiliar tastes. The American soft drinks were especially enticing; they were discouraged from buying anything American-made back home. It was a delightful treat.

The pair lingered in the restaurant, watching the various sports on all the screens until after midnight. The noise was endless as was the parade of young people, yelling at each other and the television sets, urging their teams to victory. No one spoke to them or asked them to leave; they felt reasonably at ease. But as midnight came, the task at hand grew paramount, and they carried their trash to the bins, as did the other customers. They did not see any of the other teams, which was just fine with them.

As they walked back to their rental car, the noise and harsh light became more oppressive. The sky was completely devoid of stars under the intense street lighting. Cars and trucks whizzed by from all directions. Neither man had felt so surrounded by humanity, even in downtown Beirut. Reaching the car, they felt the need to take a look at the maps, although that had been strictly against the rules. Even Aram was uncomfortable setting out into the unknown surroundings without at least a comforting glance at a map. They recognized where they were immediately: near State Road 14 north of Sylmar.

The two terrorists drove out of the parking lot and back onto the freeway. It was exactly 12:15 a.m. They had a full tank of gasoline; the small car had used less than one-quarter tank. Just after they saw the first signs for Sylmar, they reached the turnoff for State Route 14. This far north, the lights of the city diminished rapidly; they passed through suburbs and into stark rural country. In the moonlight, they saw the rolling hills of pasture and farmland, an enormous change from the big city.

In less than an hour, the sign announcing the exit for the town of Mojave appeared. They were close now. No words were spoken; they used only hand signals. This had been part of their instructions. It seemed unnecessary, but no one was certain as to the Americans' ability to listen in. When they saw the town of Mojave, however, the jihadis smiled broadly. They had arrived ahead of schedule. Memories of the scene from tapes they had watched in Beirut clicked in; all this was familiar. The dark, barren landscape; the low hills barely visible in the moonlight—all was just as expected. They cruised along, waiting to see the expected road signs that would lead them to the aqueduct.

At 1:45 a.m. they saw the sign for the road that would take them across the waterway. With a nod of recognition to Jamal, Aram drove on by. They saw no other vehicles in either direction. After five minutes, Aram stopped the car and, after checking again for the lights of any traffic, turned the car around and headed back to the turnoff. They wanted to reach the bridge at 2:00 a.m.

State Route 14 was still empty as far as they could see as Aram eased onto the road that led to the bridge. Their hearts were beating at a mad pace as they watched for any sign of the waterway. There was none. The videotape they had seen of the roadway had ended at the turnoff, so this was all new to them. But in ten minutes, they saw the unmarked metal structure that spanned the aqueduct. Aram brought the car to a halt at the side of the road; there were no markings designating the stream below. It was, in fact, not visible from the car; it could easily be mistaken for a ditch or ravine. What was visible however, was a chain-link fence that covered the bridge from one side to the other.

The two jihadis looked at each other, recognizing the task that lay ahead. Jamal got out of the car, went to the trunk, and pulled out the white athletic sock that held the precious poison: 80 grams of polonium chloride. Without a word to his partner, he walked out to the bridge but did not stay on the road. Instead, he instinctively grabbed a hold of the steel fencing and crawled along the outside, his feet barely gripping the base of the pavement beneath. He felt reassured by the sound of the water gurgling loudly eight feet below. With both hands on the fencing, the sock held in his mouth, he did not have time to worry about his own safety. The only thing on his mind was dropping the poison into the water. He silently prayed to Allah that not a speck, not a nanogram of poison had touched the cotton sock. They had been assured that the polymer bag holding the polonium had been perfectly sealed and scrupulously cleaned before it even touched the fabric.

It seemed to take only a minute for him to reach the middle of the bridge, which was only fifteen feet across. Then, holding on to the bridge with one hand, he used the other to grab the sock and shake the polymer bag into the rushing water. He heard the splash as the bag hit the fast-flowing stream and realized he had done his job. In his exultation, however, he released the sock from his grip. Soundlessly, it was carried downstream. It was too late to worry about it, he realized; he made his way carefully back to the edge of the bridge and the waiting car.

It was 2:20 a.m. when Jamal climbed back into the vehicle. Aram looked for some signal that he had been successful. In the dim overhead light from the open door, Jamal smiled sheepishly and nodded. The polonium was in the water. Instinctively, though, Aram could tell something was wrong. Tensely, he turned the car around and headed back to the highway. Once they were headed safely south toward civilization, he turned on the car radio. It was against the rules, he realized, but he had to know what had happened. Over the noise of the pop music, he glanced over at his partner and gestured for him to speak. Aram was the leader of this two-person team, so he gave the orders.

Reluctantly, Jamal told him the truth. "The bag is in the stream," he said. "I heard it hit the water." Aram waited for more detail. "But you see, I could only use one hand, so the sock . . ."

Aram absorbed this information slowly as he continued to drive, trying to assess the damage to the mission that might have occurred. "Well," he concluded, after a minute or so, "I'm sure clothing gets thrown into the aqueduct all the time. Kids, you know . . ."

Jamal breathed a sigh of relief as Aram switched off the radio, and they proceeded in silence. Only once along the way back south did they see another car, headed north. Silently wondering if this might be the next jihadi team, Aram grinned as the headlights blinked twice. It was their silent signal. He blinked his headlights once in response. All was going well, sort of. Aram saw Jamal looking at him for some sort of reassurance after his clumsiness on the bridge. The signal from the other car had in fact given

Aram some ease; perhaps everything would be all right. He smiled at the youngster and patted him on the arm.

Their next stop was at the safe house in the little suburb of Chatsworth in the northern reaches of the Valley. It was a low-income town mainly known for its adult-film industry. Residents were used to seeing strangers entering and leaving homes at all hours; the jihadis were not fearful of police interference. It was nearly 4:00 a.m. when they pulled up to the curb in the quiet tree-lined neighborhood. Across the street and down the block, two young women dressed in less clothing than ever would be seen in a Muslim country were casually leaving one of the modest-looking houses. Seeing Jamal's avid interest, Aram gave him a gentle shove to remind him of their mission. They grabbed their simple luggage from the trunk and went up to the door of the house.

Someone was waiting for them; the door silently opened before they could even ring the bell. Jamal was pleasantly surprised to see one of Nasrallah's men from Beirut, who greeted the two warriors warmly, shutting the door behind them. Jamal recognized the gray-haired lieutenant known as Mustafa, who shook both men's hands, kissing them on each cheek. "Assalamu alaikum," Mustafa said happily.

"*Wa-Alaikum Salaam*," eagerly responded the two jihadis, who were now able to relax a bit; they felt at home.

"Come in and sit down; you are the first ones back. Please, tell me how it went." He spoke in a low, moderated voice. No sense taking chances on suspicious neighbors, even here.

Aram sat first, in a comfortable easy chair. Jamal then did the same in a hard-backed dining-room chair near him. He casually looked around the room, which looked like something out of a 1940s American movie. The furniture was old and well worn, in keeping with the rest of the surroundings. The room itself was rather large with high ceilings, typical for the days before air-conditioning. An elderly woman dressed in black, complete with head scarf covering most of her face, silently brought the two newcomers small cups of tea. She turned and left the room without a word. Only after she left did Aram tell Mustafa of their adventure. He did not leave out any detail, especially noting the unexpected fencing over the bridge. Finally, he mentioned Jamal's unfortunate dropping of the sock into the channel.

Mustafa listened carefully to every word, stroking his chin at each and every item. He was deep in silent thought as Jamal felt slightly ill. What was to be the penalty for his clumsiness? Finally, the grizzled old Arab addressed the young jihadi: "You did just fine, considering the unpleasant surprise you had to deal with. Our scout mentioned nothing of the chain-link fence. Perhaps it has been added in the last few weeks. I only hope the others handle the situation as adroitly as you." He smiled at the youngster, who was able to breathe for the first time.

Though there was no audible sound, Mustafa leaped to his feet and opened the front door. Two more jihadis appeared, smiling as they entered the old-style living room. Hamid and Khatib immediately recognized Jamal and Aram from the training camp in Beirut. The four eagerly hugged and kissed each other on both cheeks. "It went well, my soldiers?" Mustafa cordially greeted the new arrivals.

"Oh yes," Hamid, the older of the two replied quickly. The tall, dark-skinned Syrian had a quizzical look on his face. "Although we were surprised to find the bridge guarded by a fence."

There was a pause as Jamal started to respond: "Yes, we also . . ."

Mustafa held up a hand to stop him. He wanted to hear from this new team first. "Go ahead, Hamid, what did you do?"

Hamid looked to Khatib, as if to say, *Did we do the right thing?* Khatib, a small, light-skinned young Lebanese, waited for Hamid to continue.

"Well, I knew that Khatib is quite athletic, so I asked him if he could reach the edge of the river by holding my hand. I turned the parking lights of our car on for just a minute, and he was able to reach out and toss the bag into the stream. We heard it splash!"

Khatib vigorously nodded his head in agreement.

There was a strained silence as the two newcomers waited for the dreaded penalty for a wrong decision. But Mustafa merely smiled and said to them: "Good thinking, my friends; well done! Come, have tea with us." He clapped his hands twice, and the old woman came silently into the room with their beverages. Wordlessly, she turned and left. *So, that was nearly two hundred grams that had poisoned the Los Angeles drinking water supply. Two more teams should be arriving shortly*, Mustafa thought. Things were going well. Soon, he would communicate with the host, waiting in San Fernando for the other four teams. With this marvelous start, the sinful city of Los Angeles would soon be feeling the wrath of Allah.

Chapter 5

Lara Edmond stepped through the double doors into the crowd at the busy mall. Her lovely blonde hair looked much the same as most of the other women's; hers, though, was totally natural. She wore heavily tinted sunglasses, even though the mall was enclosed, mainly to keep from being recognized; her face was known to many of her country's enemies.

She had not yet officially taken the name of her husband, Uri Levin. That was to wait until their first child came along. Until then, she did not want to hassle with the legal details involved. They had been married just under two years, and although the union was blessed by all other markers, they had no children yet.

Uri wanted to be a parent, as did Lara and her family. But Lara was not yet pregnant. They had completed all the testing; both were normal, though a little older than most parents-to-be. That was not an issue, Dr. Finkel, their OB/GYN in Tel Aviv, assured them. What might be, she said, were their grueling schedules. Both worked hard, long hours with Mossad, and their schedules did not often match. "This is not how nature wants it," Dr. Finkel, the graying, middle-aged spinster told them. "She likes it better when you are both at ease. Take a vacation. You deserve it."

So, they had gotten approval for a continuation of their last, abbreviated holiday trip that had coincided with an attack on this very mall in Beverly Hills just over a year ago. The pair had been diverted into an extended sojourn into Iran and a battle with determined terrorists. This trip to Los Angeles now was meant to heal the wounds of the last one. And perhaps lead to a blessed event.

Lara caught up with Uri, and the two held hands like honeymooners as they made their way past the chic shops; every imaginable piece of clothing and appliance in the world was on display. They had no need of any of it, but it was fun to see all the happy people going about their shopping with not a care in the world, apparently. The only shrieks were those of joy, mainly from teenagers who were spending their parents' money. Uri glanced at Lara, smiling knowingly.

Suddenly, both their phones squealed simultaneously. The last time that had happened was all too clear in their memories. Their current surroundings made it flash into their immediate consciousness. *Couldn't be . . .* they looked at each other fearfully. The noise of the crowd disappeared, as though time had stopped, a blanket over everything but the insistent sound of their cell phones.

They ducked into an open doorway, each turning away to answer the dreaded instruments. "Levin," Uri muttered.

"Where are you?" It was a familiar voice, but he could not place it immediately.

"Beverly Center, with Lara."

"This is Williams, at headquarters. Get down here as fast as you can. We've got a problem."

It was Bret Williams at the FBI office in Los Angeles. They had worked together before; he had greeted them at LAX when they arrived this time.

The line went dead. Uri turned to Lara; her face told everything. They had to find a taxi right now.

* * *

Bret Williams, the Homeland Security agent attached to the FBI office in Los Angeles, was brief with his greetings to the visitors from Israel. He was familiar with both: Lara, a former FBI agent, had met Uri when she'd worked a nuclear bomb threat five years ago; Uri had been on loan from Mossad. The two had worked other cases together as well; they had married soon afterward. Now they both worked for Mossad but were available at any time when the FBI needed them.

"We've got a scary situation on our hands," Bret started abruptly. "It may be nothing, but we have to be extremely cautious." The two visitors sat up in their chairs at full attention. They were caught completely off-guard at this turn of events in what was to be a vacation. "We got notice from the LAPD this morning of an upset at the water filtration plant up in Sylmar."

Uri turned to Lara, mystified. He knew nothing about this plant. She returned his gaze with a blank stare. Williams was expecting this; few people outside the city government were at all familiar with the city's water supply. Most knew, at least casually, of the enormous aqueducts that had been built in the twentieth century to bring clean water from the Sierra Nevada mountains to the populous but parched desert city of Los Angeles and its environs. The gigantic project had had plenty of detractors back in the day. Now, most of the population was not aware of the staggering volume of water involved: nearly five hundred million gallons a day flowed through the network of streams and aqueducts.

Bret ran through just a little summary of the system for his guests. Then he got more to the point. "All the water from the network that comes to Los Angeles eventually reaches a huge filtration and treatment center at the north end of the Valley, at the town of Sylmar." He presumed the agents knew the area well enough to know this meant the San Fernando Valley. The two nodded their understanding. "Anyway, the plant workers up there noticed something strange this morning. Dead birds and other small animals around the treatment tanks. Later, they saw dead fish as well. Never happened before, not in this quantity, even after some big storms." He paused to see if he was getting his point across.

"I can see your concern," Uri said. Then after a brief pause, he added, "Did the water testing show any abnormality?" He was certain this would be the first thing that had been done.

"That's the strange part," Bret said, clearly expecting the question. "The water tested fine. They checked everything: chemicals, dissolved gases, bugs—that is, bacteria—viruses and so on. Nothing showed up. The water's clean and pure; no odor, no color, no taste—nothing."

Lara was puzzled. "Sounds scary, all right. But why send for us? Neither of us knows anything about water chemistry." She glanced quickly at her husband for confirmation. He gave Bret a brief nod.

Bret had been waiting for this; he was well acquainted with their capabilities. "Well, here's the thing. We know how you've been dealing with Iranian terrorists these past few years, and . . ." He paused before continuing. His audience was spellbound; they had not the faintest idea where this was headed.

"Early this morning, one of the workers whose job it is to check for foreign matter in the aqueduct—he works in an area about an hour north of the plant—saw something white stuck on one of the screens. He got out of his vehicle and retrieved it with a grabber they all carry around. It turned out to be a sock . . ."

Lara and Uri were on the edge of their chairs. Where in the world was this going? "He reported it in to the plant director, who didn't think much about it at the time," Bret said. "But when the upset was reported— that's what we call anything unusual that might affect the water—he asked the worker if there were any identifying markers on the sock. The guy said it looked like an ordinary athletic sock, pretty new-looking, actually."

"But . . . he reported it. Did it have some manufacturer's info on it?" Uri asked.

"The plant director checked it out on the web and . . ."

"Iran!" Lara practically shouted.

"Right," Bret replied immediately. "It was made in a city named Andimeshk, by a company called Merooj. Didn't look like it had ever been worn."

"Do we import socks from Iran?"

Williams was ready for this. "We don't allow imports of anything from those guys. Not even pistachio nuts, I don't think."

"Somebody could have bought socks there, worn them home . . ." Lara was checking every possible angle.

"Possible, but not likely. And how would it get in the aqueduct?"

"Some kid could have tossed it in, you know, like they throw old tennis shoes onto phone lines, just to be, well, kids. Who knows why they do anything?" Uri was also at a loss. This looked more and more like a threat. "Have they checked the sock for traces of poison?"

"They did at the plant, yes. But most anything would have been washed out. That water flows at quite a clip. And if it was just a prank, why bother to drive all the way up there past Mojave, just to throw a sock in the aqueduct? No Iranians live up there anywhere."

"So, you think there was something in that sock, something an Iranian wanted to get into the drinking water?" Uri got right to the point.

"We've got our analytical team examining the sock fabric in every detail, mechanical and chemical. There's even some faculty at UCLA looking at a piece of it with electron microscopes and lots of other instruments that I can't even pronounce. If there's anything on the fibers, somebody will find it."

"Has anyone found anything at all so far? Anything unusual?" Lara asked.

Bret looked dejected. "No, not yet. In fact, the only thing remarkable so far is the *lack* of anything."

Lara shook her head. "What do you mean?"

"Well, with clothing, there is almost always some sign of human contact. Hair, oil, flecks of skin, dander, something. Even scrubbing with water won't remove absolutely everything."

"So, you're saying there was no human contact before it was found?"

"The guy who picked it out of the water used a long pole with a pincer on it. He also had gloves on. You never know what you're going to run into. He put the sock in a kind of plastic evidence bag they use out there, just in case it may be evidence from a crime scene."

"Why is that?" Uri asked.

"The police taught the workers to do that after we had a homicide at one of the reservoirs; drug-related," Bret explained.

Lara exchanged a quick look with Uri. These folks were not amateurs. "And that lack of human contact is unusual?"

"Absolutely. That sock had never been worn, not even tried on."

"So, someone bought a pair of Iranian socks just to throw one into the canal, I mean, aqueduct?" Lara was intrigued.

"There were some minute flecks of dead skin on the *outside* of the sock. Could have arrived during manufacture. Not enough to do any sort of analysis; we tried."

"So, someone at least handled the sock at some point, even if they didn't wear it," Lara concluded. "What about the inside? Any trace of liquid or solid chemicals?"

Bret shook his head. "No, just some of the powder they put in during packing. Totally harmless."

Uri was disappointed. "So," he said, "the sock is probably unrelated to the upset at the plant."

At that moment, the phone on Bret's desk rang, accompanied by a flashing light. Something urgent, the agents concluded. Bret grabbed the phone, answering tersely, "Williams." He then turned his back on his visitors as he had a brief, anxious conversation. He hung up within a few minutes. When he turned back to his visitors, his face had become clouded with worry. It was clear he'd heard some disturbing news; he was trying to decide if he could share it with the agents.

After a few seconds, he said gravely, "That was police headquarters. Right after the news of the dead birds around the treatment tanks, there was a proclamation from the city. I don't know if you saw it or heard about it."

Lara and Uri both shook their heads; they had not been watching any news.

"The word got out about the water, and the chief thought it best to have everyone use only bottled water for consumption until the problem was resolved. It seemed the prudent thing to do; we at the FBI agreed with the decision."

Lara and Uri nodded their agreement, waiting for the bad news they were sure was coming.

"There was a news conference early this morning out at the plant, and the head scientist there, a Dr. Regis Trombley, got up and drank a glass of tap water in front of everyone. 'There's nothing wrong with this water,' he said, and sat there for them to watch. He was fine. Later this morning, he appeared on live television to show everyone that he was, indeed, perfectly all right."

Once again, the agents waited for the coming bad news. They weren't disappointed.

"We just got news: Regis Trombley is sick," Bret concluded.

"What about the people in the city!?" Lara was justifiably terrified.

Bret ruminated, running his hands through his hair, his mind racing a mile a minute. "The water Trombley drank came directly from the tanks that receive the water from the aqueducts. The city doesn't get that water for a day or so, until after it's treated and mixed with the water already in the reservoir."

"So, it's possible the poison, or whatever it is, will be taken out before it hits the city pipes," Lara asked hopefully.

Bret looked at them with fear in his eyes. "Not likely. If it's what we're afraid it is, the medical treatment we give it won't touch it."

"What are you talking about!?" Uri was up out of his chair.

"We don't have conclusive evidence yet, but preliminary analysis of the dead birds around the tanks shows the kind of damage to their internal organs that comes from intense neutron radiation."

"But don't you test the water for radiation poisoning?" Uri was incredulous.

"Of course, but this particular kind of poison is especially insidious." He gestured for the two agents, who had risen in alarm, to sit back in their chairs. They could sense some sort of lecture coming. "I talked in detail with our chemistry guys here. If the analysis from the birds is accurate, that water may be tainted with the kind of poison that killed the Ukrainian, Litvinenko, a few years ago. You remember, the Russians didn't like his politics, so they poisoned his tea one day in London. Another unlucky dissenter got it with a poisoned umbrella tip. Sometimes people get the two incidents confused, but the poison was the same stuff: polonium."

There was a pause as the two agents searched their memories for details of the two infamous assassinations. Williams went on: "Polonium-210 is virtually nonexistent in nature; it can be made only in a specially designed nuclear reactor. Russia has the only one known in the world. They bombard elemental bismuth with a high flux of neutrons; that turns the bismuth into polonium."

The agents seemed somewhat bewildered, but he continued anyway, hoping to at least give them the necessary information.

"That polonium is deceptively dangerous to life, human or otherwise. You see, it gives off a kind of radiation called alpha rays. These rays don't travel very far in nature; they're stopped by a piece of paper or even skin. They're actually a mix of particles, neutrons and protons, not the gamma radiation that can be so destructive even years after a nuclear blast. But once inside a living being, these particles are like a neutron bomb. They destroy the vital organs quickly and irreversibly. The stuff is almost undetectable yet deadly once inside you—like when you drink water contaminated with it."

"Now wait a minute," Uri exclaimed. "How much of this plutonium do you have to drink . . . ?"

"Polonium," Williams replied gently. It was only hours ago that he became aware of the terrible details. "And you're not going to believe how small a dose is deadly." He paused to watch their faces. The agents were transfixed. "The stuff is deadlier than cyanide. More than a *trillion* times deadlier."

Lara had turned pale as she slowly grasped the impact of what they were hearing.

"You can't detect it, but just . . . what? Micrograms of it are deadly?" Uri was well beyond astonishment.

Williams paused for effect. "Not micrograms," he said quietly. "*Nanograms* or even less."

Lara couldn't help it—her mouth fell open.

"A *billionth* of a gram! How can such a small amount kill a person? Why isn't everyone in the world dead!?"

"Polonium is somehow concentrated by the body, once it gets into the bloodstream, and deposited specifically in the most thin, sensitive membranes of the vital organs: kidneys, liver, pancreas, and so on. There, the alpha rays wreak havoc on those delicate but essential tissues. And as for why we're not all dead already, the only reason," Bret explained, "is that the stuff is not found in nature. It has a half-life of merely days. It's only made in a specially designed nuclear reactor, like I told you . . . *and* there's only one reactor in the world known to produce it. In Russia. And they just make a couple kilograms a year, under strict international control."

His guests were understandably speechless. Uri finally asked the obvious question. "If Russia has the only reactor that can make this stuff, and it's controlled, how . . . ?"

Bret held up his hand. "I said the only *known* reactor." He waited a second as they absorbed that information.

"Well," Lara blurted out, "who else in the world would even *want* to make this terrible poison, let alone have the money and know-how, raw materials, and . . . oh shit!"

Even Uri was taken aback by this display of crude language from his wife, of all people. But Williams knew what had suddenly hit her like a slap in the face. The mullahs of Iran would do anything within their power to obliterate the nation of Israel, and all the Jews in the world as well. Starting with Los Angeles.

"What can we do?" Uri asked Bret, but it was a desperate question addressed to no one in particular.

"We're doing what we can. Bottled water is being flown in from every military base in the area. Distribution stands are being set up in all the neighborhoods. The dirty water is being diverted to unused reservoirs, where it can be held for months, long enough for the polonium to decay. Then it will be safe enough to dispose of in the ocean. Meanwhile, the water coming from the aqueducts will be tested by very new sophisticated analytical instruments to make sure it's safe. Then we'll feed it to single-cell creatures, like amoebas, for final testing.

"What we're hoping you two can do, since you've dealt with these guys before, is help figure out where their reactor is, so . . ." He paused.

"So, our Special Ops can take it out?" Lara had been waiting for that shoe to drop. This kind of chemical attack on civilian water supplies was nothing less than an act of war.

"Right. But we have to be damn sure of what we're doing first. And be able to prove it."

Chapter 6

Jafar Madani was entering his second year of graduate work in the esteemed laboratories of the chemistry department at UCLA. The tall, lean, unassuming young man was understandably delighted to have been accepted, having shown his aptitude with his bachelor's degree at one of Iran's most illustrious and well-known universities. Of course, it helped that he had received a glowing letter of recommendation from one of his professors, a graduate of UCLA himself some ten years earlier.

Analytical chemistry hadn't been his first choice for graduate work; he had been hoping for something a little more glamorous, like biochemistry. But he had been offered a fellowship in analytical, and it paid for his room and board as well as tuition. Things were going well; he was into the final year of the master's degree program, and his advisor had asked him to stay on for his doctorate. *Imagine*, he thought. *Doctor Madani.* How he would rise within the glorious realm of the Islamic Republic! He kept these dreams to himself. The Americans were not fond of Iran; they viewed the nation as an enemy. In any event, he didn't want to get ahead of himself. He had work to do.

Today he had a special task given to him by the department chairman. His research advisor was out of town at a meeting, something he was frequently, and there was an immediate need for forensic analysis of some fabric. A police officer had come to the department, hoping to reach his professor. Due to the researcher's absence, the chairman had directed the officer to Jafar, who was working with an advanced electron microscope that was ideal for the problem at hand.

The officer politely showed Jafar his credentials, saying that he heard that this laboratory was uniquely capable for this work. He showed

Jafar the piece of cloth and asked if he could analyze it for trace contaminants. The piece of synthetic white material was from an athletic sock, he told Jafar, and they were hoping to identify what substances might have been in contact with it. Jafar nodded his understanding of the problem and offered to do what he could. He looked at the cloth and immediately recognized the name *Merooj. How odd*, he thought. This sock had been made by the famous Iranian athletic-wear company. *But how would it have come to a police analysis in the United States?*

He asked as casually as possible, "Where did this come from, do you know?"

The officer mumbled something about a scare in the water supply, probably nothing.

"Sure, have a seat, I have to go into this secure area for the testing. It will only be a minute." Jafar went into the microscopy lab and pretended to analyze the bit of cloth for about thirty minutes. He came back with a two-foot length of strip-chart paper from a previous analysis; it had come out of the electron microscope's printer, very official-looking. He handed the multicolored printout to the officer. "I'm afraid," he said with a straight face, "that there's not a bit of foreign substance on the material. I'm so sorry."

"That's all right, buddy. We just have to check out everything. Thanks for your help." The officer took back the piece of cloth, politely shook Jafar's hand, and quietly left the building.

On seeing the policeman leave, Jafar went out the back door of the building to use his cell phone. It was one of those burner types available at many convenience stores in the United States. He had been told to use these whenever he had information that might be critical for the Islamic Republic. He had no real idea what was going on, but he knew of the sudden ban on the use of city water. If there was Iranian cloth involved in this activity, his handler must be told. He dialed the number, conveyed the brief message, then took the phone to the dumpster. After removing the SIM card and crushing it as instructed, he tossed the remains in the garbage bin.

* * *

Ali Mansoor, working in the Interests Section of the Islamic Republic of Iran at the Pakistan embassy in Washington, DC, picked up the phone message from a Los Angeles area code. He read it over twice, trying to make sense of it. It apparently came from a disposable cell phone. However, it carried the correct code that was used by unofficial sources to convey information to the government of Iran. They had no official embassy in the United States, not since the glorious revolution. Iranian students and other visitors were urged to let the Revolutionary Government know of anything at all that may be of interest. Each Iranian citizen travelling to the United States was given a secret numerical code to attach to any message.

Ali had no knowledge of any plan to disrupt the Los Angeles water supply, but he passed the message on to Tehran using the Pakistanis' secure satellite-phone system. The ministry there would know what it meant. Any action needed from his office in Washington would be conveyed to him through the Pakistan embassy.

* * *

It was 2:00 a.m. in Tehran when word came from the embassy in Washington. The night clerk at the royal palace had no idea what the coded message said, but he did as instructed and passed it on to the Foreign Office. When he saw it, the Undersecretary for Extra-National Affairs, who was working the night shift, immediately knew to what it pertained. "Extra-National Affairs" meant international terrorist activity, which was a high-priority endeavor in the Revolutionary Islamic Republic. After checking the sender's code, he dialed Defense Minister Hamid al-Shamarri, waking him from a deep sleep.

"What in the world can it be, in the middle of the night . . . ?" the defense minister mumbled groggily into the phone at his bedside.

The Undersecretary conveyed the essence of the message: the plan to contaminate the water supply of Los Angeles had been successful; the city was terrified.

The defense minister, after the briefest of thought, rose jubilantly from his bed. "All thanks to Allah, the deed is done! Death comes to the American Jew-devil!" Hamid al-Shamarri did a little dance in his nightclothes, his ample belly bouncing out of his pajama bottoms, before putting through a call to the president's private secretary. That lackey would decide whether to wake the president with this wonderful news. It certainly seemed reasonable to al-Shamarri.

Indeed, it was 3:00 a.m. when the president called his cabinet together to celebrate. Only then did he put through a call to the Supreme Leader, the holy man who governed everything in Iran, the Ayatollah Ali Khamenei.

"Inshallah," he gloated, "my presidency is forever secure!"

Chapter 7

The day passed with no newly reported cases of polonium poisoning in Los Angeles. Regis Trombley's health continued to decline, however, despite medical treatment. Samples of his blood showed miniscule but definite levels of polonium, enough to explain his lethargy and loss of appetite. In addition, there were the initial signs of renal failure, and he was receiving dialysis. Other victims were undergoing treatment as well.

Bret Williams told Lara and Uri about this in a closed-door meeting at FBI headquarters. There are organic chemicals that bound with the polonium, allowing the body to eliminate them naturally. While the two agents mulled over that bit of information, Tom Buckley entered the room. Buckley was another Homeland Security agent they had worked with in their last battle with Iranian terrorists. He was based in Manhattan, but he was called to Los Angeles when this water-contamination crisis arose.

Lara and Uri greeted him warmly; they had worked closely with Tom, albeit at long range. He had been in New York while the two agents were undercover in Iran. It had been a bloody battle, but at least the good guys had prevailed. "Good to see you, Tom," Uri began. "Wish it were under happier circumstances."

"You and I both," Tom replied, smiling ruefully. Seeing him on the street, one would never suspect he was a fully qualified field agent, capable in weaponry and martial arts. He concealed his fit five-foot-nine-inch frame in a loose-fitting business suit and highly polished shoes. To finish the picture, he wore a striped blue-and-gold tie that matched the dark-blue suit and crisp white shirt. His sidearm was concealed in a clip-on holster at his waist.

After shaking Uri's hand, he grasped Lara's with both of his. His eyes said everything. He had nothing but the highest regard for her intelligence and courage in the field. She had been indispensable in the last brutal encounter with Iran's malevolent dictatorship. It was Tom's experience with these two agents that had brought him specifically to this meeting.

With everyone seated, Bret updated them on the medical situation. "As far as we can tell, the city hasn't felt the brunt of the polonium poisoning yet. The samples from the reservoir indicate a very significant pulse of the stuff hit it from the aqueduct over a twelve-hour period. Unfortunately, that's what Trombley happened to drink. He got a significant dose, I'm afraid."

Lara had to interrupt, even though she did not know the Englishman personally. She had learned of his qualifications and experience and was certain of his well-intentioned, if hasty, show of drinking the water. No doubt, it had given the authorities a few extra hours to avoid a full-scale panic. "What can be done for him, in addition to the dialysis?" she asked urgently.

"The only thing we can do at this point is to try to remove the polonium already in his system," Williams said, this time for Tom's benefit. "The damage that's been done to his organs is already severe. But there are these chemicals I told you about called chelating agents. These organic species bind specifically to the polonium ions in the blood and lead them to the intestines and kidneys, where they are eliminated before they can do even more damage. That is, *if* these organs are still functional. If not . . ." He didn't have to continue; his message was clear: If not, Trombley would suffer a slow, painful demise as his body shut down. It was as brutal a death sentence as could be brought to an enemy of the state, serving as a message to anyone else who would try to interfere with the evil triumvirate of Russia, Syria, and Iran.

There was complete silence in the room as Lara and Uri absorbed this latest news. They also tried to anticipate what they, as agents of the West, could do to stop further aggression of this form.

"So," Tom began, starting where his colleague left off, "we need to send these guys a very distinct message. After all, we don't have anything but circumstantial evidence at this point; not even suspects. So, we can't complain to the United Nations . . ." This brought a derisive laugh from everyone. The UN was pretty much a plaything for the band of malicious countries that controlled it. "Let alone do anything that would be seen as overt retaliation. That leaves us, as usual, to handle the situation by . . . other means."

He looked meaningfully at Lara and Uri. "The secretary," he continued, referring to the Secretary of State, "has granted us—that is Homeland, the CIA, and the military, if necessary—the authority to deliver a clear message to our enemies . . . and I do mean clear . . . short of poisoning the ayatollah and his cronies." He looked the two agents straight in their eyes. "I know of no better way than to have you two deliver that message, straight to them."

The room was quiet as Lara and Uri tried to come to grips with what might be asked of them. After their last assignment, they could never be seen in Iran again, not without immediate capture and torture . . .

"Here's what we have in mind," Bret said, continuing Tom's discussion. "You two are the most capable people we know in dealing firsthand with these hoodlums . . ."

"Hang on," Lara blurted out. "We haven't got a chance in the world of showing up in that country; they'd spot us at once."

"Right," Buckley picked up the argument. "If you showed up looking like you are now. But what we have in mind is a mild makeover, if you will." He glanced quickly at Williams. They had obviously already talked this over. "With help from Hollywood, we can alter your appearance enough to make you unrecognizable to your own families. Not permanent, believe me. . . . Hollywood has to be good for something besides entertaining teenagers."

While Uri sat there gazing at his wife, imagining what they had in mind, not to mention what they would do to him, Bret broke in to distract them before they could say no. "Of course, you couldn't go as a married couple again; that would never fly."

Lara looked back at Uri, thinking, *How much worse can this get?*

"Look," Uri broke in, "even if we could get there, how could we do any kind of damage?"

"Information, that's what the two of you can supply. You know their language, their capabilities . . ." Tom was doing his best to at least intrigue them.

There was complete quiet as the couple thought about this for ten seconds. Then, when it was clear the agencies were serious about this scheme, Lara chimed in, "Just how would we enter Iran and how would we get any of this information?"

That was the sign Tom had been waiting for; he was quite the salesman. And he knew his audience; they were snared. "We have some leads," he said coolly, watching their reaction. They did have a commonality of response, more like a single organism than two separate entities. "We do have some assets there, as you know." Indeed, they did; Lara and Uri had witnessed the covert assassination of a traitor by just such a man. Right there in public.

Tom and Bret saw the hook sink in. The agents were going for it; Tom started to reel them in. "Iran is very short on IT guys. You know, computer jockeys. They've been getting their help from students schooled here in the United States, until our government saw where that help was going. It didn't cut off the supply entirely, but sure slowed it down. Anyway, now they're desperate for anyone who can help, especially well-schooled English speakers."

The two agents considered this without saying a word.

"So, what we had in mind for each of you, separately, of course, is to apply for interviews," Tom continued. "Now, I know what you're thinking: *they know us, have our photos on file.* But they don't have any DNA or prints. What we will do—or would do, if you go along with the idea—is to modify your appearances somewhat." He could see both react to that idea, and not in a good way. "Now, it wouldn't be much and would be completely reversible. Here are some sketches." He brought some computer enhancements up onscreen in front of them.

"First, here's Lara," he said, pointing at a recent photograph of her face, plus front and side views. "Now here she is, with the modifications." Lara gasped involuntarily as she gazed upon a totally different person, nothing like herself. "What you see is the effect of chemically induced skin darkening, small gel implants on the cheekbones and others at the jawline."

"That's incredible," she muttered. "How in the world . . . ?"

"There are folks out here in Hollywood who do this all the time, mostly for the film industry, but sometimes for us, like in the Witness Protection Program. Those are permanent; yours would, of course, be only temporary. At the end of the program, the implants will be removed; your skin will lighten naturally in a few weeks without the pills."

"What kind of pills?" Lara was not fond of fooling with nature.

"A mixture of melanin and DHA. Completely harmless. For your hair, we'll use standard permanent hair dye. Your naturally blonde hair will turn a dark brown to match your eyes. Oh, I forgot to mention, you'll have to wear some dark, soft contact lenses." Tom motioned back to the image on the screen. Sure enough, that woman could easily pass for an Iranian. "Here, let me show you." He reached into his desk and pulled out a small plastic tube resembling mascara. Unscrewing the top he withdrew a small brush which he drew across a piece of paper leaving a brown streak. "You just need to touch up your roots every week or so. Keep this in your purse with the lubricant for your contacts." He handed her the products, which Lara examined and stowed with her things.

"Now we get to Uri. He's already dark enough, with enough gray in his hair to look legit. We just have to do the gel inserts to alter his appearance." He switched the images on the screen to ones of Uri, as he'd look modified. Lara laughed reflexively, covering her mouth but still showing a rosy blush. Uri just shook his head at the menacing desert bandit he saw onscreen.

"We have something else for you," Tom added. He pulled out a pair of glasses from his desk. They were heavily rimmed, thick reading glasses, with obviously strong corrections in both lenses. "Try these on," he said to Uri.

Uri looked at them skeptically. The lenses looked like the bottoms of beer bottles. "What are these for? My vision is still pretty good, even though it's only one eye." Everyone in the room was familiar with his battle with Hezbollah terrorists in the tunnels beneath the Chicago River; he had won the battle but lost his left eye in the process. It had been replaced in Israel with a realistic, high-tech prosthesis that moved in coordination with his right eye. Even people who were aware of it could hardly believe it was artificial.

Tom reassured him, "these will give you that myopic look that everyone expects from a genuine computer geek. Look through them. You can see perfectly well through the center; it's only the edges that show distortion." Uri looked at himself in the mirror on the table in front of them. While Lara tried unsuccessfully to stifle a laugh, Uri had to admit that his surface transformation from forbidding bandit to harmless computer geek was genuine. There was no way he could be mistaken for the Uri Levin of Mossad fame. To his surprise, he could also see quite well through all but the edges of the right lens.

While the agents absorbed this bit of trickery, Tom sat on the corner of the desk to explain more of their roles. They were close, he felt. "We figure to have Lara apply as a skilled computer programmer and cryptographer, which she is, after all. She can pass any test they'll throw at her."

Lara peered downward modestly; she did, however, feel the tingling that went along with any new assignment.

"Uri, on the other hand, will go in as a computer technician, skilled in both English and Hebrew, in addition to Farsi, of course. Just in case they may want to hack into Mossad or Shin Bet's transmissions." Uri felt the same quiver of expectation mixed with uncertainty as did Lara. This could prove an interesting experience, but the element of danger seemed severe.

"Well," Tom concluded, "we'll give you an hour or so to think it over. How's that?"

Uri didn't let him go so easily. "How are we going to get these job offers?"

"Oh, didn't I mention it? We have some deep-cover assets in Tehran; got them not long after the revolution. They've been watching the want-ads. The 'English-speaking' part is most important, apparently. They're looking for colloquial English capability especially. I don't think you'll have much trouble . . ."

"But what about getting into the proper location? Maybe they're just looking for people to translate American newspapers." Lara was, as usual, skeptical.

"Don't worry about that. Our guys there are quite skilled at figuring out what branch of the government is looking for help. Their families were wiped out financially by the mullahs back in '79. They're doing anything they can to help. A few actually work for the personnel departments in the Ministry of Intelligence, kind of like our FBI. It's not nearly as sophisticated, fortunately.

"It was run for a long time by a brute name of Mahmoud Alavi. He disappeared couple years ago, replaced by Zarin Arani. We don't know much about him. Anyway, the ministry originates and carries out all the dirty work—assassinations and the like. They're no doubt responsible for the water poisoning. They get lots of help from the Russians." Tom was becoming more enthusiastic as he sensed a definite increase in the agents' interest.

"You mean like building the nuclear reactor for producing the poison, this polonium stuff?" Uri was getting to the heart of the matter.

"Very good," Tom interjected. The agents were going for it; he had no doubt. "We'll spend some time with you on what we know about the ministry and how they operate. Then we'll look over some of the latest want-ads. You can get the idea of what they're looking for. Once you're up to speed, we'll get you planted in Tehran. You'll be staying in separate locations for obvious reasons. No sense alerting them to a couple suddenly turning up. You'll have complete sets of papers: diplomas, certifications of employment, references, the works . . ." He looked at them intently. "You see, we were really hoping you'd say yes." Tom's enthusiasm was palpable.

Uri noticed Lara had remained quiet for the last few minutes. He felt an eagerness to do battle with the Iranians, who had now stooped to a new low: they were going after innocent civilians in a foreign country. Aside from their allies, the Syrians, who murdered their own citizens using gas and chemical weapons, this kind of behavior hadn't been seen since the Nazis were in power in the 1930s and 1940s.

He then peeked over at Bret, with whom they had grown so close during their last two encounters with the seemingly limitless Iranian despots. Bret, the innocent-looking businessman in his typical conservative blue suit and tie, appearing emotionless in his chair, listening but not adding to the conversation. Tom had been doing the sales pitch for the last few minutes.

Uri took a deep breath and said, "OK, let us have some time here to talk it over. I think we have all the info we need to come to a decision." He looked first at Lara, who smiled almost imperceptibly. Then he checked Bret and finally Tom. Everyone agreed to a time-out. The Homeland Security agents got up to leave the pair alone.

"Give me a ring on my cell when you decide . . . or need more information." Tom was nothing if not dogged.

When the door shut behind the two men, Uri could still see the concern on his wife's face. "You think our 'family' can wait a few more months?" He reached over and gripped her hand; she smiled. He had immediately seen the main cause of her reluctance. Still, they shared the animosity toward the brutal Iranian regime. If there was *anything* they could do . . .

"Did you notice Bret's hesitancy, especially there near the end?" Lara murmured.

"Actually, I did. You think he may be worried about us? He's kind of been like a mother hen."

"I don't know as I'd go that far." Lara was amused by the image. "But, yes, he probably does feel some responsibility for our well-being."

Uri chuckled, "You're right, I'm sure. But let's go ahead and tell him we'll do it, alright?"

Lara touched his shoulder in a manner that showed her acceptance and the two agents followed a young assistant to their new office.

* * *

Lara and Uri sat facing each other at their desks in the federal building. The fourth floor had a number of unmarked, locked offices for just such temporary assignments. They were studying a classified printout of a map of northern Tehran around the palace; the offices of Iran's Ministry of Intelligence lay within a mile radius. This is where they hoped to be stationed. As of now, they had already received eight promising notices; requests for their resumes met with immediate attention. The secret assets in Tehran had already submitted their documents through false email accounts in Tehran. The plan was to make appointments for about three weeks from now. By then, they should have even more opportunities for employment.

All the initial preparations for their entry into Iran had been made as soon as they agreed to the operation. Skin and hair- coloring were taken care of first, then the facial doctoring. The procedures, done by medical professionals from Sony Studios, were completed in just two hours with just the tiniest of incisions. The agents inspected each other's appearance carefully; after just a moment of amazement, they laughed and hugged one another briefly. It was going to take some time to get used to their altered faces, but they were enjoying working together. They agreed: even their own families would not recognize them if passing them on the street.

Lara had even become accustomed to her new, soft contact lenses. They required no regular maintenance. What's more, they improved her visual acuity; she hadn't realized until the eye test that she had lost some ability to read very fine print.

The two agents spoke only in Farsi. They spent hours role playing, with one being the applicant, the other the interviewer. In so doing, they would find any number of traps for each other.

"Where did you receive your computer training?" Uri would ask. Lara had to reply without noticeable pause. "And were you living at home during your schooling?" Uri would respond immediately. "Were your parents living there or were you on your own?"

They would drill like this for thirty minutes, then trade places. Many areas of concern could be revealed. Location of schools and dormitories, faculty names, and so on. They became familiar with the locations of important buildings in and around Tehran as well as the bus routes they would be using. Videos played on their computers were especially useful in this regard. After viewing the activity around the schools and markets a number of times it felt as if they had been there. It was like being back in training. Most of the previous employers and references were forgeries, of course. Requests for information would be channeled through the embedded agents using fake email and telephone contacts. At the end of each day, Bret would come down and chat easily with them, asking questions, clearly testing their readiness.

Lara and Uri continued with their training, or really, practice for ten days. In addition, they received individual exercise in their specific roles: Uri as a computer and information technology expert, Lara as a cryptologist. They were preparing for their roles as experts in an Iran that was nowhere close to the United States in these fields, but dead set on being on a par with its enemies.

* * *

It was a wet, cold day in Los Angeles, and they were getting somewhat anxious about the uncertainty of the project. Suddenly the internal phone rang. Bret and Tom wanted to see them both in ten minutes in Bret's office.

A surge of adrenaline kicked into their systems. Something was imminent. They locked up their papers and ran to Bret's office two floors up. "Have a seat," Bret announced with a smile. Tom was already seated next to Bret's desk; there was bottled water for everyone and empty pads of paper as well. At each agent's desk was a briefcase without markings, filled with papers and maps.

Bret did not waste any time. "I think you're ready to go," he stated bluntly. Tom nodded his agreement; he had obviously kept up with their progress through Bret. "We've got enough job interviews set up for each of you to keep you busy for at least a week once you get there. You'll find packets in each of your cases." He casually indicated the attaché cases on the desks. "You'll have plenty of time to go through these on your way over there." Despite his relaxed manner, there was perceivable tension in the room. Tom nervously twisted his wedding band without saying a word while Lara and Uri sat tensely, listening for every nuance in Bret's instructions.

Bret was brief and to the point. "You already have everything you'll need in terms of clothing, identification, and personal items, according to the lists you've given us." The agents had prepared their lists of toiletries to be packed for them. They knew from past experience that the items would have been procured from shops in Tehran. "You'll be going over to our King Abdulaziz Air Base on Saudi Arabia's eastern Gulf coast, for transit through the Gulf to Iran's west coast. That last part you'll do separately, so you'll need to make your goodbyes at the launch site. You'll each be picked up by ground transit for safe transfer to your 'homes' in Tehran."

"If you'll take a quick look in your packets, you'll see where you'll be staying." Bret continued. "The houses are run by our assets there and are completely secure. There's even safe telephone contact through a dedicated satellite system back to Homeland in Washington. We'll stay in touch with them at all times. Your daily sign-in times with Tom are listed on your papers; memorize those and destroy them, of course. Oh, and here are your secure phones; they're the latest of the Agency's toys."

He smiled at them convivially as he handed each of them what looked like a small, standard mobile phone. "You're to check in daily within a relatively wide time window to allow for any sort of contingency. To use it, you have to first enter the correct passcode: the date, but in reverse order; that is, year, month, day, each two digits. You get a second chance if you make a mistake—but that's it. You'll have to wait until the next day to check in again. If you miss that second day, your phone is temporarily disabled. The only way to reestablish communication is to type in the real name of your partner, last name first. You'll get a beep, then go through the daily sign-in procedure. Failing that . . . well, the presumption will be that you have been . . . um, separated from your device . . ." A long pause followed a grim look from Bret. "The phones are also the latest in trackers; we'll know exactly where you are as long as you have them with you. We'll pick you up on satellite." The two agents gave each other a knowing look, reassuring, if a little intrusive.

"There are limitations to the devices," he added gravely. "Although they are the top of the line, they're not perfect. First, they have a limited battery life. But the term 'battery' is not exactly accurate. They're powered by top-of-the-line, solid-state fuel cells. Conservatively speaking, you can count on normal usage for about two months." The agents reacted in disbelief. "I know it sounds astonishing, but these devices have been tested in a variety of adverse conditions; they are so well sealed and so efficient, well, you can count on them."

Buckley noticed a palpable sense of incredulity on the part of the agents. He then added, in a note that brought them back to a sense of reality, "They do have some drawbacks. While the locator will pick you up as long as you're not in a heavy, concrete-and-steel structure, conversation is limited to most of the populated world. Which means that about ninety percent of the globe is inaccessible to voice contact." At that, he noted a significant letdown in the mood of his troops.

"Which means you need to prepare for the necessity . . . of emergency extraction. There is, as you can imagine, a substantial chance of your exposure and the necessity of an urgent rescue." He looked at the two grim-faced agents. "Our go-to plan in the worst of all scenarios is one in which you're involved in a desperate chase. You will head for our last-chance pickup point: the city of Qazvin, two hours northwest of Tehran. Get to the municipal airport there; it's really just an empty lot on the north edge of town. There's a pretty good highway from Tehran. If you have any sort of radio, signal us through the emergency frequency you'll be given."

He paused for just a second, looking grim. "But . . . if you have no communication at all . . . then look up into the sky to the north from the end of the runway, at ten hundred and fifteen hundred hours each day." That was 10:00 a.m. and 3:00 p.m. "Our facial-recognition cameras will be on the lookout for you, especially if we haven't heard from you at your normal contact times. You undoubtedly know we can identify you from a minimum of fifty thousand feet, with ninety-nine percent certainty. The cameras will be housed in drones as well as satellites."

They sat there in silence as Tom read carefully through their instructions one more time. His brow furrowed as he neared the end. "One final thing: if you're stranded out there near the Qazvin airport and need to spend the night, take the gravel road at the east end of the airport and head north; it's the only way you can go. Two miles from the end of the airstrip, there's an oilseed farm." The two agents followed along on their copies of the instructions. "There's a thatched hut with a striped canopy and a sign that reads, 'Camping gear,' in Farsi, of course. Look for an old man with just a few teeth and a cigar. Ask for Omar; he's one of ours. That's the signal that you need help. He'll provide you with a small hut in a farmworkers' enclave. He'll give you food and water as well. You'll be safe there for one or two nights, max. That's all you should need. If you come by car, he'll show you a lean-to you can park it under.

"There'll be camouflaged pick-up aircraft, probably choppers, ready in the Caspian throughout the duration of your mission. They will pick you up from that location at the end of the runway. In case you're curious, we have that copter access through the courtesy of the nation of Azerbaijan and the transfer of a few hundred million dollars." He grimaced as though the money had come out of his own pocket. The four members of the small group all recognized the understandable gravity; this plan sounded precarious, at best.

"We plan for your departure at oh eight hundred tomorrow from LAX, so read over everything this afternoon; let me know if you have any questions. We can deal with anything tomorrow morning at six. Use your phone to sign in." Bret checked with Tom, then the two agents, who were clearly eager to get going. "I'll leave it there; until tomorrow." He smiled, but there was a slight hesitation in his voice as he said goodbye. This was no sure thing; but he was certain it was necessary and that these were the right people for it.

* * *

Lara and Uri sat quietly in the back of the government sedan that was taking them to the hotel for their last night in Los Angeles. Each was attired in the desert fatigues and footwear meant for their comfortable transport. Holding each other's hands tightly, they watched the spring rain pelt the car and the street with wind-driven fury. Low black clouds obscured everything but the splashing of puddles; the skyline was invisible in the torrent. It did nothing for their mood.

Lara's gut twisted into knots. They had been together on other dangerous assignments in enemy territory before, but this was somehow different. The unknown nature of what they were after brought down her confidence. They could have used far more time to prepare, she felt; but the power and immediacy of the threat made that luxury out of the question. Her mind raced between the horror of millions of people being trapped by monsters who were poisoning their life-giving water and the vulnerable situation into which she and her husband were headed. What would she have done if Uri were not here with her?

Uri held both their briefcases. He had similar thoughts, but he felt a fearful responsibility that he had brought this terrible responsibility onto his wife. Would she be here if not for him? This was a nagging question and one to which no answer came easily. Certainly, they were both well-trained field agents, but could they survive this perilous a mission? If anything were to happen to her, he didn't think he could . . . His years of training came back and forced him to rid himself of these negative thoughts. It was the ominous weather, he told himself. But this wasn't a Hollywood movie; the outcome didn't depend on the background. He settled back and gripped Lara's hand protectively as the car came to a stop.

Chapter 8

At their suite in the hotel, Lara and Uri first checked on the situation with the drinking water. They were relieved to find from the TV news that the downpour hadn't complicated the process of providing clean water to the people of Los Angeles. The contaminated water had been rerouted to other reservoirs and treated with ion-exchange membranes to remove the polonium. Once the poison was removed, the water would be piped several miles offshore; it would not be a threat to the ocean. Clean water from the Sierra Nevada mountains was already being pumped into the city water supply.

The bad news was that Dr. Regis Trombley had passed away from the relatively large dose he had bravely, if unnecessarily, ingested that first horrible day. There were other casualties, as well. But the bulk of the polonium never made it into the city water supply; quick action stopped the flow from the reservoir. However, more than two hundred people had been admitted to emergency rooms that first day. Fortunately, none had perished, but many suffered reversible internal organ damage. The chemical chelating agents provided to the hospitals saved the day. But the entire country was scared. Bottled water was sold at a premium everywhere, for at least the time being. With that news to deal with, they went straight to bed.

* * *

Five a.m. came without even a trace of predawn light. The rain continued to pour on Los Angeles. Water spouted out of the overburdened storm sewers. The couple slowly made their way into their clothes and through their room service breakfast. The continuing rain did nothing to improve their spirits; sleep had been elusive at best. Both, however, were glad to be starting out. They knew that once they were on their way, they could devote their energies to the tasks at hand and not dwell on the unknown.

Their car arrived right on time and hustled them to the reconnaissance shack in the military wing of the airport where the two agents went through the telephone sign-in; it worked perfectly. The device they each had received looked deceptively like the modern mobile phones in Iran. But the electronic chips inside were marvels of modern engineering, connecting them to their home base through top-secret military satellites. Even if lost or stolen, the devices were inoperable without the daily codes they had been given. They also, as a backup, recognized only *their* fingerprints. Tom answered each of their calls, wishing them a hearty good morning.

Bret and Tom arrived, all smiles as they had a leisurely cup of coffee. No need for any added anxiety. Tom gave them both a list of emergency contacts and telephone numbers; these they had to memorize on the plane and destroy. Nothing new there. Tom assured them again that their assets on the ground in Tehran were capable and trustworthy. The government men had access to the same contacts as the two agents and were there to help in any way possible. "You know," Tom told them again, "their friends and family suffered terribly at the hands of the Iranian theocracy; they're ready to wreak whatever vengeance they can. Count on them for whatever you need."

The duo had heard this assurance before, but it was still comforting to hear it again. The thought of being alone in such a hostile environment was daunting at best. Bret continued the calming lecture. "You are the best in the business as far as I'm concerned," he promised them. "If anyone could handle this situation, it's you two for sure." Looking at them closely, he had to grin. "I'd never believe it was either of you, I mean it. You look like something out of 'Lawrence of Arabia.' No way anybody's going to recognize you."

The two were already so used to their altered appearances, they seemed natural. There was a pause as Tom and Bret waited for last-minute questions from the pair, but none came. Finally, Tom shook their hands and wished them luck. Bret did the same, adding, "You can reach us any time during the flight, even after you reach Saudi Arabia."

Lara thanked him for everything and assured him they were ready. At that, they were led into the covered jeep that would take them to the waiting aircraft.

* * *

At the Homeland Security base in Manhattan the troops were busy as well. Buckley's teams of men and women were preparing the interview sites for the agents. Those locations in Tehran that had responded positively to the applications from the agents were now being struck with very specific and very troubling computer and website problems.

First, those Iranian defense contractors and government offices that had issued interviews with Uri suddenly saw their official websites turn sour. People were unable to login or were guided to other sites that seemed to pop up without warning. Even the government officials were not able to reach their own employees. The problems were intermittent; the offices were able to solve one difficulty, only to find another taking its place.

Next, those contractors and secret Iranian government installations that had asked Lara to interview were plagued with interference from outside sources. Vital information was in desperate jeopardy. Despite all the help the Iranians were able to acquire from their standard, and even high-level computer wizards, there was fear of another virus-like intrusion that had so publicly humiliated them with the so-called Stuxnet worm in 2010. Their nuclear program had been set back for months because of the Israeli/American attack on the computer-controlled Iranian fuel-enrichment centrifuges.

Homeland Security gleefully monitored the frustration occurring in the Iranian armed forces due to this double-fisted attack on their information and defense industries. They were sure to welcome the aid that the American agents were coming to provide—at least, that was the idea.

* * *

The flight carrying Lara and Uri from Los Angeles to Thule Air Base in Greenland took well into the first night. In fact, it was past 8:00 p.m. local time when they landed. The flight had taken nearly nine hours, during which time the agents had a chance to study the aerial maps of Tehran, memorize their contact information, and once again rehearse the imagined interviews with their prospective employers. They would take turns, each taking the part of personnel agent for the other. Of course, it was all done in Farsi. They had a few hours in Greenland to have a leisurely hot meal and stretch their legs. Then it was on to the US air base in eastern Saudi Arabia. As soon as they got back on the refueled and restocked plane, they settled in to sleep; they would arrive at King Abdulaziz Air Base just past noon the following day.

Lara could sleep well on the single ersatz bed in their private compartment. Uri, on the other hand, was prone to worry; he ran over what they would have to do on arrival in Saudi Arabia. Then, he worried about their night transit to the western shore of Iran and the transport by jeep north to Tehran. It would be the morning of the second day before they completely converted to their Iranian selves at their hosts' homes in the northern part of the city. They already had job interviews scheduled starting that afternoon. It was a lot to consider and worry about—in Farsi.

The couple was awakened after the nine-hour flight and offered breakfast. Lara slid open the window curtain to a blazing sun in absolutely clear skies. It was quite a contrast to their departure from subzero, totally dark Greenland. The desert landscape below them, though, was just as desolate as the arctic. They each immediately made their compulsory sign-in call; this was going to have to be a strict part of their daily routine.

Uri, in contrast to his wife, who was alert and ready for the new day, was having difficulty figuring out where he was, let alone the time of day. He had finally fallen into a deep sleep after an unknown number of hours of tortuous mental gymnastics. As he slowly awakened, he realized it was concern for Lara that was weighing on him. He simply couldn't think of her as just his spy partner. She was everything to him, and the thought of any harm coming to her was still overwhelming. Seeing her looking down at him now in his semi stupor, he could sense that she recognized his concern. She gave him a motherly smile and tousled his already messy hair.

Actually, Lara's smile was more than just tenderness; she was still getting used to his altered appearance. It was startling to see a bearded son of the desert sleeping there. But the food arrived quickly, and they devoured it. This may be their last Western-style meal for some time, they realized. As soon as they signaled they were finished, the polite young airman came back, took their trays, and informed them that they would be touching down in less than an hour; they needed to prepare for arrival.

The old nervousness came back as Uri waited for Lara to finish dressing. The small but adequate washroom was a welcome convenience. By the time he had cleaned up and changed into his desert garb, they were getting the heads-up of preparation for landing. The pair sat on adjacent seats, strapped in and holding hands. They were silent, but their minds were racing wildly. Some things never changed.

They touched down uneventfully and a jeep drove them to the building adjacent to the control tower. They carried their briefcases while two airmen brought their baggage, two nondescript cloth suitcases. Air Force Col. James Madison Cleary met them. Cleary was the commander of the Saudi base, a veteran pilot who, they had learned, had done duty in Iraq and Afghanistan. He was fifty-five years old and close to retirement but the picture of radiant health. A warm, friendly smile peeked out from under the trim, gray moustache on his upper lip.

"Great to see you folks," he shouted over the noise of the planes on the tarmac. He shook their hands and led them into his office, a rather austere affair compared with some of the generals' accommodations they had witnessed. "Sit down and let me give you a quick rundown of what we have cooking for you," he said with a Virginia twang. "We've got a couple of hours of reconnaissance to go over with you before we get you on the road. You'll be going by land vehicle to our stepping-off point on the coast. Then a personnel landing craft to take you across the Gulf. You won't even have to get your feet wet; it's got a nice ramp we can put right up onto the sand. She's got a big engine; you'll make thirty knots easy, but she has a low enough profile the bad guys won't see you on their radar. Anyway, our fleet is right there to cover your tracks and be available for any sort of contingency. Sound good?"

"Seems like you have everything covered," Uri said easily. "Want to come along?"

"Hey, we've heard all about you folks. I'd be nothing but dead weight," Cleary said, laughing. "Seriously, you'll be casting off just after dark. The boat is fully loaded with radio, radar, GPS, and everything else you could think of, even armament—I sure hope you don't need that!" Lara and Uri laughed nervously. "Anyway, they'll take you across to the Iran side of the drink where your ground transport will be waiting. About a five-hour ride but pretty comfortable; all the amenities." He paused before adding, "You'll have separate land vehicles over there, you know," focusing on Lara.

"Yes, Colonel, we know," she said.

"Well, then, good luck to you. If there's anything else we can do, let me know after your detailed reconnaissance briefing. Major Bailey will handle that." He waved to a man standing outside, who immediately entered the room.

"Agents, I'd like you to know Skip—that is, Major William Bailey. He'll be the captain of your landing craft. Skip, these are our hardy visitors. Please give them the complete rundown."

Major Bailey, who looked more like a navy man than an air force officer, shook their hands. His skin was heavily bronzed, aging him beyond his years; his hands were roughened by decades on the water. It was apparent from his manner that he was aware of these agents' history, or at least their fame. "It's my pleasure, ma'am, sir," he said modestly.

Lara did not want to mention their names, as was the order during undercover assignments, so she merely thanked him and waited to be escorted to the map room.

* * *

The recon with the major added nothing to their knowledge of the situation; it just confirmed what they already knew. They were, of course, pleased with the corroboration; nothing went wasted when your lives were on the line. There was just time for a light snack, and then they were off by jeep to the small harbor.

It was just after dusk when they boarded the modern-looking, high-powered launch. Lara and Uri boarded from a small dock near the US Navy offices along the road parallel to the beach, though there was a loading ramp that permitted entry and egress from the shore. Sentries guarded the twelve-foot high, barbed-wire fences that ran along the oceanfront. Well-lit concrete piers ran from the beach out three hundred yards into the calm sea. Five crewmen accompanied the agents, led by Skip Bailey. He watched with a practiced eye as the men on the dock tossed the hawsers up to the boat's crew.

It was an amazingly peaceful scene; the gulls squawking overhead provided the only sounds other than the gentle lapping of the quiet, warm waters of the Persian Gulf. Though it was already evening, the heat was still oppressive, especially when combined with the withering humidity. The agents had become used to the gentle climate of southern California, despite the occasional spring rains. There was, however, a beautiful sunset behind them; they could watch it as the launch slithered quietly into the small harbor. Sunset was abrupt in this latitude; it seemed no time at all until they were into the open sea, the sun already below the horizon.

The boat gathered speed quickly in the tranquil gulf. They knew the navy's Sixth Fleet was out there somewhere, silently watching over them. It was hard for them to imagine the massive forces of evil that surrounded them. There was something intangibly sinister about the quiet that enveloped them.

Skip Bailey came up as they watched the shore disappear from the port rail. "Beautiful, isn't it?" the crusty major said in a friendly manner. He was at home on the water, one could tell. "I love it out here. Going to get me a nice thirty-footer, go fishin', crabbin' in the Chesapeake when my time's up." If this mission was causing him any anxiety, they couldn't tell from his peaceful demeanor. Lara and Uri hoped to see him when the job was over, and he was there to pick them up on the Iranian side.

"You might want to grab some rest; it'll be a few hours before we hit the beach. Get some grub, too. I don't know what you're gonna eat over there." Skip gestured vaguely at the invisible shore to the east.

"That's not a bad idea, Major," Uri offered. He did want to spend most of these last few hours with his bride. *Who knew how long until . . . No sense going there*, he told himself.

"Call me Skip, please," the airman said to both agents. "I'm countin' on seein' the both of you on the way back, whenever . . ." He tipped his cap and retreated to the pilot house, allowing the pair to head into the cabin.

Lara and Uri went into the living quarters, where they were offered some fresh seafood by the young airman who was acting as chef. "No alcohol aboard, I'm afraid," he apologized. "But plenty of tea and soda."

"That's just fine, airman," Uri replied for both of them. "We need to be on our toes from here on."

"So I understand . . ." the young man stood there, apparently hoping to hear more about their top-secret mission. When he saw that was not going to happen, the freckle-faced youth darted into the kitchen to bring them some soft drinks.

The couple retired to the small private cabin they had been granted. It was normally reserved for the captain of the vessel; Skip was certainly seeing to their well-being. Both Lara and Uri found themselves exhausted; it had been a very long day. They lay down beside each other on the double bed and, holding each other's hands, fell quickly asleep.

It seemed no time at all before the gentle knock informed them that sunrise was imminent, as was their approach to the spot of beach on the northeastern shore of the Persian Gulf. They had an hour to clean up, have a quick breakfast, and enter the Islamic Republic of Iran. They dressed in their Iranian garb, with briefcases and fabric suitcases, and headed onto the deck. The sun was just rising, a flaming red orb in the east. The quiet of the night was soon replaced by the noise of the hungry gulls, clamoring for any scraps of food that might come off the launch. The gulls screamed and dove into the warm, oily-looking water, fighting for every morsel the ship might provide.

The sandy beach appeared deserted, to the consternation of the agents. Though they searched the bare sand, no vehicles were in sight. Seeing their tenseness, Skip Bailey approached them and reported that their rides were already there, hidden just out of sight, waiting for them to hit the beach. The major grasped each of their hands and, with some barely concealed apprehension, wished them well. His words were reassuring, but his face revealed a hint of concern. Uri wondered if it was just his imagination, but a glance at Lara showed she sensed it as well. *What did he know that he's not telling us? Too late to worry about it now.*

The crew turned the boat, backed up to the shore, and ably lowered the ramp onto the hard sand. At the same time, two Iranian-made jeeps pulled out of the scrub bushes and came to a stop no more than ten feet away. "Greetings, friends!" the apparent leader of the Iranian team said in English to the Americans, primarily to Bailey, who seemed to recognize him.

"Nice to see you, Salib," Skip replied grasping the rebel leader's outstretched hand. "These are our friends, who you will know as Heydar and Daria." He nodded to first Uri, then Lara.

The two agents greeted the rebel leader in Farsi: "Our pleasure to meet you, Salib," they said politely in unison; immediately following with the phrase, *"Hāl-e shomā Chetore?" How is your health?*

The group of rebels smiled and laughed at the agents' fluency with the language. The six Persians, all men, shook hands eagerly with Uri, bowing gracefully to Lara. She nodded to them in return.

So far, so good, Uri thought. *Now, what was Bailey's apprehension all about?* His goodbye to Lara was quick, without betraying any emotion. No sense giving away any personal details. The jeep carrying her and three Iranian rebels drove off without hesitation.

Uri's driver introduced himself only as Ali, a name as common in Shia countries as John in the West. He was a young, slender Persian man, dressed in desert fatigues showing neither rank nor citizenry. Uri sat upfront with Ali, his suitcase and briefcase between his legs in the open jeep; the two other soldiers climbed in the back with just a wave to their new comrade. "It will be many hours before we reach our destination," Ali informed him. "If you need we will stop along the way. We should be there before dark."

Uri glanced at the sun, already climbing well above the horizon. "Oh, don't worry," Ali told him. "We will bring up the top before noon. The weather will be quite pleasant." Uri smiled in return.

There was little conversation in the noisy, rough-riding jeep; he was going to be sore tonight, Uri thought glumly. At least he would get a night's sleep before his first interviews. He ran over the first day's schedule in his head. He had committed everything to memory by now. The first few interviews were with minor government bureaus. They all needed help setting up spreadsheets and personnel accounts. He had been impressed that they had access to relatively new software; he would be able to step in gracefully, he hoped.

Many of the personnel advertisements were also seeking graphic designers and people to set up websites. He had received valuable schooling in this during his "crash course" over the last few weeks. Others were looking for what were listed as Information Technology professionals but were people skilled in uprooting false and disruptive incoming transmissions, "scams" as they were known worldwide. Here, he would have some valuable assistance from Homeland Security. Homeland was prepared to transmit professional-looking opportunities to any company or government office to which Uri was applying. As soon as one of these transmissions was received and opened, it would cause havoc on all the office computers; Uri would be right there to solve the problem in a couple of hours. What better test of his IT skills?

His knowledge of English was also a benefit. He had a counterfeit degree from an American university and was able, of course, to pass any test his interviewer gave him. Knowing what sort of problem each interviewing agency would have been dealing with lately was an advantage. He had been thoroughly briefed during training, not only about the issues that plagued them but also the fixes.

They had been driving all day, with only three rest stops, each at a market where they were able to buy some fresh food, not the packaged variety common on American highways. Uri noticed that the sun was rapidly setting; it was now striking him from the driver's side window. Looking out at his surroundings, he realized they had entered the suburban area south of Tehran. Even as he watched, the groups of farm dwellings slowly melded into residential communities; cars in driveways became more frequent. Children were apparent everywhere, either coming home from school or going to evening prayers. The scene was strikingly similar to the images from the global satellites and drones he had seen during his training. He quickly became more alert; he was about to enter his new life.

Chapter 9

It was late Sunday when they entered Vali Asr, one of the longest streets in southern Tehran. Ali left the four-lane highway and entered a relatively new development of upper-middle-class homes. They appeared well maintained and spacious. Modern-looking supermarkets and restaurants appeared on many of the street corners. If it weren't for the clothing on the pedestrians, Uri could imagine himself in a suburb of Tel Aviv or even Los Angeles. Except, of course, for the omnipresent billboards displaying huge pictures of the ayatollah and his sycophants, most brandishing weapons even as they smiled at their captive audiences.

The late spring twilight had settled into night as Ali followed the instructions of his GPS onto one of the quiet streets. Most but not all of the driveways were occupied by vehicles, many of them small, white sedans. He pulled into one of the driveways nearly identical to its neighbors. They all tumbled out of their jeep, stretched, and with Ali in the lead, strode up to the front door. Uri noted very few people out in their yards or on the sidewalks. Ali knocked gently on the door, which opened, revealing a woman in casual western dress but with a head scarf. Seeing Ali, she beamed with pleasure and kissed him on both cheeks. Simultaneously, she scanned the other men, seemingly knowing the two who were Ali's compatriots, but then stopping to peer intently at Uri, the only one carrying a suitcase and briefcase

"This is Heydar, Tala," Ali said to the woman at the door, in Farsi, of course, even as she stood still, scrutinizing Uri. "Heydar, meet your hostess, Tala." The woman did not offer to kiss the newcomer, but she did reach out her right hand to him. He took it gently but firmly.

"It is my pleasure to meet you, Heydar," she said to Uri. "Please, come in and make yourself comfortable." Her eyes never left him as he entered what was to be his new home. "These are my parents," she said, indicating a rather elderly couple who sat rigidly in stiff-backed wicker chairs. A television set blared in the background; some sort of Persian game show was in progress. As Uri sat in a dining-room chair at the edge of the room, placing his bags on the floor, Tala had a conversation with Uri's travelling companions, who started to leave. But first, Ali came over to Uri, offering some quiet words meant to calm him down a bit. Apparently, his uneasiness was obvious; the whole transition from Los Angeles to Tehran had taken place so fast.

Once Ali and his companions had said goodbye to Uri, Tala came over to him, sat next to him, and smiled. Her gaze never left his face, making him even more self-conscious. "You have been to Tehran before, Heydar?" she asked in Farsi.

"No, I've not had the pleasure," he responded glibly. "This is my first time here."

"Oh, your Farsi is quite good!" she exclaimed with delight. "Just a hint of a Lebanese accent."

"Very good, yes," he said. "I grew up in that area."

He could see her trying to put everything together; he wondered just how much she actually knew about his background and mission. Her eyes continued to explore his face, now and then drifting to the rest of his person. He could feel himself coloring under her scrutiny; he hoped it wasn't showing.

She turned and said something quietly to the old couple introduced as her parents, then turned back to Uri and removed her head scarf, which had been covering most of her face below her eyes. "These are not actually my parents, as you might have guessed. They are a distant aunt and uncle, but the neighbors, you know . . ." She paused. "They lost everything when the Shah . . . well, I'm sure you know all that."

Actually, he didn't, and silently cursed his handlers for not briefing him more completely about his accommodations. But he was also struck by her dark beauty. She was one of those Persians with mixed northern European blood: jet-black hair and flashing blue eyes. He hoped his room was far from hers. She rose, as did he, as she said, "Let me show you to your room; I hope that you will be comfortable here. We are certainly pleased to be able to help you with whatever . . ."

She turned toward the staircase at the side of the dining room and led Uri up to the second-floor landing and his room at the end of the corridor. "You will have your own bathroom; it's connected, you see, at the far wall. Oh, and you will need your own mobile, of course." She handed him a modern mobile phone with a Tehran area code, along with username and password written on a piece of paper. He accepted it gratefully with a nod and a smile.

Uri was pleasantly surprised to see a double bed, closet, desk, and dresser, complete with mirror. There were two simple chairs in the room as well. He didn't check the bath; that could wait until he was alone. He was certain it would meet his needs. He immediately went through a silent check for listening or viewing devices in the room; it came out clean. Then he went through the sign-in routine on his secret phone, tapping in his code as arranged. He got through immediately, but Tom did not answer the call. Uri left a message and fell into bed.

He was amazed by how long he slept and how exhausted he must have been. He awoke to a gentle tap on his door; his breakfast would be ready for him whenever he was ready. He showered quickly and dressed in a sport shirt and slacks, the same outfit he had seen on other workers in the government offices. After a pleasant breakfast of feta cheese, jam, and lavash bread served with sweet Persian tea, he was off to his interviews. With his briefcase under his arm, he headed for the bus station as per his instructions.

His first appointment was at the Ministry of Defense Auxiliary, in a building not far from the mountains that bordered the city on the north. He found himself attired very much like the two-dozen or so Iranian men already on the bus, none of whom were speaking to each other; he could have been in any large metropolitan area. He saw the building well before the bus stopped. It was white granite about eight stories tall, with metal lettering on the face. Getting off the bus, he prepared himself for the first scrutiny he would have to face, remembering to first put on the fake glasses that made him look both harmless and studious. He strode into the building along with eight other men all hurrying to work. The guard, who was carrying a large sidearm, casually checked the ID cards of the other men, allowing them into the entry hall. Uri, of course, had no such ID card, only the forged government identity card that all citizens must carry. He noticed he had begun to sweat at this first checkpoint.

The guard asked him for his papers; he replied, showing his identity card and his appointment time in the Office of Ministry Applicants. The guard checked Uri's academic-looking picture against the bearded man standing before him; apparently satisfied, he went through a list of names on a sheet attached to a clipboard. Finding the name Heydar al-Nabi, exactly as on his sheet, he gestured toward the elevator and said to Uri, in Farsi, of course, "Room 203," then unnecessarily, "Second floor." Before Uri could take even a step, the guard handed him a temporary pass on a chain that was to go around his neck.

Uri got off the elevator directly in front of the door to the applications office and, since he was early, sat in a hard-backed chair just inside the door until a hawk-faced man in a brown uniform curtly told him to come forward and sign in. He did so, opposite his name on the pad that rested on the front desk. The receptionist, if one could call him that, merely grunted as he looked at the pass hanging on Uri's neck. Uri sat back down, briefcase on his lap, and waited just a few minutes until he saw another applicant come out of the inner office. The man at the desk just gestured with a curt nod for Uri to proceed.

This is it, Uri thought as he took a deep breath and headed into the office. He carried his briefcase in as confident a manner as he could as he strode in and found a middle-aged woman sitting behind the desk with a welcoming smile. She was wearing a modest dress but with no head scarf. *They are making some progress here after all*, Uri thought as he sat directly in front of Ms. Hadani, as her nameplate indicated.

"And how are you today, Mr. al-Nabi?" she said in a friendly manner. She took note of his thick glasses but, to his great relief, did not laugh.

"Fine, I'm delighted to be here," he replied in a similar tone. Her attitude put him immediately at ease.

She scanned the papers in front of her, which Uri could see were his application forms. "Well," she said promptly, "you appear to have just the training and experience we were looking for." A bright smile appeared on her full lips. "You have dealt with, what shall I say, computer 'glitches,' in your past employment?"

"Indeed, I do have some familiarity with those kinds of problems," he said with as much modesty as possible.

"Well then, could I ask you straightaway to take a look at some pesky issues we have just recently run into?"

Uri's heart skipped a beat. *Could Homeland already have broken in, so to speak?* "Certainly. I could give it a look. Can't guarantee anything, of course. What sort of problem is it?"

"We haven't even been allowed to log in to our home website for the past couple of days. Our people are not able to figure out what's going on. If we can't log in ourselves, it means others cannot as well. As you can imagine, our chief is not at all happy about that." She smiled. "I wonder if you are familiar with our operating system." She slid a couple of pages over the desk to him.

Uri tried to control his delight as he saw one of the systems he had just been trained to use. He waited just a second before replying cautiously, "Actually, yes, I do have some fluency with it. What seems to be the problem?" Uri knew at once what the problem was—at least, he hoped so.

"Well, as I understand it, our systems analysts have been getting this strange error code. We've been forced to use an older program that's not very efficient. People are having trouble getting through . . . well, let me get Sa'id to talk with you." She pushed a button on her desk, and within twenty seconds, a chubby, dark young man with a harried look on his face opened her door.

"Yes," he said curtly, evidently too busy to deal with formalities or introductions.

"Sa'id, this is Heydar, our latest applicant for the computer technician post. Can you show him the little issue that's been bothering us?"

"Oh yes," Sa'id said smugly. *If his team couldn't deal with it, good luck to this odd-looking stranger.* He didn't bother to shake Uri's hand. "Follow me."

Uri followed the bouncy little man out the door into the hallway. He strode briskly down the hall to a room that had a sign on the door that said enigmatically, "Operations." Not holding the door for Uri, Sa'id led him to a modern personal computer with a large flat-screen display. Sitting down next to Uri, he fiddled with the keys until he reached a screen that said simply, "Access denied. Error message AH 919."

"This is our home website, as you may have been told. In the last few days, no one can get in, not even ourselves." He looked at Uri with an expression that held nothing but contempt.

But Uri had been told to expect this. The Homeland guys had inserted a virus, thanks to one of their moles, into the operating system that would not yield to anyone who didn't know the new access code. "That could be tough," Uri said thoughtfully. He'd better not solve this problem too easily, or it would be exceedingly suspicious. He tilted the screen toward himself, just out of Sa'id's view, then rapidly typed in a code that should, he said, allow entry into the webpage. As Uri anticipated, he got the same error message that Sa'id had. The pudgy Persian smirked happily.

"Hmmm," Uri grunted, seemingly stumped. "Better try something else." While Sa'id grinned at some colleagues, Uri quickly entered the correct code and said to his new acquaintance, "This looks more promising." Sa'id's mouth dropped open as he looked upon the freshly opened webpage.

"Welcome to Operations," it stated in bold capital letters in Farsi.

"That's it," the fat young man said, eyes bulging with wonder. "How did you . . . ?"

"I'm afraid that was just a temporary measure to assure that the webpage was not corrupted," Uri said, casually exiting the page with a flutter of his fingers. "I would need to spend a little more time to assure a secure connection."

"Please, go ahead . . ."

"I would, but I do have some other appointments pending, I'm afraid. However, I left my phone number with Ms. Hadani at the desk . . ." He rose, grabbing his briefcase. *No sense looking too eager. They'll call.* He felt confident as he took Sa'id's lead and headed for the door. The phone number he gave Ms. Hadani was the mobile phone given to him by his hostess, Tala.

The first things he did as he left the building, after returning his visitor's pass and signing out, was to open his briefcase, remove the goggles, grab his secure phone, and report in to Homeland.

He made a concise report of the day's events, including his certainty of a callback to his "audition." He finished the call with his plan to his remaining two appointments; they were with a small computer-software company and a government-run education facility. Uri felt upbeat as he headed for a small falafel restaurant for some lunch. He wondered how Lara was doing with her assignment. They were not allowed to make direct contact but were to be apprised of each other's progress through the secure link each evening. Their separation brought on a pang of loneliness that tempered the feeling of achievement from the morning's events.

The afternoon appointments were relatively unexciting compared with the success at the Iranian defense ministry office. Neither interview yielded the kind of computer glitch that Homeland had provided to him in the morning. His interviews were mundane, merely filling out some forms and a promise to "get back to you in a few days." Either the computer bandits in the Homeland office in Manhattan had failed in their attempts at these locations, or the low-level offices in the afternoon's meetings had just ignored the issues for the time being.

It was 4:30 p.m. when Uri headed back "home" for dinner. He was eager to see if he was correct in his assessment of the call from Ms. Hadani and the update from Tom Buckley at Homeland.

Chapter 10

Tala was there to greet Uri when he arrived fresh from the interviews on his first day of "job hunting." She was all smiles but did not offer to shake hands or make any physical contact at all. Uri, on his part, did not offer anything other than a smile in return. She was not fazed by his apparent coolness. In fact, she was quite upbeat as she informed him that dinner would be at 6:00 p.m., if that suited him. Uri thought only a moment before agreeing, saying he would just clean up and be down in time.

He hustled upstairs to have some privacy as he looked first at his secure phone for messages from Homeland. As promised, Tom had left a brief dispatch about Lara, merely saying she had safely reached her target and was proceeding as planned. Uri knew her location; it was out in the western part of the city, an area called Ekbatan Town. Her safe house was in a relatively new development in this city of over eight million, with a semirural setting complete with trees, parks, and shopping centers. It was reassuring news for Uri.

Tom then reacted very positively to Uri's news about his first interview. "Take them up on any offer to return," Tom said. "If they make you a proposal of employment, mull it over, but take it. That office handles employment for the information- technology offices in their defense establishment. Couldn't be a better start. Then cancel all your other appointments. None is better than this one."

That was great news for Uri. He would now check his mobile phone for messages, especially from Ms. Hadani. If he heard anything, he would immediately send word back to Buckley. Having plenty of time to shower and change for dinner, he checked his Iranian mobile phone. Sure enough, there was a brief message from the operations office asking him to come back first thing in the morning. They were very pleased with his first interview and were actively considering him for an open position. Without a pause, Uri sent a text back to Ms. Hadani, informing her that he would indeed be back the next morning at 8:00 a.m., and that he was positively impressed with the office and its opportunities.

That left Uri just enough time to message Tom with the positive news. He then proceeded to clean up and change for dinner, in the best of moods.

Arriving at dinner, he found the elderly aunt and uncle sitting next to each other at the square dinner table, leaving Tala and Uri to also sit adjacent to each other. The aunt, who was now introduced to Uri as Sarina, nodded politely. She was dressed in traditional Persian clothing, dating back to prerevolutionary times: a modest dress, no makeup, with her hair tied neatly in a bun. She appeared to be in her late sixties.

The uncle, introduced as Mohsen, smiled broadly at Uri. He appeared to be about seventy, his face creased heavily, apparently from many years in the blazing Persian sun. He stood and gave Uri a powerful handshake, giving his guest the feeling of a potential suitor to his niece. "Welcome to our humble home," Mohsen said. Uri replied in his best Farsi, "The pleasure is all mine." Tala beamed at him from her chair at his right.

They then got down to the business of the meal: chicken skewered kebab-style served on rice with a beautiful assortment of steamed vegetables. Plates of fresh bread with olive oil lay in the center of the table, one for each of the four diners. There was a bottle of what appeared to be dark-red wine at Mohsen's left hand, from which he poured everyone a glass. All four then drank a toast to the guest; Uri found the "wine" to be, in fact, grape juice, but it was fresh, cold and delicious. The meal followed suit, as tasty and nutritious as he had enjoyed in some time. It was followed by a large platter of fresh fruit and nuts, including pomegranates and pistachios, among Uri's favorites.

They lingered at the table as Mohsen described his life in Iran before the revolution. It was clear that he knew, at least vaguely, of Uri's allegiance to the Western democracies. He seemed safe in speaking of his devotion to the Shah. He spoke of the large plantation his family had owned for generations; they were wiped out, of course, by the fanatics attached to the Ayatollah Ruhollah Khomeini back in 1979. His estate that had hired, fed, clothed, and paid for the schooling of hundreds of Persians over the years was seized and allowed to go fallow by the ayatollah's followers. All his offspring had been killed or transferred to parts unknown as the Iran that he had known was transfigured into a prison camp. His story reminded Uri of the way most of his own ancestors were treated by the Czar, then the Ukrainians, the Nazis, and finally the Stalinists. Of course, he did not share this with the family, but the looks he received from Tala and Sarina seemed to indicate they recognized his sympathy.

The little family realized it was getting late and their visitor had an early morning in store. What exactly he was doing, they didn't know, or at least weren't pursuing it; but they allowed him to head to his room. He graciously and sincerely thanked them for the meal and said good night.

The next day came after a refreshing night of sleep. He made his way downstairs even before the call to breakfast. He was eager to see how his return visit to Operations would go. But first, he called his appointments set for the day and delayed but did not cancel them. He wanted to leave his options open, for now, at least. Tala came downstairs, surprised to see her guest already waiting. Sensing his urgency, she put together a quick Iranian breakfast of honey, freshly drained from the honeycomb, along with a thick, spreadable cream and warm bread. While he was polishing that off, she poured him a cup of thick, dark Persian coffee, but without the usual sweetness so often found in Iran. She knew enough about him to realize he was quite Western in habit.

Stepping outside into another day of bright sunshine, Uri, dressed in similar clothes to the day before, hustled to the bus stop and retraced his steps to the same government building. He slipped on his glasses and entered, meeting the same guard as the day before, who recognized him immediately. Uri signed in and headed for the second floor.

It was exactly 7:58 a.m. when he entered the door to Room 203. There was Ms. Hadani, dressed in the same outfit as the day before, and sporting a wide smile. "So good to see you," she greeted him. "We were really hoping you would show."

Uri returned the smile. "I am delighted you wanted me to return. I think I can finalize the adjustments I made yesterday—if that is agreeable to Sa'id."

"Indeed," she replied. "He is waiting for you; follow me." Uri was careful to focus his gaze directly ahead, not wanting to clumsily trip by glancing through the contorted edges of his lenses. She led him into the same room as the day before, meeting a trio of office workers who were fruitlessly trying to log in to the home webpage.

Sa'id, the chief of the group, greeted Uri with a hearty handshake. "We are indeed happy to see you! We're not having any luck logging back in."

"Yes," Uri replied knowingly. "There is a safety lock that keeps the unwanted away from mischief." He sat down at the computer he had used the day before. He appeared to be studying the screen in order to distract the onlookers from what he was really up to. His hands glided rapidly over the keyboard in a well-practiced maneuver. Before the office computer team realized what had happened, the web page rose magically on the screen.

"It's all set now," he offered lightly. "Here, have a go at it." He cleared the screen and allowed Sa'id to try it.

Sa'id sat at another machine and attempted to log in. The rest of the men murmured in amazement as the web page appeared. "I don't understand what you . . ."

"Oh, I put a lock in the code after I cleared the chaff out of the program yesterday to make sure no one got into it again. But now I secured the software; your office staff can log in with their same passwords, but no one else will be able to. I made sure of that."

The five men standing there looked reverentially at the bespectacled stranger. Sa'id, meanwhile, went quietly to speak with Ms. Hadani. She called Uri into her office, all smiles. "We can't offer you a high salary. There is, of course, a mandatory probation period, but we would love to have you come work with us. When can you start?"

"How about right now?"

"Oh, that would be wonderful! We just need to take care of some of the usual paperwork. Please come sit in here. I know you have most of the information we require already, so it won't take long. Meanwhile, Sa'id will prepare your desk, machine, and phone for you. I know you will love it here."

Uri took his briefcase to the table she had set out for him; he filled out the forms as he had been taught during his training. The Homeland staff had prepared him well; it took less than thirty minutes to complete the work. He was welcomed by the rest of the team as he put his new desk in order, learning how to use the phone and log in to the computer with his new password. By then, it was time for lunch; he joined the others in a trip to their favorite spot, where they dined on some of Uri's favorite Mediterranean dishes, washed down with local sparkling water.

Uri was very deferential to the others. He listened politely as they told him of their schooling, their girlfriends, and their ambitions. He could see he had entered their world as a sort of father figure; he offered little but took note of what they offered. *Every bit helps*, he thought.

They returned to work, everyone in high spirits. Uri learned that this section of the Operations Division had been searching for a capable computer person for some months. One of their highest priorities, it turned out, was for someone fluent in English. Uri had already learned from Ms. Hadani that her section had been assigned the task of analyzing dispatches stolen from US Department of Defense documents relating to Iran's growing military capabilities. She hastened to assure him that theirs was not the only office in the government that had this assignment; there were many across the spectrum of the Revolutionary Government. Here, the focus was on information that had been gleaned from computer-coded internal messages among defense department offices in Washington, DC. It was all written in highly technical English, which was proving to be a complicating issue for the Iranian military operatives. It would be a great feather in their cap if they could break down these coded messages sooner, and with better accuracy than any other division.

So, Uri was not surprised when Sa'id first asked him, as they sat down to business after lunch, if his English skills matched those with the computer. Uri pointed with some modesty at his resume that showed he had learned his English while studying in Lebanon.

"Yes," Sa'id replied, "I noticed your Farsi had the unique characteristics of that region."

"Why don't you let me have a look at some of the English-language messages that Ms. Hadani spoke to me about?"

"Oh, she mentioned those, did she?" Sa'id seemed a bit disappointed. "Well, I suppose that would be a good place to start," he agreed somewhat sullenly. He had wanted complete control over his new asset. He shuffled through some papers on his desk, all marked both "Urgent" and "Most Secret" in Farsi.

Uri, his glasses perched on his nose, perused quickly through the first document. It was a rough conversion of the coded message into idiomatic, technical English. "Well," he said calmly in Farsi, "this one deals with a new medium-range defensive missile the Americans discovered in 'our capabilities.' They feel it could take out some of their better midrange offensive rockets." By the word *our*, Uri was referring, of course, to Iran.

Sa'id sat there stunned by this immediate translation and analysis. "You got all that from this page of transmission?"

"Well, I have a pretty good knowledge of English from my time in Lebanon. And I know a bit about military hardware as well. It's all in my resume."

Sa'id rushed over to a cabinet and retrieved some sweets, which he offered to share with his newfound expert. Uri demurred as the pudgy Iranian gorged himself with sugary treats, grabbing more top-secret American internal communications. "Can you look through these—well, as much as you can—today? It will be most helpful to us." He was overjoyed with his new assistant. What this could mean to the Republic! Not to mention his own career.

"Of course," Uri replied, thinking to himself how much Tom Buckley would be able to make of this new connection. He got to his desk and started reading the American DOD messages. He spent the rest of the afternoon reading and analyzing the documents, surreptitiously hiding a few notes in his briefcase. They would be undecipherable to anyone else. At the end of the day, he made a big show of returning the stolen American transmissions to Sa'id, saying he would try to finish by the next day. Sa'id grinned with pride as he said to Uri, "Shab bekheir, Heydar!" Uri responded likewise, saying good evening to his new boss.

Uri returned slightly early from work, savoring what had to be considered a roaring start to his job. He was eager to leave a coded message for Tom at Homeland Security.

He arrived home in the late afternoon; the heat of the day was just beginning to subside. The beautiful Alborz mountains that rose from the northern edge of the city produced a wonderfully cool breeze that in the winter became very cold. It was far different from the sticky heat of the Persian Gulf region that Uri and Lara had suffered through so recently during their last mission. In fact, Uri knew Tehran's weather to be quite similar to that of Denver in the States: warm and dry in the summer; cool and dry in the winter. But it also suffered from the air pollution that plagued the American city. The mountain range offered protection from severe weather but also formed a boundary to adequate ventilation. Clear skies and a plethora of automobiles had led to toxic buildup of nitrogen oxides, known as smog. Hopefully, Uri would be gone before the late summer episodes began. Meanwhile, though, he had more than enough on his plate to keep him from fretting about the weather. He just enjoyed his little walk from the bus stop to the little house that was to be his temporary home.

"Good evening, Heydar," Tala greeted him, opening the door for him even before he reached it. She was all smiles, dressed in a flattering flowered print dress that reached well below her knees. She was, he noticed, wearing heeled pumps that showed well-formed ankles. Don't even think about it, he told himself. "We have a nice roast for dinner tonight; I hope you will like it."

"Yes, I'm sure I will; your meals have been outstanding." He excused himself, saying he would like to lie down for a bit before dinner.

He headed upstairs, needing some time to properly phrase his necessarily brief dispatch to Tom. Hopefully, he would get a quick reply, perhaps even an update on Lara. He put together a synopsis of the day's events, especially a description of the stolen conversations from DOD and his assignment in the translations of them. He sent it on its way to New York, knowing it was some eight and a half hours earlier there. Tom would see it at the beginning of his workday, allowing him to draft a quick reply.

He took a slow, refreshing shower, then checked his in-boxes, both on his local phone and his coded business receiver. It had been only twenty minutes since his transmission to the United States. His Iranian cell phone showed only a greeting from Ms. Hadani at work, welcoming him to the group. However, there was already a detailed response from Tom. His team had hoped for precisely this kind of opportunity to infect the Iranian military efforts. They would first verify Uri's ability to accurately track the US efforts. Tom would transmit, through the same channels that Uri had seen at his new office in Tehran, a "secret" description of a US military rocket test to be conducted in the Pacific the next day. In fact, the message continued, such a test would be run, or appear to be, for all eyes in the sky to see. There would be a launch and an explosion downrange. It was just a test of an existing missile, but an observer would have no way to know that. Then, the "secret" transmissions would report a successful hit on a retired cargo ship with complete details on its position. Satellite data available to the Iranians and their Russian allies would confirm just such an event at that exact geographical location. In fact, a missile firing would occur at the appropriate time followed by a preset explosion on a target ship. This should verify Uri's credentials and ability to break into the Americans' coded messages. He was delighted with this plan; and he knew his new Iranian bosses would be as well.

There was just a short message about Lara: she was still getting settled and had not yet gained employment. Otherwise, all was well with her. Uri lay down on his bed and allowed himself a short rest before dinner; he then came downstairs in fresh clothing. Even with the windows open to allow the evening breeze, he could smell the delicious aroma of a Persian roast. The rest of the family was already seated as Tala brought in the main dish: beef chuck covered with, of all things, rose petals!

"What else do you have in there?" he said, smiling.

"You mean besides the rose petals?" She laughed. "Well, there's sumac, cumin, cinnamon, and lime powder. In case you ever want to try it yourself."

They all dug into the fragrant meal. It was clear to all that Heydar was in a good mood. "You had a good day at work?" Aunt Sarina asked casually.

Uri just relaxed his shoulders and replied, "You could say so, yes, I suppose so. And this roast makes it even better." Tala beamed at him in recognition of the compliment. *Don't get carried away*, Uri thought to himself. He didn't say more as Tala brought in the dessert, fresh fruit from the local farms. "Is it safe to walk around here in the evenings?" he inquired of everyone, not just Tala.

But it was she who immediately answered, "Oh yes, very safe. You can see the mountains in the moonlight, too. Very beautiful." She looked at him as if to ask if he wanted company.

"Thanks, that's just what I need to settle down from a busy day. If you'll excuse me . . ." He stood and headed for the door. He had brought a light leather jacket downstairs. Outside, he went over the day's events once more. *Tomorrow should be even more interesting*, he reasoned. If Tom came through with that transmission and it reached the Operations desk . . .

The evening sky was indeed spectacular. A gentle breeze wiped away the day's smog, revealing the spectacular north mountains in the late twilight. With the traffic noise abated, he could hear the urban bird population in the nearby park. Finches, gulls, and other waterfowl made quite a racket as they dove for leftovers; the Caspian Sea lay just beyond the mountains. Uri walked over a mile through the hilly suburban neighborhood without incident, finally realizing he was quite tired and ready for bed. He headed quietly back to the house and, using the key Tala had given him, made his way noiselessly into the already darkened living room and up the stairs. He dropped onto the bed dressed only in his white

T-shirt and trousers, almost falling asleep in the first few minutes. It was now about 10:00 p.m.

Suddenly, he heard a gentle tap on the door. He rose and opened it to see Tala standing there in the dim light from the single bulb in the hall. She was clad only in a thin cloth robe that was nearly transparent. She had a tray with cups on it, which she held out, smiling at him. "I thought you might want some tea before bed."

What the hell have I got into here? Uri thought anxiously. *This was not in the plan.* He hurriedly thought to find a way out of the situation gracefully. "Oh, that's very kind of you, but actually, I'm already falling asleep. Long day, you know." He tried to appear casual, not in the least intimate.

"That's all right," she replied seemingly unfazed. "Maybe another time." Uri just nodded as he gently closed the door. From now on, he promised himself, he would wear the geeky glasses at home as well as at the office.

* * *

Uri looked forward to the following day at the office. This was to be his first real test to see if the fake secret messages would establish his credentials. He arrived at work tingling with anticipation; he hoped it didn't show. Perhaps it would be seen as the typical first-day syndrome: a new employee trying his best to impress his superiors. He deliberately arrived ten minutes late so the Iranian decoder team could already have received and attempted to analyze the message that they had hopefully stolen from their signal-intercept system.

It started out well. Sa'id had already arrived and appeared very excited to see Uri. "Heydar, come quickly; we have a fresh transmission for you. It's marked 'Most Secret' by the Americans! We are so far unable to unscramble it. Can you have a look at it, first thing? It appears to be delivered to one of their agents identified by the pseudonym 'U37FGI.'"

Uri was exceedingly pleased by this news; this was in fact the moniker Homeland was to use for false dispatches aimed specifically for him. He did his best at looking bewildered at the enthusiasm displayed by Sa'id and his team. It was made easier by the thick glasses that made him seem so innocent. "Yes, of course, let me take a look." He set his briefcase on his desk and fired up his computer as Sa'id handed him the raw message. Uri took his time, glancing around at the eager faces surrounding him. Sa'id, recognizing what he saw as discomfort on the new recruit's face, gently asked the others to give him some privacy. It was, after all, in everyone's best interest to get the stolen dispatch decrypted as soon and as accurately as possible.

Uri put on his earphones and tapped in the keystrokes he had preset to give him the information on the proposed test. He put on quite a show for the team around him. Though they were all pretending to be busy with their own work, it was clear to Uri they were anxiously waiting for his decryption. Uri did his best to demonstrate frustration, followed by an eager display of success as he printed out the preassembled analysis.

Sa'id was the first to rush to the printer. His jaw dropped as he read the transmission. Then, with a huge smile, he clapped the newcomer Heydar on the shoulder and announced to the little assembly: "The Americans are going to test a new midrange rocket in the Pacific, right under our noses! We will be able to see the whole thing with our satellite. What a coup for our team!" Then a little more subdued, he reminded Uri: "Let's hope this comes off as anticipated. We don't want to look like fools." Uri could only trust the same thing. He wanted the success in the worst way.

The next day was Thursday, with the demonstration planned for 2:00 a.m. Pacific time in the United States, which would be 1:30 p.m. in Iran. No doubt, thought Sa'id, to give the Americans a clear view of the impact. He told his superiors immediately; they were a bit skeptical, it seemed to him, but they would pass the information up the chain of command. Sa'id received word back an hour later. There would, in fact, be a satellite in place at that time to view at least part of the exercise: the impact.

Sa'id was ecstatic, if somewhat apprehensive. This could either be a major success for his small Operations team or an embarrassing black eye. If the test failed to come off as promised . . . well, he thought to himself, there was always the excuse that the Americans had failed in their launch attempt. He brought the team together and gave them the rest of the day off, with the insistence that they all show up early the next day to make sure the Americans did not for any reason postpone the test. He looked at Uri with the silent caution that he scan the airwaves for any word of a postponement. Uri caught the drift at once and nodded his acceptance. He would be at work early to check any and all telecommunications from Midway Island. It was there that the test would be supervised. He tried to look calm and confident as he packed up and headed for the door.

It was not yet 1:00 p.m. as Uri caught the bus that would take him to his neighborhood. It was his plan to take a long walk around the parks and bazaars within the Vali Asr area. He didn't want to show up early and allow his eager hostess a suggestion that he was available for any extracurricular activity.

It was another beautiful spring day in the northern part of Tehran. The markets were busy, and he could hear children playing in the schoolyards. There were happy sounds all around, tempered only by the silent admonitions from the somber ayatollah and his acolytes from the ever-present billboards. The smog had even cleared off early due to the northerly breeze off the mountains. Uri sat in a park, made sure he was not being watched, then checked his messages. He was especially concerned for any word from Tom regarding the planned missile launch; there was none. Checking again for unwanted visitors, he sent a cautionary note asking for immediate communiqué of any change in the coming procedure. He was certain that Tom would not allow him to suffer the embarrassment, or worse, of a no-show.

Uri strolled around the parks and food stalls for another two hours until it was the proper time for him to show up at home. He put on his goggles, as he thought of them, and walked slowly to his residence. Tala was right there at the door as he entered, feigning exhaustion. "A troubling day?" she inquired immediately.

"Tiring, to say the least," he offered with a weak smile. "And I must be there early tomorrow as well."

"Oh, that is too bad," she said, somewhat disappointed. "I thought you might like to go to a movie . . . or something."

"Not tonight, I'm afraid," he said, hoping she would get the message.

"And why the spectacles?" she inquired.

"Oh, I was so busy, I even forgot to take them off," he said sheepishly, as he headed slowly for the stairway to his room.

"Dinner will be as usual, Heydar," she called after him; he just nodded with a tired sigh.

On reaching his room, he removed his shoes and searched his secret phone for anything from Tom. He didn't have much reason to think he would hear this soon; it was only about 6:00 a.m. in New York. But there it was: *Everything on schedule. Proceed as planned.* Brief and to the point. He washed up, put his shoes back on, and without even changing clothes from his workday, walked slowly down to dinner.

To the casual observer, Uri looked like a tired working man after a long day, looking forward to a restful dinner and sleep without much else on his mind. The three members of his "family" looked at him sympathetically; they recognized a person who had had a tough day. Tala smiled and, without a bit of rancor over her rejection the previous night, said, "You still have on your glasses, you know."

"Oh yes, I guess I'm even more tired than I realized."

"We will just have dinner and let you go to bed. You have to be at work early tomorrow?"

"Yes, I'm afraid so." Uri had not given them any idea of what he was up to; they only knew him as an antigovernment agent whom they were ready and willing to support. But he could tell they were extremely curious about his real role. However, he continued the performance as the tired and listless office worker. Inside, he was a ball of nerves, ready to follow through with the missile firing set for the following day. While he picked at his food, his mind whirled with every detail of the test. It simply had to go off as planned, or his role as the expert analysis agent would be destroyed.

"If you'll excuse me, I really do have to go to bed. I have to leave for work at five in the morning, so I will just pick up something for breakfast at the booth in our building downtown." He rose, folded his napkin, and trudged wearily to the stairs.

"You will come with us to prayers on Friday, will you not, Heydar?" Aunt Sarina pleaded.

Uri had completely forgotten about the Friday Jumu'ah services. He immediately turned and replied, "Of course, I will be most pleased to join you." He was fully prepared to join in the Shia religious observance. The family, especially Tala, beamed at his response. He would spend the day with them, dinner and whatever else they had in store.

The next morning came early. Uri slept little, going over and over the day's plans. On rising, his first business was to check his phones. There were no messages. Tom was not one to risk unnecessary communications. He headed to the bus stop in the predawn semidarkness. Even the normally chatty birds nesting in the trees had not begun their standard conversations. Only the earliest of commuters rode the bus at this hour. He had plenty of room to sit and consider all the things that might go wrong. He transferred as usual midway on his commute, now standing for the short remaining trip. He practically burst through the door as the bus reached his intersection, half jogging to his building, his briefcase under his arm, his identification badge already around his neck.

The guard merely nodded to him as he hastily signed in and bounded up the stairs. Aside from Sa'id, he was the only one already there. His boss seemed as full of nervous energy as he, just as eager to see this intelligence coup come to fruition. For different reasons, of course, but he could smell a promotion if it were to come off as planned. As far as Sa'id knew, no other part of the Iranian military had a hint of this missile launch. In fact, his superiors were very skeptical of the veracity of the intercepted message concerning the event. Sa'id was certain they would be as curious as he to see if it indeed came off as he anticipated. They had, as far as he knew, never been privy to such information.

Uri gave a brief greeting to the excited Sa'id as he headed to the small refreshment counter to get something for breakfast. The food stand on the second floor was surprisingly similar to those in Israel or any American office building. He got a cup of hot coffee and a packaged breakfast bar. That would serve him until near "launch" at 1:30 p.m. local time. He came back to the office as the others arrived, as excited as he at the upcoming event.

Ms. Hadani was the last to arrive, as nervous as the others. She glanced at Uri, who was making himself busy, scanning all the incoming news on the non-classified wire. There was nothing at all to suggest that the few Iranian military observation planes or satellites had seen any activity in the mid-Pacific. Finally, at one o'clock, Uri went back to the little food stand to get some juice and snacks in preparation for the upcoming shot. He did not dare to check his secret phone for messages from Homeland. It was too late now to do anything about it.

At precisely 1:33 p.m., there was a burst of electronic chatter on the military wire. An American missile launch had been detected in the Northern Mariana Islands by both planes and satellite; it appeared to be headed in a southeasterly direction toward an unknown target. The room erupted in cheers; Uri was at the center of the congratulations. Sa'id quieted everyone as they awaited news of the path and impact. As Uri had predicted, the path was maintained, and at 2:58 p.m., an impact was reported just east of the Marquesas Islands. First reports were of a vessel being struck; it was moored in open water, and there were no distress calls as it quickly sank.

There was near pandemonium; the room exploded as if it were New Year's Eve. Uri was pummeled by his coworkers. All they awaited was official word from "upstairs," verifying the news. Uri welcomed the applause as casually as possible; after all, he had done nothing more than report a captured enemy signal. In less than ten minutes, the phones were ringing. The people in headquarters, housed on the sacred sixth floor, were asking Sa'id—no, ordering him—upstairs ASAP with all of his pertinent intelligence on the launch. Sa'id started on his way to the elevator, then turned back and told Uri to come with him and bring the deciphered, classified intercept. Uri, trying his best to hide his elation, did as told.

As they arrived upstairs, it was clear that this was a monumental event. Never had the offices of the Operations branch broken into the securest of American transmissions. If they could do this, there might be no limit to the extent of their reach. Plans for an incursion, even for a cooperative venture with the hated Israelis, might be made available. The operatives in the sixth-floor offices were on their feet, many in military uniform, applauding the pair as they arrived. Uri had surreptitiously turned off the power to his secret phone before they entered the offices; he didn't know how sophisticated their detection systems were.

How had this new arrival, Heydar, performed this feat? Uri did have some declassified documentation to try to satisfy the curiosity of the gathered group of military and civilian administrators. Amid the celebration, one man stayed seated at his large, gleaming desk. He wore what Uri recognized as the bars of a brigadier general in the Revolutionary Guard. The general stared at the unimposing new middle-aged man steadily, directly into his beer-bottle spectacles. There was a long silence as the two men gazed at each other. Then finally, the silver-haired general broke into a broad grin, rose, and grasped the newcomer's hand, his other hand reaching around Uri's shoulders. "You have indeed done a great service to the nation, my friend," he growled.

You should only know, Uri thought as he accepted the plaudits of the gathered officials. They insisted on knowing more details of his successful signal interception, which Uri deflected with obscure explanations with phrases like "elliptical transmissions" and "hole-in-time technology." But the room was too drunk with elation for anyone to try to understand what the rock star of the moment was talking about. They settled for a highly condensed version of his manufactured schooling and experience, taken directly from his resume. The festivities lasted well past 3:00 p.m., when the work day was scheduled to conclude.

Sa'id and his now-famous employee headed back downstairs to their offices. There, his teammates were all over him, complete with cheers and congratulations. Sa'id calmed everyone down, reminding them that the workweek was now concluded; they would commence again on Sunday, as usual. As everyone packed up to leave, returning all classified documents to the safe in the outer office, Ms. Hadani's interoffice phone jangled loudly. Something was up. Everyone stopped and waited for the office manager to answer it. After just a brief pause, she drew Sa'id and Uri over to her desk. Covering the phone, she said just loud enough for all to hear: "It's the chief of operations—at the Castle. They want to see you, Heydar, first thing Sunday morning. Bring all your gear."

There was no doubt in anyone's mind; Heydar was being transferred to headquarters, in the Castle. After just one week on the job! The staff looked on in awe as he packed his meager possessions into his briefcase. Sa'id signed and Ms. Hadani cosigned the release that was taped over his locked case. That gave the guard at the front door authorization for "Heydar" to leave the building with it, as long as the release form hadn't been torn open.

Uri knew something about the Castle. It was a medieval structure just northeast of the city in the foothills of the mountains. The ancient fortification had been converted into a secret office building strongly believed to be the location of the headquarters of Iran's military apparatus. Before Uri left, Sa'id told him that transportation to the Castle would be available for him on his arrival at work Sunday morning.

The speed with which all this was happening was making Uri's head spin. He could hardly wait to brief Tom on these events and get his reaction to them. What instructions would he receive? Uri was glad they had two full days for the plans to develop and be transmitted to him.

Chapter 11

Lara made her incursion into Tehran without incident on the same day as Uri. After a long trip in the blazing sun the jeep carrying her and her friendly escorts finally made its way into the southern outskirts of the bustling city of Tehran. She had to admit, at least to herself, that she felt unusually vulnerable here in these surroundings on her own. She knew, of course, that the network of counter-revolutionaries had been going strong for more than twenty years, so she wasn't, strictly speaking, alone.

The US Department of Homeland Security had overseen activities in Iran ever since the department was established a year after the heinous attacks of September 11, 2001. The DHS had nearly a quarter-million employees, with an annual budget of over $40 billion. Most of this allocation of personnel and money was spent on issues involving the Middle East. Originally, since the 9/11 terrorists were all Arabs, the focus had been on the Saudis and their allies. Now, however, the center of attention had shifted to Iran. Knowing these facts gave her some degree of comfort. The hidden assets the United States had in Iran were behind her, even though not always immediately visible.

The transport from her landing spot on the Persian Gulf Coast to Tehran was a jeep, similar to Uri's. There were in her jeep, however, two Iranian women agents, schooled in the States. That gave her a great deal of assurance. She was also pleased to find that her residence was in a very modern area on the western edge of the city, with parks, museums, and apartment buildings. Pulling up to the door of her new home, she found it to be in a quiet neighborhood southwest of the downtown, with a plethora of schools, shopping centers, and monuments.

To her great relief, two women greeted her on arrival at the two-story dwelling just three blocks from a modern mall. The women, who introduced themselves as Faezeh and Sara, were very different in appearance. Faezeh was a large middle-aged woman with brown hair and intense black eyes. She seemed to be the person in charge. Her companion was almost the opposite. She was a small woman, about thirty years of age, with a mild, soft-spoken manner. They both greeted her in English with almost no detectable accent, each giving her a warm, friendly hug. Lara returned the pleasantries but using her excellent Farsi. The two Iranians gasped in astonishment at her facility with the dialect; they recognized that from here on, the conversation would be carried out in the Iranian language. No other occupants of the house were apparent; it was just as she had been briefed.

Lara's escorts brought her bags from the jeep, and after a brief exchange, excused themselves and headed back to their vehicle. "Sit down, please," Faezeh said pleasantly to her new housemate. Sara just nodded in agreement. Lara felt immediately at home with the two and saw no imminent difficulties. They chatted for about twenty minutes, Sara bringing in a platter of hot tea and Persian cakes. The two hosts detected Lara's tiredness almost immediately; she'd had practically no sleep for the past twenty-four hours. Looking at Faezeh for affirmation, Sara suggested to Lara that she might wish to see her room and "freshen up."

What a great idea, thought Lara silently as she smiled agreeably and followed Sara up the stairs to a small second floor that had four closed doors on the hall. Lara was grateful to find that her room was to be the last along the corridor, with an adjoining bathroom that also opened from the hall. There was a double bed, mirror, and washstand in the bedroom, along with a desk, chair, personal computer, and television in the corner. "Delightful!" Lara uttered in honest approval, to the clear pleasure of her hosts.

"We can have dinner at eight if that suits," Faezeh suggested.

"Of course, that would be great," Lara responded, noting that allowed her a couple of hours to shower, rest, and change. Faezeh nodded and placed Lara's bags on the floor by the bed. Lara was so relaxed at this point, she hadn't even realized that she had left the bags right where her "chauffeurs" had put them on arrival. She lay down on the bed, set her internal alarm for one hour, and fell instantly asleep.

Just about an hour later, she heard a gentle tap on her door. *So much for my internal alarm,* she thought to herself. "Be right there," she remembered to say in Farsi. She found she was even thinking in the Iranian language these days.

Lara first unpacked her bags, placing her clothes neatly in the bureau provided. There were the work clothes that had been picked out for her: the western-style loose-fitting long-sleeved shirts and equally loose-fitting tan slacks that came down to just above her ankles. For her off-work hours, she had brightly colored blouses and full skirts. No skin or body curvature must show at any time, of course. To top things off, so to speak, she had a variety of plain and flowered head scarves, in keeping with modern Iranian custom.

She dressed quickly, then remembered to wet her contact lenses. She had gotten used to them amazingly well; but she took every opportunity to use the special fluid she had been given. That item taken care of, she trotted quickly down the stairs. The table was already set as Faezeh came in from the kitchen with a platter heaped with skewers of what appeared to be beef and lamb, interspersed with onions, carrots, and other vegetables. The entire platter was covered in rose petals, giving it an amazingly charming appearance. There was also a delicious-looking salad and a pitcher of cold, sparkling water. A plate of warm, homemade bread and olive oil sat in the center of the square dining-room table. *I couldn't have ordered anything better,* Lara thought. She noticed the implied but not obvious intimacy between the two women: the way they seemed to know what each other would choose to eat, the warm friendliness they shared. She presumed them to be a couple, which was just fine with her.

Faezeh controlled the conversation. There was no discussion of her mission, background, or capabilities; only talk of the city, transportation, and sights. It was as if she were any tourist visiting Tehran for the first time. Lara was feeling more and more comfortable. Dinner proceeded with a slow, friendly pace until Lara noticed by the hall clock that it was approaching 9:00 p.m. She made her excuses to her hosts, thanking them for the wonderful meal, but noting she had appointments beginning early the next day, Monday. They understood completely and rose as she did, wishing her a sound sleep.

"But first," Sara interrupted, "we must give you your local mobile phone. It was purchased from a reliable vendor here in town." She smiled knowingly. Lara accepted it gratefully; this was as expected, even though it seemed a bit odd to have this connection with her hosts.

Before going to bed, she needed to check in with Tom, see if there was any news for her or word from Uri. Sure enough, there was a message on her secret DHS phone, tailored to appear like a commercial Iranian model. If ever questioned as to why she had two mobile phones, she was to say that one was not operating well, so she had purchased the other but had not transferred all phone numbers as yet. If anyone other than Lara tried to open the DHS phone, it simply would fail to function; it was just like Uri's in that regard.

She was pleased to hear that Uri had arrived safe and sound around the same time as she. He was living in a neighborhood a few miles east of her in a similar private home. They, of course, were not to communicate directly. The news was reassuring; she could imagine him nearby. She responded with the code for "everything normal." On that pleasant note, she got up and opened the single window in her room. The cool nighttime breeze was already wafting down from the nearby mountains; along with the wonderful songs of the nightingales, Lara fell quickly asleep.

Chapter 12

Six thirty a.m. arrived too soon. Lara awoke refreshed and immediately checked for messages; thankfully, there were none. She then switched to thinking about her first appointment that morning. It was for an experienced cryptologist, something in which her resume showed she had abundant training and experience. Of course, that was true, except that most of it was gained at the NSA, the US National Security Agency. She had, in fact, two years' experience unscrambling Iranian intercepts the agency gathered. She had no real way to know what lay in store for her; this particular job she was interviewing for was with a company carrying the nebulous title "Information Systems Specialists."

She found that Faezeh and Sara had prepared a wonderful breakfast of cereal and light cream along with dates and figs, fresh from the market. She had her choice of sweet tea or strong, hot Persian coffee; she chose the latter for a quick wake-up call. Then it was off to her job hunt.

Two bus transfers brought her into the bustling downtown. Granite and concrete towers loomed overhead, along with the incredible noise of cars, trucks, and motorcycles. It seemed as if everyone was honking at the same time. She also noticed a slight brown tint to the air, accompanied by an acrid smell. Smog had found Tehran. Visibility was limited to about a half mile.

It was relatively easy to find her target; it matched precisely with the tourist map she had used in training. The ten-story office building had a modern directory on the wall. Information Systems Specialists occupied the top two floors. She rode up the elevator with a pack of six men, all dressed in western-looking suits, all of whom got out on the lower floors. When she arrived on the ninth floor, which was as far as this elevator went, she found a small lobby in front of glazed-glass walls. Two uniformed men armed with automatic pistols pinned her with their stares as she exited the elevator, carrying her professional-looking briefcase. Lara was clad in the most modest of business suits, the skirt reaching well below her knees. Her hair was almost completely covered with a headscarf that did not, however, cover her face. It was a costume for women widely accepted these days in urban Iran.

In fact, a similarly dressed woman sat at the desk just a few feet in front of the elevator door. She was the only one smiling, other than Lara, who was trying her best to put on a brave front. Her pulse, had they been able to monitor it, would have given her away. It was racing at around 120 beats per minute.

The receptionist asked nicely if she could be of service. Lara put her briefcase on the table in front of her and looked through it for her official invitation for the interview. As she did so, both armed guards, glowering, brought their weapons up to a ready position. Pretending not to notice, Lara drew out the invitation for the receptionist to examine. There was no nameplate in front of her; in fact, there was no identification of any kind that Lara could see. However, as she bent down to examine Lara's papers, the badge on her blouse showed her name as Mrs. Khorasani. The gray-haired middle-aged woman said nicely, "Oh yes, Daria, we've been expecting you. So glad you could come by," as though this were some sort of social engagement.

Lara smiled in return as the guards relaxed a bit and dropped their weapons from the ready position. "Let me first give you a temporary pass so that you may come and go as you wish." She brought forth a name badge on a metal chain, which Lara immediately put around her neck. "Now then, please have a seat while I have your instructors tell you about your interview."

Two men appeared almost at once, though Lara did not see Mrs. Khorasani push any buttons. The young men, Ali and Habib, as their name tags identified them, emerged from the double doors behind them. Lara sprang up from her chair, bringing her right hand up to greet them. The two men, however, made no move to shake her hand, so she dropped it to her side and just smiled at them. Mrs. Khorasani nodded at Lara as if to say, "They're very young, forgive them."

Lara bowed politely and followed the two men through the double doors into a room with a glass-windowed door. They pointed to a chair in front of a desk, on which there was a sheaf of printed text next to two blank pads and three sharpened pencils. The larger of the two men, Ali, said to Lara bluntly, "You are to decode this. You will have fifty minutes." He moved his considerable bulk just enough to let Lara pass. She nodded politely to both men and sat, without again offering her hand. She took a second to place her briefcase on the floor in the far corner of the room, clearly out of her reach. Habib, a small man with steel-rimmed glasses, glanced at Ali, then both exited the room without another word. But she could see them sitting just outside the door, brazenly watching her as she scanned the document.

It was apparently an instructional briefing, headed in English as: "Ministry of Defence and Armed Forces Logistics." She noted the British spelling of the word Defence and recognized it as a training manual from prerevolutionary Iran. From there, it was all in Farsi. Lara almost smiled as she started into it; she had read this document as part of her initial training in the language and had actually translated it from this same exact basic, alphanumeric code. She did not, however, show any emotion as she furrowed her brow and began; she knew the two young men were watching her attentively.

Lara did use some theatrics as she paused several times at each line of text, scratching some notes on the spare pad. After forty minutes, she read through her three pages of the decrypted manual, carefully checking each word. She then looked up, saw both her escorts scrutinizing her intently, and nodded for them to come in. They did, and as Ali took the pad from her, he told her authoritatively to wait for them to return. Lara did so, casually looking around the bare room. There was one window, through which she could see a courtyard with a fountain in the middle. A group of finches was busily drinking, bathing, and quarreling, keeping her from worrying needlessly.

Fully thirty minutes later, Mrs. Khorasani arrived at Lara's room, accompanied by a bushy-mustachioed man in a brown uniform emblazed with medals, reminiscent of Soviet-era officers. He carried the insignia of a colonel. "This is Colonel Bijan Soroush, aide-de-camp to the general," the receptionist informed Lara. "He inspected your decryption." She smiled at Lara; apparently, it was good news.

His medals jingled as the colonel reached out across the desk to shake Lara's hand. He was a slim, well-groomed, highly-refined man, no more than forty years of age. His thick mustache seemed oddly out of place, but this was, after all, Iran. She was pleased when he shook her hand as if she were a male colleague, firm and dignified. He spoke to her in quiet, educated tones. "Well, Ms. Haddad, I must say I am very impressed, both with your decryption and your knowledge of technical Farsi. Where is it you were educated?"

Lara rose to meet him. "As you see on my introductory papers, I was trained formally at a military base in Esfahan. The exact name and location, I'm afraid, are classified; but you will see that all the appropriate documentation is as required."

"Yes," he said, nodding approvingly as he scanned the dossier that had come in with her application. "I don't happen to know any of these people personally, but I certainly know of them. Very capable. And, I must say, you made quick work of the decryption. It's almost as if you had written the original." Fortunately, he laughed, covering her almost instantaneous blush, visible through her darkened skin. "Well, why don't you take a few minutes to get some refreshments while we find you something a little more challenging?"

Lara smiled her approval of that idea, took her briefcase, and left for the washroom. She did not dare to take anything from it as she washed up and straightened her hair, making a mental note to touch-up her roots. *Who knew who was watching and listening?* After an appropriate amount of time, she returned, grabbing a cup of drinking water on the way back to her little office. There was Col. Soroush, holding another sheaf of papers, this one with a noticeable blue band around the edge of every page. Lara knew immediately this signified highly classified documentation in any military establishment.

"This may give you a bit more challenge; we've allotted two hours for it . . . you did say you're fluent in English, is that not so?"

Without bothering to answer, Lara took the classified document to her seat and quickly scanned it. She knew at once what it was, or at least, what class of coding she would be dealing with. It was a Distributed Common Ground System, or DCGS, software developed by the RAND Corporation for the CIA. There was no way she was going to be able to decrypt this without access to the software package hidden in her agency cell phone. And there was no way they were going to let her take it with her! She thought for only a few seconds, looking at the clock on the wall, as she said to the colonel, "This will take some time to decode. And I'm afraid I have another two interviews set for today. Is there any way you can possibly reschedule this for tomorrow morning?" She smiled as she handed the papers back to the intense-looking army officer.

Col. Soroush thought about that for just a few seconds before deciding. He did not want to lose this potentially valuable agent. "Yes, of course. That is perfectly acceptable. We will see you tomorrow at the same time, eight a.m.?"

"Absolutely, Colonel, I'm looking forward to it!" she replied brightly, full of enthusiasm, only partially faked. Meanwhile, she repeated the coded title of the document to herself, forcing it to memory: *IAPG-SYSXXOPG 195446-96.* She said her goodbyes and headed for the door; she was impatient to get to a sheltered spot where she could write it down.

Instead of heading toward the bus stop and her next appointment, for which she had plenty of time, Lara took off her ID badge and placed it in her briefcase, then walked to a park that was out of sight of the office building. On the corner was a newsstand where an older man with a face bronzed by the sun held copies of the morning newspaper. She bought one from him, her eyes covered with sunglasses. Then, sitting on a vacant bench with the newspaper in front of her, she reached into her briefcase for her secret phone and dialed Tom's private line. Dozens of pigeons and gulls searched in vain at her feet for some scraps of food as she irritably waited for the outgoing message to finally finish.

It was near midnight in New York, but she hoped Tom would get it by at least 6:00 p.m. in Tehran. That would give her all night to deal with his response. She gave him all the details of her interview, including the top-secret memo she had seen just briefly, and of course, its coded title. Then there was nothing more she could do about the DCGS translation for the next few hours, at least. She walked around a bit to cool off before her next interview, then hopped on a bus, following her prearranged transport to a location just a few miles away.

The first of the afternoon's appointments was a disappointment, especially when compared with that of the morning. Despite the organization's promising title of Governmental Systems Analysis, its province was quite mundane. It handled only the most routine of semiofficial business, dealing only with employment insurance and the like. But in order to maintain her status as a worker from another province seeking employment, she went ahead with the interview. It turned out to be nothing but a pro forma affair, as the man she needed to see was out of town. Could she reschedule for the following week? She accepted and left the building.

By then, it was already 3:00 p.m., and Lara hadn't had anything to eat since early morning. She perused the neighborhood and settled on an outdoor café displaying falafels and kebobs. Noting the time, she decided to try to reschedule the last appointment, which turned out to be fine with the representative she reached on her local mobile. They would be happy to see her the following Monday.

To Lara's extreme delight, as she checked her classified phone, there was a message waiting for her from Tom. Brief and to the point, he told her the title she had transmitted to him was indeed that of a top-secret joint program between the United States and Israel. The two governments had agreed to develop a defensive missile program that was a substantial advance on the successful "Iron Dome" platform. The Iron Dome protected Israel from the Iranian-supplied short-range offensive rockets that Hamas was using to terrorize Israeli citizens in the south of the country.

He told her that he would have the coded epigram decoded, translated into English, and sent to her agency phone via CSCS, Commercial Solutions for Classified Systems. She was to learn the document well enough to translate it into Farsi and then "burn it." That is, once she had it memorized, she would remove it from her hard disk and any other temporary locations. There would be key errors in the transcription; it would be highly suspicious, and dangerous, otherwise.

This was indeed fine with her; she immediately replied to Tom that she would await the promised message and carry out his orders. So, Lara was in high spirits as she headed home. It would take all of the coming evening to memorize the translation promised from Homeland.

Lara arrived at her neighborhood bus stop at the height of afternoon traffic; it was also the height of the afternoon smog, and her eyes were burning. She hustled to her home away from home and her friendly hostesses. Both Faezeh and Sara eagerly awaited her; she apologized and excused herself for a few minutes. The smog, she explained. "Oh yes, it must be quite annoying for visitors," Sara offered knowingly.

Lara headed for her private bathroom and flushed her eyes with the cleansing solution, washed her face and hands, touched-up her roots and returned to the living room. "Everything is just fine," Lara assured the two women. But if they were waiting for more specifics, they would be disappointed; Lara had nothing more for their ears. In fact, she was eager to get to her phone to see if Homeland had come through with the promised transcription.

Dinner was a pleasant affair. The food was delicious, as usual. Conversation was limited to the traffic and the smog. "Yes," Lara commiserated, both were irritating, but she was able to deal with them. Sara had prepared a small cake, but Lara apologized, saying that she really had some pressing business to deal with, as well as an early appointment in the morning. The lightly built woman seemed a bit hurt by this rebuff, but she seemed to understand that their guest was under severe restrictions in her social life. Lara made as polite an exit as possible, heading for her room and her mobile phones.

First, to get them out of the way, she dealt with the remaining rescheduling issues on her local phone as best she could; then, with her heart beating a tattoo in her chest, she checked her agency phone. To her great relief, she found a long document in English waiting for her. She had to immediately acknowledge receipt or it would self-destruct, she knew, so she did that before proceeding. She then translated the English document into Farsi, writing it on a blank pad she had in her briefcase. After checking it over twice, she erased the message from all locations in her agency phone. It was a bit over 800 words, well within her capacity for memorization, especially since they were her own words, Farsi translated from English.

She noted as she was learning the memo that no essential information was detailed; nothing that could be useful to the Iranian offensive-missile program. Still, the knowledge that the United States was teaming with Israel to fortify an already powerful defense system would be frightening to the ayatollah's regime. The present Iron Dome system was proving a mighty asset against their illegitimate attacks on civilian targets.

Lara stayed up past 2:00 a.m. memorizing the manuscript verbatim. This was an exercise all agents at the FBI and NSA had to be able to handle, even in the most uncomfortable situations. When she was able to accomplish this feat three times in a row without error, she tore the paper into bits and flushed them down the toilet. For safety, she did the same with the top four blank pages underneath. She then lay down, but before allowing herself to sleep, she repeated the exercise. She was ready.

Morning came early, but Lara allowed herself an hour extra sleep, setting the alarm on her local phone for 6:30 a.m. She awoke fresh and ready for the day's activity; this was an exercise with which she was quite familiar from her work in the field. Her contact lenses freshly watered, she came rushing downstairs and gave her hosts a brief farewell, saying she might even be back early, but she would have to miss breakfast. Sara, however, convinced her to take a buttered muffin to eat on the bus.

Traffic was pleasantly light that morning, as was the smog, she was happy to find. She arrived fifteen minutes early for her appointment. Lara slipped on her temporary ID badge and walked in the door. Both Mrs. Khorasani and Col. Soroush were there waiting for her, the document in the colonel's hands. The pleasant receptionist asked Lara if she would like some coffee, and to appear perfectly at ease, Lara accepted the offer, following the colonel to the same little office she had occupied the day before. There was already a fresh pad of paper in front of her, along with three sharpened pencils. Lara took the coffee from Mrs. Khorasani and sat primly in the chair, after thanking her for the coffee.

Only then did she glance at the front page of the document the colonel laid on the table. She was relieved to see on the cover leaf the descriptor: *IAPG-SYSXXOPG 195446-96*. Lara was ready. However, she first rose from the chair, placing her briefcase in the corner as the day before. The colonel glowered at her, a little incredulous that this woman was really about to perform the given task without any aids at all, not even a dictionary. But Lara just smiled and said pleasantly, "I'll wave when I've finished," indicating she was certain he would be watching. His eyebrows lifted just a bit as he and Mrs. Khorasani left the room, the colonel taking a seat just outside the glass window in the door.

Lara adjusted her chair just a bit, not glancing up, and started reading the now-familiar top-secret manuscript. She knew she was performing before an audience, so she pretended to have difficulty at first, then surprise at finding the nature of the stolen document. Her speed increased as she appeared to become familiar with the content. It took her just over an hour to complete the translation; but to finish the charade, she went back over it, crossing out a few words, and replacing them with "corrections." Only then did she wave at the colonel, who was indeed watching from a chair just outside the door.

"If it's all right," she said brightly to the colonel, handing him the entire pad, "I'd like to freshen up a bit."

"Yes, of course," he replied, not quite able to accept the fact that she had finished her translation.

Lara headed to the washroom with her briefcase, washed her hands, and took the opportunity to cleanse her contacts before returning. She found the colonel talking agitatedly with Mrs. Khorasani and another military-appearing man but in civilian clothes. As she arrived at their chairs, the discussion ceased, and the colonel introduced the dignified-looking newcomer as "Mr. Gharoub, from our G-6 Section." He did not hold out his hand, so Lara did not offer hers. But she noted that the Iranians made no secret of their intelligence section, G-6, having adopted the nomenclature of the Western militaries.

"Please, come have a seat in my office," Col. Soroush said pleasantly, leading the little group down the hall to a tall wooden door with his name on it. They all took their seats, except for Mrs. Khorasani, who, after a quiet word with the colonel, excused herself and headed out the door, silently closing it behind her. The colonel seated himself behind the desk, with the civilian from G-6 sitting on his left. Lara waited patiently, very curious to see their reaction.

"I must say, Ms. Haddad, your translation was quite impressive," the colonel began without prelude. Mr. Gharoub remained impassive. "I have to tell you that, with a few minor exceptions, yours was essentially the same as our own staff's." He looked over at Gharoub, who simply stared at Lara. "How were you able to translate the document so well, without reference to any decoding aids?"

Lara smiled knowingly. "Oh, you see, as I told you yesterday, I've had training at one of our secret bases outside Esfahan. I'm afraid I can't disclose any details, as you must know, but we had access to the particular DCGS the Americans used here." She gestured at the document on the desk. "Once you've transcribed a few of their communiqués, it comes easily."

Gharoub listened intently; he seemed quite impressed, Lara was certain. He might even have an idea what particular base she was referring to—the one used by the notorious Sheikh Abidin responsible for the slaughter of so many Americans. But he said nothing; he simply sat there with just the hint of a smile crossing his lips. He then motioned to Col.

Soroush, who beamed at Lara, rising from his chair and escorting her to the door.

"May we reach you by phone later today or tomorrow?" the colonel asked pleasantly.

"Yes, of course," Lara replied, handing her temporary pass to a delighted Mrs. Khorasani, who was sitting at her desk. Lara felt almost giddy as she left the building. It was now past 1:00 p.m., and she was beyond hunger, having little to nothing for breakfast. She found another snack shop with kabobs broiling in the display case, sat down and quickly devoured one as she considered what might happen next. There was another small park in the next block, out of sight of the office building. She found an empty bench and phoned Tom to report on the morning's events, including the presence of Gharoub from G-6. Then, feeling relieved of immediate responsibility, she strolled around the park, scattering leavings of her lunch to the eager avian scavengers at her feet. Then it was time to head home; the afternoon smog had made itself known to her eyes in a major way.

It was just past 4:00 p.m. when she arrived at her dwelling, to the eager greetings of her hosts. "How was your day?" both women asked at once.

"Oh, fine," she said calmly. "Just a bit tiring is all." In fact, her late night and tense morning interview had taken their toll. She needed a short rest before any thoughts of dinner and conversation. With regrets, she asked the ladies if it would be all right if she showered and changed before dinner. Eager to please, they assured her that would be fine. Lara went upstairs, sat on the bed and kicked her shoes off. Then she checked her local mobile phone for any messages. There was, in fact, a brief one from Mrs. Khorasani: Mr. Gharoub from Military Intelligence, G-6, would very much like to see her in the morning at his office at another location. If she could return this call, she would receive further instructions. But it was made very clear they were going to make her an offer of a position with their section! Thoughts of rest vanished as she hurried to return Gharoub's call before the end of the business day. The mysterious man answered on the first ring; there was not even a secretary.

Lara tried not to appear overly excited as she spoke to him but realized it was likely in vain. In any event, he was brief and to the point as he repeated his invitation. If she was interested in his offer, could she simply show up at the same office building tomorrow morning at, say, nine o'clock? There, a car would pick her up for transport to his offices. She noted that no names or addresses were transmitted in this open telephone conversation. She accepted the offer, hoping her heartbeat was not too evident. Then, breathing a sigh of relief and elation, she checked her agency phone.

There was indeed a message from Tom, received just minutes earlier. It was now around 4:00 a.m. in New York. *Call at once*, the message said. She took a deep breath, checked the hallway for visitors, then went into her bathroom. With the water running, she called in.

"Any news?" Tom asked without prelude.

"In fact, yes. I've been offered a job with their G-6! I'm getting the formal proposal tomorrow."

"Outstanding," he replied. "FYI, this Gharoub is one nasty customer. He's high up in the Revolutionary Guard, been with them since the beginning. He's a full general with their version of Black Ops. We've been trying to get him for years." By this, Lara presumed Tom meant "trying to eliminate him." "Do whatever you have to—within limits, of course— but get inside if you can. I don't need to tell you this is a high-risk situation."

"Any idea what's going on? I mean, what sort of Black Ops are we talking about?"

"There's word that their offices are not happy about how the Los Angeles affair turned out—if you get my drift." She did; this was turning out to be just what they were after.

"I got it, and I'm on it. Any word from you know who ?"

"That's a positive." Her heart leaped. "Nothing certain yet, though. I'll keep you informed. Let me know how tomorrow goes."

Chapter 13

Lara was met the next morning in front of the office building she had been to the previous two days. A black Mercedes limousine with heavily tinted windows sat idling at the red curb, a uniformed man in mirrored sunglasses standing at the passenger door. He was carrying a leather briefcase and wearing a .45 caliber sidearm on his hip. Seeing her arrive from the bus stop, he stepped forward and, without smiling, asked quietly, "Ms. Haddad?" He was holding her photograph in his left hand. The guard from the front desk, whom Lara recognized, nodded subtly to both Lara and the man in sunglasses. Seeing her acceptance, the man opened the passenger door for her, then stepped to attention. The front desk guard smiled briefly at her, then saluted as she entered the limo. The passersby seemed unconcerned with this chain of events, moving on their way without any show of alarm.

She sat in a wonderfully comfortable seat, by herself, as the uniformed man at the curb entered the right-side front door, and the Mercedes slid silently away. The limo was delightfully air-conditioned; the smog that she had actually become used to suddenly vanished, much to her delight. The uniformed escort removed his cap, exposing a military-style haircut. He turned, opened a sliding-glass panel, and politely asked Lara if she would like some refreshments. The trip would take only about twenty minutes, but there was hot coffee and bottled water just below, right at her fingertips. "The general will be delighted to see you," he added, referring of course to the mysterious Gharoub.

"Thank you, but I'm fine," Lara responded as she watched the downtown area slowly change into more opulence. They were headed north into the higher elevation of the foothills of the Alborz mountains, the highest of which showed snow above the haze that enveloped the city. Just as the escort had promised, in less than twenty minutes, the limo glided gracefully toward a gate that blended into a high concrete wall, covered with barbed wire. There was no plaque, no sign of any kind identifying the drab, gray building that lay behind the grim walls. It could have been a prison or military compound; no way to tell.

The driver pulled up a circular driveway, the heavy limo crunching loudly on the pea gravel. Immediately upon their arrival, two uniformed guards sped to Lara's door, as if propelled by a silent spring. One opened her door, the other offering a gloved hand to help her from the car. She accepted it gracefully, thinking, *This must be what it's like to be royalty.* Both men tipped their caps, greeting her in Farsi.

"Welcome to the Ayatollah Khomeini Revolutionary Military Headquarters," said the first.

"All glory to the Revolution," offered the second.

Taken somewhat aback by all this pomp, Lara simply muttered a thank you to both men, smiling at their courtesy. As they entered the building, Lara noticed that, for the first time, she did not have to show credentials or sign the log. The guard at the desk, dressed in a forest-green uniform rather than the standard brown of the men outside this fortress, rose and tipped his cap. He did not salute a civilian woman, Lara noted.

Her escorts led her swiftly down the hall to a tall bronze door, in front of which stood another officer dressed in forest green, his chest covered in medals and ribbons. As Lara approached, he slapped his right hand to his left chest in salutation. If all this ceremony was meant to impress her, it was certainly doing so.

One of her escorts knocked on the metal door, waited just a moment, then swung it open to reveal a room the size of the Oval Office, with a grand Persian carpet in front of a gleaming walnut desk. General Ali Gharoub rose, and with a show of shining, artificially white teeth, offered his hand as he strode around the desk to meet her.

"Ms. Haddad," he exclaimed, "how wonderful of you to come!"

She noticed, in the stark light of the grand room, how painstakingly he had dyed his naturally gray hair to a shiny black. This was a glaringly egotistical man.

"It is my pleasure, General," she replied, smiling indulgently.

"Come here, please, and be seated. Let me tell you why we are so obviously pleased to see you." He gestured to a small table to the left of the bronze doors, waving his hand dismissively at the guards. She sat as the others left, closing the door behind them.

"I'll get right to the point, Ms. Haddad. We were clearly impressed with your cryptological abilities." The general paused for effect, but there was no need; Lara was overwhelmed if not downright intimidated. She struggled to keep her composure.

"Thank you, General, I'm happy to be of service to the Revolution." She almost bit her tongue.

"To come right to the point: you must be aware of the humiliating exposure we suffered in Los Angeles . . . the water supply debacle."

"Of course, General," she offered demurely, lowering her eyes in acknowledgment of his embarrassment.

The general smiled at her courtesy; this was indeed a dignified, intelligent, and attractive woman. Perhaps even . . . he did not pursue his carnal thoughts further. "I have to tell you, it is incumbent on us to now recover from this disgrace in front of the world with a strike that will show them of what we are capable." The precision of his little speech made it clear that he had given it much thought and preparation. She could scarcely wait to see what was in store.

"Of course, General," she repeated.

"You can be of the utmost service in our next foray into the devil's nest. I speak, of course, of our coming strike at the hive of American Jews that resides in the cesspool of California."

"You . . . I mean, we are once again going to attack the waterworks of Los Angeles?!"

Gharoub smiled indulgently at the young woman. She was, quite clearly, as aware as she could be of the activities of his undercover team.

The close call they'd had at the Los Angeles water plant had made news all over the world. There was, as yet, no official public knowledge of Iranian involvement, but the speculation was rampant. The Iranian Revolutionary Government was widely assumed to be fully ready and capable of carrying out such an attack.

The motivation was clear: recent attacks on maritime activities in the Persian Gulf left little doubt as to the perpetrators, official denials notwithstanding. Iran had been carrying out such Black Ops against its foes, both foreign and domestic, ever since the successful revolution of 1979. The bold, if totally illegitimate, takeover of the American embassy in Tehran was just the first of many such audacious attacks. Each such success led to more daring assaults on the enemies of the Revolutionary Government. Now Iran was showing its hold over the international waterway with more and more overt acts: holes appeared in the hulls of foreign vessels; crew members disappeared; cargo was sent to the bottom. There was little doubt of Iran's seemingly de facto ownership of the international waterway. These acts, if responsibility could be proven, were technically acts of war. But who was to prove them? Or take any steps to stop them? The Western nations showed little interest in engaging in a conflict halfway around the world. In fact, recent history had provoked strong distaste for another Vietnam, Iraq, or Afghanistan. The dominance the West had enjoyed over emerging countries had disappeared since World War II. The image the United States and its allies now held was one of slave-masters, not aid-givers. Iran was using this image to its distinct advantage.

"No, my dear, not exactly," he replied quietly, trying to sense her interest and nascent complicity. "But we do have a project just coming to fruition that will show how vulnerable the West is to the forces of Islam."

Lara could scarcely contain her intense curiosity. She hoped her blazing inquisitiveness came across as appeal and not fear. Her body language spoke of growing attractiveness and not repulsion. In fact, she was hoping for a chance to participate in whatever this fiend had in store. She could sense that her compliance was making its mark. Her innate perception as a woman among male colleagues picked up more than professional interest from Gharoub. Even with her artificially darkened skin and deliberately unattractive facial implants, he showed lascivious interest. Well, she had dealt with this before; it was something she could handle, or even use to her advantage.

Gharoub did indeed perceive a positive inclination for what this attractive and apparently available young woman was hearing of these felonious activities. Criminal activities did often provoke sensuality, he had found. No harm if he could combine his favorite pursuits. With this in mind, he proceeded to describe the plans for the second assault on the California water supply.

He sketched out his plan for a commando-style strike against one of the reservoirs serving the San Francisco Peninsula in northern California. Her first assignment would be to carefully watch for civilian and military radio transmissions on this subject. She would be responsible, along with other staff, for capturing any warnings about the water supplies in the area, especially those in highly classified code. She agreed with Gharoub's assessment of the importance of such messages toward the success of Iran's goal: the public display of the impotence of the United States against the Revolutionary Government. They had a very friendly end to the meeting, with the general summoning one of his aides, Captain Maloof, to show her to the communications room and her new office.

The captain was a fortyish man in civilian dress with horn-rimmed glasses and a somewhat timid smile. It was clear from the first that she would now be his superior in matters dealing with the decoding of incoming and scrambling of outgoing messages to the United States and its allies, specifically those dealing with Project Neptune, the name assigned to the disruption of America's drinking water infrastructure.

Lara was somewhat overwhelmed by this level of security. But she quickly realized that there no doubt was parallel infrastructure in place. Gharoub couldn't be so foolish as to put all his eggs in one basket, so to speak.

The rest of the day was spent setting up her office, detailing the computer arrangements and her lines of communication. The space was set up in a manner similar to a large insurance firm. There was a large open area, two stories tall, in the center of the space filled with rows of desks and chairs; these were occupied by clerks and secretaries. The private offices lay along the walls, with the higher-ups having totally private rooms with wooden doors.

Medium-level workers, like Lara, occupied cubicles along the windows, with glass enclosures at eye level. She had a comparatively private space with a medium-size desk, computer, phone, filing cabinet, and a single window facing the parking lot. The partition facing the open area was glass from above eye level, so the privacy was not total. But the ceiling was covered with sound-absorbing tiles, so she was able to concentrate on her papers. There were two visitors' chairs in her space in addition to her swivel chair; she sat facing the opposite wall so as not to be distracted by the people in the rest of the open area.

Maloof immediately introduced her to her staff: two young women to help with office supplies and meals, and a young man, Mobin, who would take care of her transportation. She would be picked up and delivered between the downtown offices and her new base in this fortress in the foothills. She merely had to put in a request at any time. It was a lot to get used to; she was handed a stack of documents to peruse at her leisure. Some she could take with her; others had to remain under lock and key in her office. She put together those she could take home and stuffed them into her briefcase. These mostly had to do with office protocol. The others, mainly classified material, had to be left on her desk or in the file cabinets. All of the latter were marked with the usual blue bands on the edges or margins.

When all these details were taken care of, she had Mobin arrange for her transport downtown. She could have been driven home, but she said she had some errands to run and preferred to take the bus home when she finished. She did not want anyone to know precisely where she lived. In fact, she wanted to get home as quickly as possible in the hopes of speaking with Tom about the day's events. It would be early morning in New York, but he would most likely call as soon as he could, certainly before 7:00 p.m. in Tehran.

That taken care of, she opened her briefcase for the guard and left. She noted that no one here had name tags. The military were all in uniform, and the civilians were known by the guards on sight.

The bus trip home from the downtown office building was uneventful, though her head was spinning. Each day, she decided, she would get off at a different stop so as not to set a pattern; she could use the walk for exercise. Lara had to resist the urge to put anything down on paper, so she focused instead on the late afternoon sunshine and diminished smog. The cool mountain breeze had begun early, and with it the sounds of the birds hunting for scraps of food left on the streets and sidewalks with which to feed their newly hatched young.

Lara finally arrived home, brimming with items to bring to Tom's attention. After assuring her hosts that all was well, she headed upstairs to clean up and rewet her contact lenses. Then, in a hurry, she left a message with Tom that she had important news. It was now around 5:00 a.m. in New York. Luckily, Tom was an early riser. She lay on the bed, with her agency phone set to vibrate, in her hand. Sara would tap on her door when they were set for dinner.

It was less than an hour when the vibrating phone interrupted her light sleep. Tom was alert and ready to hear what she had for him. Lara, who had been rehearsing the news in her head, launched into the details of her day, starting with her new position at the Military Intelligence headquarters. She quickly then got to the most important issue: the impending attack on the San Francisco water supply. Tom was silent as she described her conversation with Gharoub about Project Neptune. There was a pause as Tom processed this; he would have to act quickly if the enemy was this far advanced into their plans.

"First thing, Lara," he said, controlling his emotions at this disturbing development, "is to get some dialogue going . . . see how much detail we can get out of them. Let's say we send out on a line we know they're monitoring, a 'CSfC' message. These, they'll bring to you, hopefully, since you've shown your capability with them. There will be some factual information in the translation you can give them, with a hidden stenographic message only for you. We can keep up a dialogue with them this way. You can translate the CSfC for them and keep the other part for yourself.

"You can then give them a coded message to transmit back to their agents here in the States, indicating how to proceed. We'll keep up this artificial 'secret' dialogue until we're sure we have their plans and are ready for them. In other words, we'll keep sending out CSfC's that you will translate for them. Each will have one of these stenographic messages for you. As long as they have every reason to believe in what they get from you, and we'll be sure they get confirming data on our movements, we'll be able to stay one step ahead. At least, that's the plan for now . . . are you reading me?"

"Yes, I get it . . . but you know I won't be the one coding and sending the outgoing signals to their agents, right?"

"That's all right . . . as long as you get to see them and can decode them yourself. After all, they have to depend on you knowing what's going on, correct?"

Lara thought about all this for just a moment, the details of this hide-and-seek game rushing through her mind. "Affirmative, Tom!" She was eager to give this a go. The stenographic part, the code within a code, was one of the latest tricks the NSA had come up with since 9/11. Hackers who had broken into a coded message, say, one that was in a CSfC transmission, would still not be able to decode, or even detect, the stenographic portion.

"We'll send them a test signal right away; hopefully, they'll bring it directly to you."

"Sounds good, Tom! Oh, any news from my partner?"

"He's getting a good start. Not much more I can tell you right now."

With that, they terminated the connection. All of this had taken less than three minutes. Lara's heart was going at least double-time as she tried to process all that had just transpired. Of course, nothing could be written down; she would have to memorize it, then go over it all in her mind later that night.

Chapter 14

Lara's next day, her first full day at her new position, started with a surge of adrenaline. Her new aide, the timid Captain Maloof was showing her the various files pertaining to Project Neptune, the coming attack on the San Francisco water supply. The most important files, he informed her, were the coded messages coming in from the teams of attackers getting in place on the peninsula. Then there were the intercepted signals from the Americans, presumably concerning any anticipated attack. These were apparently sent to agents and other assets the Americans had in the field. The Iranians so far had not successfully decoded and translated them.

As he was showing her the pertinent files, Maloof mentioned that the key aspect of this office's work was to confuse the Americans as to where the attack was to take place. It was taken for granted that they were preparing to repel any assault before it reached the actual water supply, as during the first attack in Los Angeles. "You see," he pointed out politely, "the general feels certain the West Coast is considered by the Americans most vulnerable." Lara said nothing, waiting for the captain to reveal as much as possible; but her palms started to moisten. She pulled out a handkerchief and pretended to stifle a sneeze as she wiped her hands.

"Excuse me," she said, "it must be the air-conditioning. I'm not quite used to it yet."

Maloof smiled obligingly. "Yes, it happens quite often to newcomers to Tehran. You are new to the big city, I understand." She nodded and put the hanky away, leaning back to the files. It was clear she wasn't about to start a nosy conversation. The captain got the hint and went back to the briefing.

"You see," he continued, "one of our main jobs here is to mislead the enemy as much as possible. So, we have to offer them information eading them to believe the attack is coming from somewhere other than the true location."

He saw the interest he had raised in his new colleague. "Please," he said, "let me buy you a nice hot cup of coffee; it may alleviate your discomfort." He pointed at his nose to eliminate any misunderstanding of his intent.

"That's a good idea," she said obligingly, rising from her chair. Lara was certain Maloof was going beyond his authority in disclosing this information to the newly arrived decoding expert, but she listened patiently without showing the mounting interest she felt. He was trying to gain favor with her, it seemed, and she was willing to go along, at least for a while.

He led her to a nearby room with American-style coffee and tea urns, paper cups, and the usual amenities. Early as it was, there was no one else in the room. He poured her a cup of coffee along with one for himself, then brought over some sugar and cream.

Sitting across from her at a small table, Maloof said, "The general and his staff know the Americans are assuming we will make an assault on San Francisco's waterworks, that being the second-most-populated city on their coast. So, we're giving them hints as to where specifically it will occur."

Lara, with mounting apprehension, stiffened but said nothing. She was quite willing to hear anything he was willing to disclose.

He lowered his voice unnecessarily in the empty room. "In fact, we have fake assault teams already in place in an obvious location. It's much the same as the Americans themselves did in their famous D-Day invasion of Normandy during World War II. You know to what I'm referring?"

"You mean the false landing at Calais, I presume."

"Oh, you are up on your military history, I see. Of course, you must be, with your background." He reddened, feeling clumsy. "Well, in this case," he said, regaining his composure, "we've sent teams to the San Francisco Peninsula as bait to draw the Americans to that site." He smiled conspiratorially as he groomed his moustache with his fingers.

Lara simply sat there, listening; her new assistant seemed right out of a movie from the 1930s. He appeared to be waiting for some sort of recognition, so she nodded for him to continue, knowing he was already way out-of-bounds in sharing this information. "You see," he continued in a very low voice, "the attack will, in fact, be on the San Francisco supply, but it will occur far upstream, on the east side of their San Francisco Bay. It will be at the so-called Hetch Hetchy reservoir at the western edge of the Sierra Nevada mountains. The Americans will never suspect such a brazen move."

Lara nodded in tacit approval. "Very clever, I must say. But won't the Americans detect the poison before it reaches the city?"

"That's the beauty of the plan. You see, there are several sources of the city's water, this being just one. We are leaving them hints pointing at a more obvious location just south of the city. There are several reservoirs in the southern suburbs where maintenance workers have access to the water and piping." He was obviously delighted with her undivided attention. After a few moments waiting for a response, he stood and politely said, "Well, you must have many things to do, getting started. Please let me know if you have anything you want to discuss. You have my phone number; my office is across the main hall, with the other officers."

"Thank you so much, Captain," she replied gracefully.

"Abdel, please. We will be working together so much." His face colored slightly as he rose, pleased with this affable meeting. Lara smiled in return but did not offer to shake hands. He allowed her to return to her desk and then strode briskly away. *This is going to be a fine relationship,* he thought to himself, quite a pleasant turn of events.

Lara went quickly back to her desk eager to get on with the filing of the paperwork General Gharoub had left for her. Her mind, though, was reeling with what the shy captain had just disclosed. She filed it away in her mind. Then she used all her energies the rest of the day getting settled, totally absorbed in the necessities of organization. She would have plenty to tell Tom after she returned home later that afternoon.

The day went by quickly; there was a fast lunch, four more hours of ntense work at her desk, then it was time to leave. She waited for her ransport downtown along with about ten of the other privileged staff who lid not have to take public transportation. These were nearly all male officers and senior female personnel, kept segregated from the others as much as possible. One man, however, also waiting curbside, stood out from he others. He was a major, Lara noted from his shoulder bars, standing rigidly in his finely tailored uniform and highly polished shoes. She could not help but notice how his muscular chest and shoulders strained at the seams of his jacket. He looked like an advertisement for a physical fitness program. She never noticed, as she turned away, how carefully *he* examined *her* as her ride appeared.

Chapter 15

General Gharoub was standing at his window, peering out on the huge complex, with the mountains looming in the background. This was such a marvelous country. And its greatness was just beginning to be realized by the rest of the world. *How fortunate I am to be here to see this, to be a part of the marvelous events about to unfold*, he thought as he took a large pull on his Cohiba Behike cigar. *The best money can buy*, he thought as he savored the strong, spicy tobacco. It tasted especially good realizing this Cuban delicacy was unavailable in the United States, at least legally. Life was indeed good and about to get better; much, much better.

There was a light tap on his door; he knew who it was. He had asked, or rather told, his second-in-command, Maj. Sarash Asani, to come see him this morning. In answer to a gruff bidding from Gharoub, Asani opened the door and strode eagerly into the room. He was a confident-appearing man of about forty, trim and muscular in his tailored uniform. He was regarded within the facility as quite the ladies' man. The general gestured wordlessly for the major to take a seat as he himself put down his cigar and planted himself in his large, comfortable chair behind his gleaming desk. The two men studied each other for a moment before Gharoub began. While it was not unusual for Gharoub to ask his top aide to see him, this summons seemed somehow special. A smile crept across the general's face as he leaned forward; he spoke quietly: "Sarash, my friend, I have had a thought about our plan."

There was no doubt in the major's mind about which plan was under discussion. It had to be the attack on the San Francisco water supply; that was the main effort under consideration. He leaned forward in his chair. This must be something new, some change in strategy.

"You know how much I prefer distraction and deception to a blunt attack," Gharoub said, his thick, black eyebrows raised in delight.

"Yes, of course, General. It is the hallmark of all your operations."

"That is why I have decided to throw another curve at the Americans. Tell me what you think of it." There was a slight pause as the major pondered what his chief had in store.

"You know, of course, that we have guarded our main strike with a false attack at another site." The major simply gestured with one hand to show his affirmative answer. "Well, I have thought it more prudent to have *several* points of attack with which to confuse our enemy." He waited a few seconds for the major to process this idea before continuing.

"That, of course, is a prudent idea, but won't it tax our forces to call so many more men into the fray?" The major always thought of practical matters; that was what Gharoub liked about him.

"Indeed, yes, you are, as usual, correct. One team at the outlet of the reservoir on the peninsula, and the other at the Hetch Hetchy plant. A singularly captivating name for a waterway, don't you think?" Gharoub laughed, amused at the unusual name. Asani chuckled along with him. "Well, what if we were to generate reports that other locations were under attack? There are many places along the water supply routes that could be used. We could dilute the enemy's response if they had to defend ten or more sites, wouldn't you agree?"

"Yes, of course, but how could we produce these distractions?"

"Good thinking, my friend! What I had in mind is to create minor interruptions in the water supply, just enough to require teams of the municipal water district, suitably clad in their distinctive gray overalls, to race in to inspect and repair any disturbances."

"Yes, but what . . . ?" Asani appeared puzzled by the impact of such a move.

"With ten or more technicians in identical jackets at all these sites, it will take an hour or more for the authorities to find which, if any, are the saboteurs." The major slowly caught on to the genius of this approach. How, especially at night, were the authorities to search and identify all these seemingly authentic workers, spread over tens of miles of waterway? By the time they had found the culprits, the poison would have been inserted and spread through the system. It was an ingenious addition to the scheme.

Chapter 16

The ride home was a little slow, but Lara was in good spirits. Dropping down from the mountains brought her into the afternoon smog, which was heavier than usual. The gulls and pigeons, unfazed by the polluted air, swooped noisily down into the streets and sidewalks, hungry for the tiniest morsel of food.

The noise and dirt of the city did not distract Lara, nor did it affect her attitude. Her first real day at work couldn't have gone better, and she was eager to talk to Tom. She hoped he was already awake, though it was about five in the morning in New York.

Her hosts, Sara and Faezeh, were waiting at the front door as she came up the walk. They had looks of mixed eagerness and apprehension, like parents after the first day of school. But Lara was in too much of a hurry to chat; she made excuses about the grimy air and needing to freshen up, then headed to her room. She did, in fact, wash her face and clean her contacts as soon as she got upstairs. Then she sat down on the bed and called Tom. To her great relief, he was already awake and ready to hear from her. She quickly went into the details of her office and went right to her meeting with Maloof. She heard a gasp as she told him what Maloof had revealed about the San Francisco attack.

"That's not what we've heard from other sources," he told her. "I wonder if he's really in on the true plan."

"He works for the general and was assigned directly to me, so unless they suspect me . . ."

"That's unlikely since you have access to all their communiqués, so we'll have to give it credibility, at least for now. It is a major concern—"

"Oh, speaking of majors," Lara interrupted. "I noticed a uniformed man today I haven't seen before. He was wearing a major's bars . . ."

"What did he look like?"

"Thirty-five to forty, looks like an Iranian movie star, sort of, or a bodybuilder. Broad shoulders, perfectly groomed, and straight as a ramrod."

"Wow, that's Sarash Asani, number-one assassin. Watch out for him! And he's a notorious Lothario to boot. I wonder what he's up to."

"Sounds like you're asking me to find out . . ." Lara's interest was piqued.

"I'm serious, Lara, this man's dangerous in many ways. Do what you can, but be on the alert. This guy has no scruples—none."

"You make him sound like a monster," Lara teased. There was no immediate response; Lara was a bit frightened. "I'll be careful; you know I can handle myself."

"What can I say? I know you've been in some tight spots before, but this guy is like a predatory animal. No joke."

"All right, you've got me totally scared. Please, don't tell you know who about this . . . unless it becomes necessary."

"Your actions are secure with me, don't worry—unless something goes wrong. Then I've got to get him involved. Your security is our number-one concern right now. So, like I said, stay alert, no chances taken, all right?"

"You're the boss. I won't try anything crazy."

"Good luck, Daria. Keep in touch."

And that was it. She was essentially free to head into the lion's den.

* * *

Lara's next day started out similar to the last. Wearing the standard clothing for the female workers in the office—a peasant-type blouse with a long, full gray skirt down almost to her shoe tops—she headed into her office with a brisk stride. Her darkened hair was pulled back in a severe bun. Her lightweight black tunic reached to her midthigh, and an orange head scarf fell around her neck. All that was showing was her face and hands. *At least I didn't have to wear a beekeeper outfit*, she thought.

She went straight to her desk and finished the last of her organizing. Then she was free to tackle some of the real work: decoding the messages that had been intercepted from the Americans in the past few weeks. She immediately spotted a few of the transmissions that Homeland had sent as fodder for her to use to convince the Iranians of her skills. She translated these first: they were innocuous tabulations of the high-altitude overflights and reconnaissance satellite paths that were already known to the enemy. The accuracy of her work should cement her status as a most capable cryptographer. She finished these close to lunchtime, put them in her out-box for pickup by the courier, and prepared to head to the lunchroom.

Suddenly, a large figure in uniform appeared at her door. She instantly recognized the sinister major about whom Tom had warned her: Sarash Asani. He tapped lightly on the glass and entered, his uniform cap under his arm, a warm smile on his face.

"Sorry to startle you," he said in a friendly manner. "I am Major Asani. Sarash, if you would. I work for General Gharoub. Perhaps you know of me."

Lara, a little unsettled, tried to maintain her composure. "A pleasure, Major, I'm sure. How can I help you?"

"The general himself would have introduced us, but, unfortunately, he is away on some urgent matter in the field." He handed her a simple business card with his picture in the top left corner and his title below: *Maj. Sarash Asani, Head, Counterintelligence Division.* A phone number was printed at the bottom right.

Lara compared the photo with the man standing before her, smiled, and offered him a chair. She did not extend her hand to him. He returned the smile and sat down, placing his cap on his lap.

"You are Ms. Daria Haddad, are you not?"

"I am, yes. How can I be of assistance?" she repeated.

Asani was not put off at all by her curt manner; he continued unfazed. "The general has given me glowing assessments of your capabilities; I am indeed overwhelmed with your skills, even at this early time in your employment here." Again, the warm, toothy smile. "There is much you can do to help us in our fight against the Western interlopers. Believe me, we can certainly use your assistance. Here is a letter of introduction from General Gharoub." He handed her an envelope with the general's embossed name and title. She opened it and removed a smoothly creased letter stating exactly what the major had told her, followed by a request to give him any aid that she could. It was signed in his hand; she compared it with a memo she had from him on her desk.

Lara could not help but be pleased with this introduction. The head of counterintelligence might be of even greater use to her. Warning or not, she would like to see what this man had to offer. "All right, Major, I would be happy to do whatever I can."

"Please excuse me if this seems at all forward, but I would like to discuss what I have in mind in a less public place. The Divan restaurant on Fayazi Boulevard. Do you know of it?"

"Yes, of course. I have not been there myself, but I understand it is quite nice." She had indeed heard of it; it was one of the most expensive restaurants in Tehran. "When did you have in mind?"

"Tomorrow night if it is convenient, say, seven p.m.?"

"I would like to check with General Gharoub, if you don't mind."

"Not at all," the courteous Asani responded. "You have his direct line?"

"Yes, I do, thanks. I'll phone him this afternoon."

"Well, then," Asani said smiling broadly, "until tomorrow. Oh, would you like my driver to pick you up?"

"Thank you, but I prefer to take a taxi, if that's all right."

"Of course," he said happily, rising from his chair. "Until then. Oh, if there is some problem, you can contact me at the number on my card."

* * *

Lara finished work that day without further interruption and cleared her desk. There were no messages of any importance in the transcriptions she read through in the afternoon, mainly arrival times of packages that were already available to the Iranians from their satellites and drones. She logged them in anyway and then headed home as usual, eager to relay the day's events to Tom. Sara met her at the door, curious about her day at work. Lara's position in the secret fortress in the foothills of the mountains held a fascination for all the residents of Tehran. Few, however, had ever even seen it, let alone been inside.

Of course, Lara told her nothing about her job. But she did offer her the news of the dinner invitation she had for the following night. Major Asani, it happens, was a local celebrity, often seen hosting starlets and other lovely young women at various nightclubs. Sara was near breathless. She immediately offered Lara a lovely crimson head scarf for the evening. It would go well, actually, with the floral blouse she had decided to wear; she accepted gracefully. But first, she had to keep her word about phoning General Gharoub about the dinner plan. She went to her room, and after washing up and cleaning her lenses, she used her local phone to reach Gharoub. One of his lieutenants answered on two rings. She explained the details of her meeting with Asani; the lieutenant asked her to wait for him to confer with the general. After what seemed like twenty minutes but what was actually about five, he returned to the line to say that all was well, and she could accept the invitation to dinner.

That bit of business finished, she placed a call to Tom on her secure phone. Typical of him, he answered instantly; she knew well how vital her assignment was. When he heard of the invitation to dinner, he seemed delighted. "By all means!" he exclaimed. "I wonder what's on his mind . . . you know what I mean."

"Of course." She laughed. "I'll be careful. It's a very public place, you know. And no alcohol."

"All for the best. Call when you get home, OK?"

"You bet, Tom," she said, as if she were a teenager on her first date. Refreshed and relaxed after these calls, she changed and went down to dinner, hoping not to have to field any more details of her day at work.

Chapter 17

The next day flew by as Lara plowed through more mundane communiqués intercepted by the Iranian field offices. She did contact Major Asani's staff and left a message saying their "meeting" that night was confirmed. The lieutenant who took the call sounded as though he was used to hearing of such meetings. *Oh well.* She left work slightly early in an attempt to beat the traffic and be at the restaurant, which was in a well-known mall, on time. Arriving home in a hurry, much to the amusement of her hosts, she hustled upstairs to wash up, change, and make it to the restaurant on time, or close to it. There was no time to call Tom; she had really nothing to tell him, anyway. She looked herself over in the mirror; the red head scarf really did set off the rest of her outfit. She looked a bit glamorous, she thought, but certainly not provocative.

Not wanting to advertise where she was living, Lara walked to a small shopping center three blocks from home before making a call for a taxi. The cool air coming down from the mountains felt pleasant on her face, especially after a day in the office air-conditioning. Only a few people were out in the darkling twilight, and she was able to gather her thoughts as she walked. This was the first real chance she'd had to consider what Major Asani was up to. She certainly hoped it was work-related and not a date.

It was already past 6:00 p.m., so Lara hoped the traffic would allow her to be reasonably prompt. She didn't want to appear too eager; at the same time, there was no point in being rudely late. The taxi appeared in ten minutes. She gave the driver the name of the large mall where the Divan was located but not the restaurant name. As she feared, the traffic was bad, and she arrived at the mall ten minutes late. She paid the driver and made sure he was gone from the mall parking lot before she headed to the elegant restaurant, one of the finest in the city.

She entered and instantly saw a beaming Major Asani waiting patiently for her. This time, she allowed him to take her hand as a staff member led them to the VIP "Red Room." Lara couldn't help but be impressed with the opulence that exuded from this remarkable location. Only four tables were set in this two-story chamber; they were led to a table for two in the back of the room, away from the door but not isolated. The high ceilings and ornate chandeliers seemed to keep the carpeted room luxuriously quiet. Huge portraits of Persian kings and, of course, current political and religious leaders hung on the walls between the enormous, finely draped windows. Through the north-facing window, she was able to see the snow-covered Alborz mountains under the bright full moon. It was quite impressive.

Their table, like all the others, was black-lacquered, as were the chairs. A fine white linen cloth along with two matching napkins graced the table, she noted, as the host deftly held her chair for her. Only after he left did Asani speak to her. "You look lovely," he said, his eyes gleaming.

Oh no, thought Lara, *not a pass, please.*

"Please don't misunderstand. I mean that only as a compliment, nothing more." He smiled as though asking for understanding. She returned the smile graciously.

He quickly changed the subject when he saw her discomfort. "Would you allow me to order for us?" he asked as the impassive waiter silently slid menus in front of them.

"Yes, that would be fine," she said, noticing he was wearing a glistening chest full of medals she hadn't seen before. She didn't know whether he was trying to impress her or the waitstaff.

"Would you like to start with a cocktail? Nonalcoholic, of course," he added quickly. Alcohol was legally banned in all of Iran. Which meant it existed only on the sly.

"Yes, do they serve *ma'osh sha'ir*? I prefer the lemon flavor." This was a fermented zero-alcohol brew she had tasted at her temporary home.

Asani instantly ordered two of the fruit-flavored drinks for them; they appeared almost as quickly, in cocktail glasses with slices of lemon on the lip. They appeared for all the world like drinks served to teenagers anywhere else. As Lara sipped the ice-cold drink, Asani quietly indicated to the waiter the items on the menu he would like to order. Lara had a chance to glance at the prices; they were astonishing for Iran. A modest dinner would cost the equivalent of $100 a person! He was going all-out, it seemed.

The waiter left them, and the major proceeded with small talk, asking about her accommodations and how she was finding life in the big city. "Just fine," she replied. Her hosts had been selected for her by the Homeland assets after she had been selected for the interview. She had decided to stay on with the two women after she was chosen for the job. Lara neglected to tell him where precisely this was, but implied it was within the city in an agreeable location. This seemed to satisfy him, as the first course of their expensive dinner arrived.

Grilled chicken appetizers served on pastries came first. They were delicious—tasty and delicate. Lara was impressed. The portions were small, just as Lara preferred. A cold pitcher of rosewater was brought to the table at the same time as their cocktails were removed, and their wineglasses filled with the subtle liquid. They had barely finished the chicken before the next course appeared: lamb shank in a saffron sauce. Again, the portions were small and carefully presented on colorful vegetables. Lara hardly had time to compliment Asani on his choices before their plates were removed and the main course appeared. This was the beef kebab kateh: skewered filet mignon cubes served on crispy rice and steamed vegetables. Once again, the portions were small enough for Lara to comfortably eat all she wanted.

"Be sure to allow for dessert," Asani said with a gracious smile as she finished. "It's fantastic."

"Oh, I don't know . . ."

"At least give it a try. You must." He signaled to the waiter, who promptly had the attendant remove the dishes, after which he presented them with dishes of fruit-colored ice cream surrounded by slices of local resh fruit and sprigs of flowers. It was breathtaking. Against her better udgment, she managed to consume about half her portion.

It was only after the table was cleared that Asani assumed an attitude hat indicated he had something to present to her. The few other diners in he Red Room had already left, and they were quite alone. Major Asani had apparently arranged for the bill beforehand. Lara held her breath, hoping it was not what she feared. "You know," he said quietly, leaning over the able, "your performance so far is even more impressive than your excellent credentials led us to believe. I say this with all sincerity; you have surpassed our highest expectations."

Lara raised her hand in silent protest.

"No, I am serious." He paused and looked carefully around the room, then said in even a lower voice: "You know, of course, of our coming plans?"

Lara just nodded, taken aback by this change in the direction of the conversation. She assumed he was referring to the coming attack on the San Francisco waterworks. In the few seconds of silence, she directed her full attention at the major as she waited for his next words.

"We failed dismally in our last attempt, as you know." Lara did not respond; she hung on the ensuing presentation. *He must have had this place checked out for bugs*, she thought to herself. "Well, I know you've been informed, at least casually, about our coming campaign in the . . . north." Her body language indicated agreement. "Well, for us to fully utilize your skills, I feel you should see our capabilities in this regard."

Lara went into high-alert mode; she hoped he did not detect it.

"Tomorrow, I would like to take you on a tour of our facilities so you can see for yourself what we intend to do. It should help you; that is, as you do your job, to see what our . . . adversaries . . . know and do not know."

This was almost too good to be true. Lara was transfixed.

"Of course, Major. I should be very interested to learn our plans."

He seemed relieved at her response.

"Well, then, I know you have an early day at work tomorrow; shall we say noon for our little tour? I will pick you up at the general's office."

He rose and stepped over to take her chair as she placed her napkin on the table. She agreed, albeit somewhat reluctantly, with Asani's offer to drive her home. He walked her out to the curb where an official-looking limousine was waiting, complete with a middle-aged female chaperone. They drove her to her home, Lara on a seat next to the woman, the major on the opposite bench. With a minimum of conversation, they glided swiftly into her residential neighborhood.

The major held the door for her as she exited the limo. Lara could already see her two hosts watching through the window curtains. "Until tomorrow, then . . ." Asani said, standing politely, tipping his cap as she headed to her house.

"Oh my!" exclaimed Faezeh as she entered the house. Sara was smiling broadly at their guest's royal arrival. They knew Lara was not about to disclose the nature of her business with the famous major, but the women were eager to hear of her sumptuous dinner. She agreed to share the details of the famous Divan restaurant and the exorbitant meal. Neither of them had ever been there, but they were well aware of its lavishness. They gasped as she went through the various courses of the feast and the graciousness of her host. But that was it. She excused herself, saying she had to get to bed as she had an early day coming up.

Lara fled to her room, eager to call Tom and deliver the news of her remarkable dinner date. He answered on the first ring; he was in his office as it was now near noon in New York. "My gosh, you sound excited," he exclaimed as she blurted out some of the more astounding details of her dinner conversation. "So, he's actually going to take you on some sort of tour tomorrow? You must really have impressed them with your capabilities. Call me as soon as you can afterward. We need to set wheels in motion here before they get started on their next campaign. By the way, he didn't indicate any other reasons for . . ."

"Tom, he was a perfect gentleman. But he does know exactly where I live now; I hope the ladies have adequate cover."

"Chances are, they already knew that; I'm fairly sure you've been under surveillance since you started working there."

"Of course," she said. "I know our agents here have done a thorough job of 'vacuuming' the house and my hosts here. I'd probably be in prison by now otherwise." The color rose in her face as she recognized the fragile nature of her presence in this hostile country, let alone the nature of her workplace.

It was the way with intelligence work everywhere. She often remembered the astonishing case of Israeli spy Eli Cohen, who, in the middle of the twentieth century became the most trusted aide of the brutal Syrian leader Hafez al-Assad. So trusted was Cohen that Assad, defense minister at the time, actually gave him a tour of their military positions on the Golan Heights just before the Six-Day War in 1967. Cohen's information allowed the Israelis to destroy the fortifications and occupy, then later annex, the strategic seven-hundred-square-mile clifftops. The Heights had for years been used by the Syrians to bombard the Israeli farms below and act as a secure buffer against their hated foe.

She also remembered the tragic end for Cohen when his true identity was disclosed. He was hanged in a public square in Damascus, his body open to public viewing for days before being taken down. She felt chills every time she thought of it. Long after her conversation with Tom ended, she lay sleepless, thinking of the day ahead.

* * *

Lara's night was filled with wild dreams; she awakened to find her covers twisted and strewn around the bed. Her body was covered with a patina of cold perspiration. But by morning, she had recovered herself, and by noontime, she was ready for her excursion with the dapper major. Asani showed up right on time. To the intense interest of the onlookers in her department, he escorted Lara, dressed in her usual conservative apparel, to the front door of the building where his staff car was waiting. To her great relief, the major made no attempt to touch her, not even helping her into the car; a female lieutenant was there for that duty. She also sat next to Lara in the spacious car; the major sat in front, next to the driver.

There was little conversation, and that was limited to the usual discussion about the brown cloud of smog that hung over the city. It was even more evident from their location in the foothills to the north. The drive lasted about thirty minutes. Lara could tell they were moving east along the north edge of the city but could not see street signs and deliberately did not make an attempt to view landmarks.

They arrived at an unmarked structure that looked like a typical industrial warehouse. The driver parked in one of several spaces at the front of the building marked "Reserved" in Farsi. As they disembarked, Lara noted Major Asani's name printed in bold letters at the top of the sign. When they reached the front door, the female lieutenant entered only as far as the reception area, where two armed guards were positioned. The major signed in for both Lara and himself, and after a stiff salute from the guards, returned by the major, the two were admitted into the large work area. There, Lara was greeted by a vast area filled with casting, drilling, and other machinery, a storage space filled with industrial liquid and solid containers, and high-pressure gas cylinders. Silent workers moved carefully around the factory floor, covered in protective clothing. They looked like the teams who had cleaned up after Chernobyl and Fukushima, clad from head to toe in coveralls, hoods, boots, masks, goggles, and gloves. They showed no interest in the visitors, who were immediately clothed in gear similar to the workers. At least their costumes allowed for vocal communication.

The sounds of industrial equipment, muted somewhat by the soundproofing evident on the walls and ceiling, permeated the building. It was difficult for Lara to hear the major's voice, let alone make sense of what he was saying. He slowly guided her around to an enclosed area, a sort of building within a building. They were met by an armed guard who, before allowing them to enter, verified the major's identity with a retinal scan, requiring him to remove his goggles for just a few seconds. The door opened with a click that was audible even above the ever-present noise of the equipment.

The door closed behind Lara and Asani with a sound that was as frightening as the structure itself. The industrial noise from the factory instantly vanished, leaving just a low, sinister hiss from the air vents. Inside the room was an enclosure made of glass or Lucite. Lara saw six workers clothed even more securely than those in the rest of the plant. They were covered in beehive-type suits with white gloves and boots taped securely on to the sleeves and legs. She could see their faces inside the helmets, covered with masks; small microphones allowed for voice communication.

Asani pointed to a conveyor belt on which clear four-ounce bottles moved slowly. The bottles were filled halfway with bright yellow crystals. The ghostly looking workers carefully checked each bottle as the product moved slowly along to a packaging location at one end of the enclosure. After a minute or so of this fearful display, the major indicated to Lara that they were to move back outside.

He motioned Lara to follow him as he strode out of the enclosure back into the factory and into a quiet, unoccupied space with tables, chairs, and vending machines. They sat, Asani now opening his face mask, motioning Lara to do the same. "Well, what do you think of our little factory?" he asked proudly.

"Was that yellow powder the . . . ?" she uttered quietly.

"Indeed, it is! That's the stuff that will bring the Americans to their knees! Polonium chloride, it's called. A *million* times more deadly than cyanide," he said proudly. "Each grain of those crystals in their water can slay thousands of our enemy!"

Despite knowing what he said was, in fact, true, Lara was still terrified by his words, combined with the close contact she had just had with the yellow poison. Her face revealed the pallor of one who has just been exposed to a mass murderer. Asani was clearly pleased with her reaction; a slight smile crossed his face. "Now do you see how we can humble the mighty Americans?" She just nodded grimly; he took it as an affirmation of his deadly power. "Well, let us get back, and I will give you more details of our plans . . . and the important job I have in store for you!"

Lara followed him back to the entrance, where they were helped out of their protective gear and then scanned with some sort of radiation monitor. They were whisked back to their office building, Lara still in a mild state of shock. She was about to thank the major and head back to her office when he held up his hand, a slight smile on his face. "I wonder if we might have a word or two in my private office." It was not an order but might as well have been. They were in the hallway that ringed the north side of the building; she presumed his office was along here, near General Gharoub's.

"Of course," she replied after just a moment. He had caught her off-guard.

"Fine, it will just be a moment." He motioned to a corner office at the end of the hall, and Lara crossed in front of him with the slightest of hesitation. Knowing his reputation, she was on her guard, the hair on the back of her neck aroused in a self-defense mode. She saw his name on the wooden door along with the title "Chief, Military Intelligence" in bold black letters. He opened the door for her, revealing a portly, middle-aged woman in a lieutenant's uniform sitting at a secretarial desk. Lara was not introduced to her as the major just nodded, guiding Lara to his inner office, the secretary glowering like a prison warden.

From his inner office, she was greeted by a spectacular view of the mountains, unobscured by the smog. Far to the north, snow covered the higher peaks. At his direction, Lara took a seat in front of an elegant teakwood desk trimmed with ebony, with just a few manila folders neatly stacked on one side. Asani took his seat behind the desk after first gently closing the glass-paneled door to the anteroom. Lara noted the secretary silently watching the proceedings; there would be no monkey business, it seemed clear.

"Well," the major began, "what did you think of our little tour?" A self-satisfied smile appeared once again. He knew quite well how impressed she had been at the display of the terrible polonium poison-production facility.

After just a moment for her to completely register what was going on, Lara replied as she knew was expected of her. "Major . . . what can I say . . . it was astonishing, to say the least. But first, if you don't mind, I would like to wash up a bit . . . you understand?" She saw a private bathroom inside his impressive office.

"My apologies. Of course," he said, clearly embarrassed by his lack of courtesy. He stood, extending his hand toward the washroom. Lara stood, taking her small shoulder bag with her, and headed in. Her first move after closing the door behind her was to make a cursory look around for any obvious cameras or listening devices. Seeing none, she turned on the water, washed her hands and removed her contacts; her eyes were burning from the smog as well as the thought of the chemicals in the poison plant. Finishing quickly, Lara returned to the major's office. She now felt able to handle whatever he had to offer. She smiled obligingly as she sat again in the comfortable chair, his desk in front of her, the mountains visible to the left.

"Let me get right to the point," Asani began, his elbows on the desk, his chin resting on his hands in a manner keeping with a highly important message. "I am deeply and thoroughly impressed with your work here." She nodded graciously at his opening remarks. "You, of course, know our purposes, and now see our capabilities." His thick, black eyebrows raised as he gazed directly at her. "We are going to strike the Americans with a deadly blow, one that will cause them to remove all the economic sanctions they have placed upon us. What's more, they will no longer threaten us with military retaliation, for they will acknowledge our capability to strike the heart of their civilian population centers. They know full well the inability of their coddled populace to handle as elementary a menace as poison in their drinking water. If an enemy can strike there, what choice do they have?"

That insidious grin spread across his features. Lara could envision his thoughts of hundreds of thousands of civilians writhing in agony as the polonium in the water wreaked havoc on their organs. She squirmed unconsciously in her chair at the terrible scene.

Asani paused just a few seconds to give her a chance to feature the grisly aftermath of such an attack on a large metropolis. "You can assist our cause greatly, you know." While she writhed inside, she assumed a pose of uncertain curiosity. "Your ability to decipher the Americans' transmissions is vital to our broad plan."

Lara's head was whirling with this offer. Even though she didn't yet know the details, it was obvious that she could have a significant impact on the Iranians' vicious plans. She waited for the major to continue with his nightmare scenario.

"You see," he continued, assured of her full attention, "we have two main attack divisions: military operations and military intelligence. Operations are handled in another facility; our job is intelligence." He paused at this point to see if she had any questions. Seeing that she was ready to hear more, he began again. "Our whole attack depends on secrecy and deception, as you can imagine. We must not allow the enemy to anticipate our strategy. They know we are coming, but if they don't know where or when, the uncertainty will dilute their response enough that our troops will succeed!"

Lara waited anxiously for more. What did he have in mind for her?

After another pregnant pause, he continued. "You have shown a remarkable ability to read deeply into the heart of the Americans' missives dealing with counterintelligence. Your translation of that *IAPG* message we intercepted showed us nuances that our earlier attempts missed entirely." Lara remembered the test message she had handled in her interview; there had been some Americanisms in it that would not be obvious to the foreign eye.

"That's the kind of perception we need in our job of reading their minds, so to speak. Your job, or I should say, *our* job, is to translate the messages we intercept from the enemy's network . . . Oh yes, we are able to read almost everything they send." This last was added when he saw her eyebrows rise in surprise. "But we need to be sure we know exactly what they mean, not just what they say." Lara did not speak—she waited for more. "We noted your ability to read into their vernacular, almost like a native. Your training at Esfahan . . . yes, I know you aren't allowed to elaborate . . . but it was as precise as the reports in your dossier claim. Our best English-speakers here were highly impressed!"

Lara could not help but blush, hoping it would not show too much beneath her darkened skin. Just how much was he going to reveal? she wondered. Tom was going to be very interested in her transmission tonight.

Asani glanced at his desk clock and abruptly closed the briefcase that he had placed on his desk. "I had not realized it was so late," he said, slightly embarrassed. "I didn't mean to keep you. I know you have matters to deal with on your desk."

"It's quite all right, Major," Lara replied in the friendliest of tones. It had been a most productive lunch date from her perspective. She rose and shook his offered hand; he opened the door for her, smiling as usual.

Lara noted the matron at the desk in the outer office scowling at her as she headed out the door and down the hall. Right now, her head was filled with questions about the major's next move.

Chapter 18

The rest of the day passed quickly as Lara sorted through the stack of intercepted radio and telephone conversations that had reached her desk. Some, especially those with the *IAPG* label, grabbed her attention; she placed them in a special folder. They would get immediate attention the next morning. She needed to speak with Tom tonight if at all possible; he would no doubt have some instructions for her after hearing Asani's startling remarks. She packed up her things, leaving all classified material in their proper folders, stored in the file cabinet. A uniformed guard, she noticed, was just outside her door, carefully watching her and a few of the clerks as they packed up and left.

There was the usual rush to the transport that took the employees downtown, and then the smoggy bus ride to the stop near her home. She carried just her bag containing her phones, notes, and personal items, none of which caused any unusual concern from the guards. As she walked the last few blocks from the bus stop, she recognized a few commuters; several nodded their greetings, which she returned. *Good*, she thought, *I'm just another bleary-eyed city dweller.*

Sara and Faezeh were waiting at the door, as usual, as she hurried past with just a smile and brief greeting. They knew her routine by now: she needed to wash up and rest before dinner. But Lara's mind was filled with observations and questions for Tom. Even before washing her face, she took off her shoes and, with the water running, dialed him. It was later than usual, so she felt sure he was already at work, waiting for her call.

Sure enough, he answered on the first ring. She had plenty to report, and he was eager to hear all of it. The first item was her visit to the poison factory. Lara could hear him lightly sigh as he absorbed the ghastly news.

Well, it wasn't like we didn't know it was coming. But her recounting of the major's instructions to her afterward evoked a sharp "Yes!" Tom was pleased at this development.

As soon as she completed her story, he told her why. "They've no doubt picked up some of our coded transmissions; you know, the IAPG notes like the ones they've seen before. What we've been doing now is informing some ghost agents of our plans." Lara knew to what he was referring: instructions purportedly meant for double agents in Tehran, informing them of the Americans' plans for derailing any coming Iranian attacks. There were, of course, no such agents. The messages were being sent by a friendly source, intended for capture by the Iranians. Now Lara would have the opportunity to translate them and hopefully learn of the Iranians' response. It was relatively standard spycraft, albeit with another layer of deception—Lara's involvement.

"We're pretty sure where they're headed with this latest batch of polonium: San Francisco. But there's conflicting information as to which pipeline they're planning to strike. On the one hand, we have sources that say it's one of the lines coming from the reservoirs south of the city in the hills; there's a number of them. But then, as you reported, we just got confirmation that they're headed for the main source of water for the whole central coast: the Hetch Hetchy reservoir that catches the water from Yosemite. It's huge, well over a hundred-billion gallons."

Lara knew the famous Tuolumne River carried the water that originated from the melting snow of Yosemite National Park. Over 10,000 cubic feet per second of the precious fluid headed for cities and farms more than 200 miles away.

"That's a scary scenario," he continued. "If they were to contaminate the reservoir or its outflows, we'd have a major disaster on our hands!"

"Do the Iranians even have enough polonium to pollute all that water?" Lara countered.

"They do." The answer came back startlingly fast. "By now, they could have sufficient heavy-water reactors to stockpile a hundred pounds of polonium, enough to poison the whole state . . . and more."

Lara sat there, aghast. "What in the world can we do?"

"We have to stop their attack. But in order to do that, we have to know where it's headed. They've been feeding us loads of information, most of it fake. So, it's essential that we find out which to believe. We have two fronts in that battle. First, at your end, they're going to have you leading their team translating the IAPG messages we're sending. These will be designed to make them believe we're buying their false signals . . ."

"But how will we know which those are . . . ?"

"That's partly the job of our other team, the one that will be sending messages *deliberately* aiming at their defenses, messages that even their primitive decoding squads can deliver to their military arm, affirming our fake plans to intercept the troops they're pretending to send. In the end, it all depends on whose intelligence is better at misguiding the enemy. Which, of course, depends on whose agents are better at deception. It's a tough game; always has been."

Even with her background in military intelligence, it made her head spin. "But you'll have backup plans . . . right?"

"Of course. We're not laying all this on you! We're confident that our NSA guys are better at this than the bad guys by a long shot. And our field agents are better at their jobs than theirs could ever be. In any case, our backup plans have more layers than they might even imagine. But you and your partner are our first line of defense."

"Speaking of him . . . how is he doing?"

"He's hard at it, as you can imagine. I can't give you any details, for obvious security reasons, but he's on a parallel path." These words immediately brought to Lara's mind the question: Was Uri part of the team delivering the false offensive military instructions? It was a clever combination of deceptions: one arm aimed at convincing the enemy that *their* defensive strategy was working; the other that their offense was hidden from the Americans. It was clear to Lara that her job, eliminating the threat of the polonium from its source, was the first and most important line of defense. She didn't need to hear it from her boss.

"I get it, Tom. And I'll be on it."

"I know you will, and I have every confidence in you. Stay in touch." He ended on that upbeat note that told her he did, indeed, have that confidence. It was the hallmark of a strong leader.

Chapter 19

The next few days of work passed quickly. Lara stayed in the good graces of Captain Maloof as well as Major Asani; it was clear that both were eager for her attention and of their competitor's interest.

The following Wednesday, Asani brought her a captured American radio transmission labeled: *IAPG-SYSXXOPG 2035166-06.* "We just received this!" he said excitedly. "Signals Branch says the probable source is inside the country, perhaps near the northern Gulf. Not that it matters; it could have originated anywhere. The general thinks we were lucky enough to pick it up off a retransmission." His face beamed with this opportunity of making further inroads with his new colleague.

Lara saw the *IAPG* marker, knowing immediately it originated from Tom's team. "I'll give it top priority," she said promptly, realizing they would remember how quickly she had translated the first one. She was already clearing her desk as the major left her alone, but not before giving her a conspiratorial grin.

She recognized the coding details on the first reading, and then went back over it to make sure she'd gotten all the details correct. Tom wanted the Iranians to read and believe everything in this "secret" message. Why, she didn't know—yet. But she would call him tonight to check. Meanwhile, she wanted to get the translation to Asani within a reasonable time and, hopefully, learn his reaction.

The document was titled, "Peninsula Water Supplies—Access Points."

Wow, she thought to herself, *was this real or manufactured bait for the enemy?* There were four potable-water pipeline-entry points listed; that was clear. She read the document carefully, which seemed gibberish to the untrained eye, translating as she went:

Crystal Springs Reservoir, San Mateo, Skyline Boulevard. Easy access, not totally obscured.

Lower Crystal Springs Dam, Highway 92. Hiking trail, good cover.

San Mateo, Highway 92. Major station, full access, unguarded night entry.

Mid-Peninsula Water District, worker entry point, easy access, poor cover.

There were no maps or other details provided; apparently, these features were available in the public domain. Lara's heart was beating double-time as she typed her translation in Farsi on her government-issued computer. She saved it in her official documents folder and sent a copy to General Gharoub at his private email address. She had been assured on her first day that it was a totally secure address in a high-security government server.

She didn't have to wait long. An urgent phone call came from his private secretary in less than twenty minutes. She, along with Major Asani and Captain Maloof, were to report to his office at once. Lara hustled down the hall, carrying a copy of her translation in a plain manila folder inside her briefcase. She hadn't had time to thoroughly digest the contents of the intercept; but that was as it should be for someone who had just decoded such an important enemy message.

The two officers were already sitting in the general's office when she arrived. Closing the door behind her, she noted that each had a printed copy of her translation. "Gentlemen, and Ms. Haddad, you have in front of you a most interesting piece of paper," the general stated, getting right to the point. "Our Bandar station picked up this bit of news just this morning, and thanks to Ms. Haddad, you now see what the Americans know, or think they know, of our coming plans." He smiled, grooming his moustache with his fingers. "You see, this information was deliberately placed in their laps, so to speak, by our military intelligence branch near the Turkish border."

Lara tried to assimilate this latest bit of spycraft. So, the Iranians were attempting to assure the Americans that their bit of false information had been accepted. She would have to tell Tom his ploy had worked.

The general dismissed his agents shortly after this bombshell, and Lara headed to her office to look over her papers. After just a few minutes, she looked up to see a smiling Major Asani standing in her doorway. "Sorry to disturb you . . ." he began.

"Please, Major, have a seat. You seem to have something important to share with me." She was courteously pleasant with him.

"Yes, indeed. You seemed so interested in our little factory tour the other day," he began, clearly referring to the polonium poison plant, "that I thought you might like to see something even more critical . . ." He looked around to make sure no one was lurking nearby.

Lara, intrigued by this overture, gave him her full attention, leaning forward in her chair.

"Do you have an hour or two to spare this afternoon? I have something you will find even more interesting . . ." The major left the conversation hanging at this intriguing juncture.

"Of course, Major! I'd be very excited to see whatever it is you have for me." She had no need to feign her enthusiasm.

"If you might grab your bag and come with me now—I have already cleared our little trip with the general."

They were already on their way to the main exit of the building before Lara suddenly stopped in the reception area. "If you don't mind, Major, I would like to wash up first."

Asani obliged politely as Lara went into the visitor's restroom and rinsed her contacts, taking the moment to make sure her secret phone was securely tucked in its little pouch in her briefcase. She wanted to be certain that wherever they were headed was well recorded by the Agency's satellite.

As soon as they settled into the comfortable staff car that was waiting at the curb, Asani, sitting courteously at the other end of the spacious rear bench, began to explain this sudden trip. "General Gharoub has been very impressed with your work, the speed as well as the accuracy of your translations. When I told him of our trip to the, um, factory and how interested you were, he suggested this little jaunt to a location that you may find even more . . . fascinating."

Lara noticed that he glanced at the female lieutenant sitting opposite the driver. She was the apparent chaperone on this little junket. "At any rate, you will see another link in the little surprise we have in store for our . . . enemies." There apparently was no more to tell her before they reached their destination.

The route followed a paved two-lane road north of the city, just below the foothills of the Alborz mountains. The air was crisp, even in the early afternoon, and Lara was fascinated by the display of subalpine firs. After thirty minutes, the car came to an abrupt stop at an electrified fence and guard booth. Two armed sentries stood just beneath terse-looking "No Entry" signs; adjacent to these on the fence were the distinctive, universal "Radiation Hazard" signs. Lara's pulse was near panic level.

Major Asani showed his credentials to one of the sentries, who, along with his partner, examined them closely for a full minute, then used his walkie-talkie to communicate with an unseen person, no doubt inside the gray concrete building in front of them. After some more scrutiny, the guards allowed the driver to enter the premises and park the luxury car. On exiting the car, Lara noted the distinctive Iranian government flags displayed on the doors.

Lara and Asani were led into a sparsely appointed reception area, its walls adorned only with portraits of the current leader of the government and his predecessors. They each donned full-body protective suits along with radiation monitors, the type that measures actual dosage of alpha, beta, and gamma absorption. Only then were they permitted to enter the huge gray structure that obviously housed a nuclear reactor. A loud hum was as pervasive as it was insistent. Whether it was the sound of monitoring or air-cleaning equipment was not clear, but it was both annoying and frightening. They were led straightaway to a platform that overlooked a large pool of intensely clear water. Though the water was apparently quite deep, an insidious glow emanated from the region at the base of the concrete reactor itself, perhaps ten feet or more beneath the surface.

Lara knew what she was seeing: it was the Cherenkov radiation, which supersonic particles emanating from the reactor produced after being absorbed by the reactor's cooling water. The sinister glow might assure the observer that the water was absorbing the deadly radiation, safeguarding the people. It was like watching the creation, and hopefully nullification, of death itself. She glanced over at Asani's face and saw, rather than the fear that she herself felt, a gleam of satisfaction at the visible evidence of his nation's deadly game of nuclear transformation.

They stood there, mesmerized by both the visual and aural demonstration, until a guide escorted them courteously into a small classroom. There, the radiation badges were scanned to make sure nothing more than insignificant dosages had been absorbed. Then a professorial-looking gentleman took to the podium as the major and his guest took their seats.

"Hello, honored guests," the gray-bearded man said politely. "I am Professor Sabani. It is my privilege to explain to you the workings of our unique reactor." A slideshow commenced on a screen next to him. "What we are doing here is nothing less than transforming one element into another, something man—and woman—have struggled to do for centuries." The professor had all the attributes of a television pitchman; Lara smiled inwardly as he continued.

"In our heavy-water cooled reactor, elemental bismuth is bombarded with high-energy neutrons. After a few days, the product of this impact decays to the element known as polonium-210, one of the most poisonous materials known to man . . ."

"Yes, well thank you so much, professor," Asani interrupted. "That is all very interesting, but we must be on our way. We have a busy schedule as you know." He smiled graciously, nodding to Lara that they must depart. They exited the classroom, glancing briefly at the very pleased professor.

They moved quickly to the reception hall, where the major told their driver to bring their car around. Then, seeing the hall empty of other people, he said quietly to Lara, "I have shown you these facilities, the bottling plant and this reactor, in appreciation for all your excellent work in translating all the important messages from our enemies. And now I want to bring you up-to-date on our plans for the near future."

Lara held her breath for what must be coming.

"We are planning, as you know, a strike on the San Francisco municipal water supply. The general has been assessing all the incoming messages from the Americans, and we now know that they are anticipating our strike to come up the peninsula . . ."

"But where else could it come from . . . ?" Lara affected a puzzled demeanor.

Major Asani again checked the hall for any observers; this, after all, was one of the most secure buildings in Tehran. "The other likely path for an attack would be from the Hetch Hetchy reservoir, on the west end of their so-called Yosemite National Park. It captures all the precipitation from the park itself, an enormous amount of water, as you can imagine. Practically all the winter rain and snowfall in central California. It supplies the drinking water for more than ten million people!"

Lara feigned astonishment; it was easy enough in view of the enormity of what he had just announced. She even let her mouth drop open just a bit, to the major's delight. "But isn't the lake, or reservoir as you call it, under severe observation? How could your men possibly get the, uh, poison in . . . ?"

"You are very quick, indeed. Yes, ordinarily that would be difficult," he said, scanning the hall again for intruders. "But, you see, just this year, the park authorities have yielded to growing pressure from the public for more access to recreational facilities, especially in the hot summer months. Fishing and swimming have been allowed for some time. But they have just announced that, beginning July Fourth, pleasure boats will be allowed on the lake—for the first time since the building of the dam that created Hetch Hetchy. And it will be literally impossible for the authorities to inspect every motorcraft and sailboat on the lake at any given time. The opportunities for contamination of the lake, and thus the San

Francisco water supply, will be incredible. Hetch Hetchy will drain all the resources of the US government, if you will pardon the play on words." He grinned, pleased with his display of humor.

"So," she extrapolated, "with the Americans assuming you know of their plans to protect the peninsula . . ."

"How quick you are, indeed. Yes, they will assume we will choose the reservoir as our avenue for contamination." At that moment, their driver entered. Their vehicle was ready for them. After they each removed their protective gear, the major opened the door for Lara, and they proceeded to the waiting car.

Chapter 20

Uri spent what should have been a relaxing weekend at home; however, it was just the opposite. Friday, the Muslim holy day, was taken up with meal preparation and religious services. It was not, strictly speaking, the same as the Judeo-Christian Sabbath. In fact, the Prophet Muhammad had reportedly shunned any relation with the Jewish day of rest. Muslims were encouraged but not required to return to work after the afternoon prayer and sermon. In order that no suspicion be aroused, Uri had been instructed to spend the weekend with his ersatz family. If they were to run into relatives or neighbors, "Heydar" would be introduced as a distant cousin from the southern part of the country, in Tehran seeking employment. Tala had been looking forward to some time with her "cousin" so that she could show him some of the sights of the big city; she had made that abundantly clear.

Tala and Sarina did all the shopping for the weekend on Thursday. Friday morning, the family prepared for the afternoon prayer services and dinner. There would be guests for the meal, some friends of Sarina and Mohsen, who would arrive an hour or so after they returned from the mosque.

Uri made his early morning call to Tom. It was a convenient time, because it was Thursday evening in New York. Tom was delighted, of course, to hear of the success of their deception with the peninsular water plants and gave Uri instructions for his upcoming week at the Castle. That was first on the agenda. With the water running noisily in Uri's bathroom during the brief four-minute call, Tom told him that his assignment would no doubt be with Iran's Black Ops division, which was known to be headquartered at the secret fortification in the foothills above Tehran. The Castle had been constructed over the last decade as a highly fortified command center for most of the anti-American operations run by the Iranian

Revolutionary Government. The exterior had been under constant US surveillance all during its construction, but the interior was still largely a mystery. There were, however, multiple cable connections, both electronic and optical, that were constantly monitored as well as possible.

The division was headed by the notorious General Hossein Alirezeh, who had been with the revolution since the beginning, in 1979. He was, in fact, one of the young "students" who were responsible for the takeover of the American embassy on Taleghani Street in Tehran, now an anti-American museum. The compound occupied a full city block, decorated with gratuitous murals and slogans such as, "Death to America." The Great Seal of the United States, badly damaged, was an attractive novelty for the scores of Iranians who visited the compound daily, now laughingly known as "The US Espionage Den."

General Alirezeh was, as expected, a highly secretive individual. Photographs were nearly nonexistent. But he was known to be in his mid-seventies, physically fit, with a full head of artificially colored black hair. His ruthlessness was unequalled; he reportedly had several of his own family killed when they questioned his antipathy toward the United States. This, after a multibillion-dollar program of famine relief from the United States at the turn of the century.

Lara and Uri knew all this long before they embarked on their mission. The focus of this short conversation with Tom was Uri's specific task at the moment. He was to be America's eyes and ears inside the Castle, at least through the current drinking water terrorism campaign.

He would begin by making contact with the Americans, using the code he had deciphered in his initial interview at Sa'id's office. Uri would make a response in a CSfC appropriate for a field agent. Tom's men would pick it up and reply to this agent, identified once again as "U37FGI."

What Uri would communicate, as this nonexistent American agent, was that there was no impending threat to US drinking water supplies, at least on America's Pacific Coast. Uri would then intercept a return message, in code of course, from Homeland to Agent U37FGI thanking him for this reassuring information. This should establish a solid line of communication.

"What about the real agent U37FGI?" Uri wondered. Tom replied that this person was rumored to have been lost to "SAVAMA," the Iranian secret police that had evolved from the Shah's notorious SAVAK somewhere along the way, but without divulging any information. "Sort of murky, then . . ?"

"Right, that's the way things are over there; works to our advantage." Uri could almost see Tom smiling as he said this. "Make contact Sunday night if you can,"

"Will do. What about 'Daria'?" Uri inquired hopefully.

"Doing well. She's on a parallel path. But let's keep this short for now."

That would have to do it, Uri could tell. At least no bad news. Maybe there would be some good news next week.

* * *

Uri made some excuses dealing with work, aiming to keep some distance between himself and the amorous Tala until it was time for the Jumu'ah, or Friday afternoon prayer service. Each of the little family did their ritual washing, separately, of course, then dressed appropriately. Uri had with him his white "thobe," or long prayer shirt that he wore over jeans and slippers. He also wore a white knitted skullcap. He noticed, thankfully, that Mohsen was attired similarly; the two women were dressed in modest, dark clothing complete with head coverings.

At 2:00 p.m., the four of them: Tala, her "aunt" and "uncle," and the somewhat reluctant Uri headed for the local mosque just two blocks away. Other couples and small families made their way slowly to the service, some carrying simple prayer rugs. On the way, they chatted briefly with friends from the neighborhood, introducing "Heydar" as a distant cousin from the desert-like south of the country, in Tehran to look for work. This was a common theme: families in the big city helping relatives seek a living in the urban environment. They all wished him well, not knowing his experience or schooling and not about to pry.

At the mosque, Uri and Mohsen slipped off their sandals at the door and entered the men's section toward the front of the large hall. Head blocks made of stone were already in place as they each did the preparatory movements and uttered the appropriate prayers before prostrating themselves. Though Uri had sufficient practice, he still felt as if he were being stared at, the stranger from another district. Finally, the prayers began, the women out of sight in the rear of the hall, away from the men. Mohsen did not look at Uri at all; it had been clear from the outset that he was aware of Uri's true identity and was doing everything necessary to help this agent of the United States bring back a democratic Iran. He played his role perfectly. At the end of the service, in which Uri fully participated, a sermon was delivered by the local mullah, one that wished for peace and ascension of Ali, the true heir of Muhammad.

An hour or so after their arrival, all rose, greeted their neighbors, and recovered their sandals. Uri and Mohsen met Tala and Sarina outside, greeting them with wishes for a pleasant weekend. They began walking back home at a very slow pace, greeting a few of their neighbors, all of whom seemed to at least know of the presence of Heydar, who nodded and smiled at them. Along the way, Tala pointed to a monument outside the mosque, motioning for Uri to follow her. Sarina and Mohsen did not seem to notice; they continued on their slow pace toward home.

Tala pointed to some ornaments on the monument, but her voice was uncharacteristically low. "I know I may have seemed unusually forward toward you. It is part of the plan." Uri pretended to look at the monument as he considered her remarks. They were totally unexpected, especially in view of her behavior. He felt it best to go along as if nothing unusual were occurring. But if this were true, why hadn't Tom even mentioned it? Uri was extremely suspicious.

"Agent U37FGI—that is I. That is me," she said in English. Uri halted in his tracks, stunned by her statement. How would she even know this name, let alone the context? "All right," she added after a pause, "not exactly me, but I worked for him; he told no one, not even his contact in America, Tom Buckley."

This time, Uri spun around, at a loss for words. *How did she know who Buckley was, let alone his name?* He would have to check with Tom as soon as possible. For now, he would go along. "All right, tell me more," he said, walking around to the back of the monument, taking a peek at the people on the street; no one seemed suspicious.

"It was the way with us," she said. "His name was Harry; he was Israeli, like you." Uri felt a film of perspiration form all over his body. *How could she know all this?* "We pretended to be lovers; it would explain the closeness between us. We were not, but no one suspected the collaboration. Even Sarina and Mohsen, they just assumed we were . . . intimate. That's what I was hoping to set up with you. I know you are married, and quite happily," Uri was flabbergasted. He would just have to listen and see where this led. He could then check in with Tom.

"There is another plan against the American water supply system; you must alert them to it."

Uri circled the monument before replying, "Can we talk about this later, after the guests leave?"

"Certainly," she said, smiling. "They will not stay long. They are going on a trip tomorrow early." She then added an afterthought: "Tell him about the Boris affair two years ago." She looked him straight in the eyes for an instant. Then, "It was me."

Uri nodded, pretending to look at the far side of the monument as they returned to the sidewalk, his brain whirling. He did not discuss the matter further; they caught up to Sarina and Mohsen and walked in silence the short distance to their house. Once there, Uri said he would like to change clothes and take care of a few matters from work before dinner, which would be at five. He did, in fact, change back to his casual attire but then immediately checked in with Tom. He left a message that he needed to talk to him tonight; that is, this morning, Friday, in New York between 6:00 a.m. and 7:00 a.m. It was urgent, he added unnecessarily. Then he went downstairs to greet the visitors for tea before dinner. It took all of his charm to discuss his brief time in the city, then as quickly as possible switch the topic to the guests, their family, and their life in Tehran. It was about 7:00

p.m. when the guests made their excuses, saying they were taking a trip to the mountains tomorrow, a Saturday, and needed to pack. They left on an agreeable note, pledging to get together again soon.

Seeing that the time was now right for calling Tom, he started to head upstairs, just as Tala reminded him of the "walk" she had suggested that afternoon.

"Of course, just let me wash my hands and put on my walking shoes and socks," he replied casually. She nodded; of course, she knew he would be contacting Tom, informing him of the startling news she had given him after the prayer service.

Up in his room, the water running, he reached Tom on the first ring. "What's happened, Uri?" the chief said instantly.

"Agent U37FGI . . . my host says it's her! She knows all about you!"

There was a stunned silence on the other end of the line as Tom tried to process this information.

"Are you there, Tom?"

"Yes . . . yes, of course . . . it's just that . . . how in the world!?"

"She said to tell you of the Boris affair from a couple of years ago. Does that make any sense?"

There was another pause before Tom replied. "Yes . . . he was a Russian agent working for the Iranians. Our team, those working for the agent you mentioned, helped . . . dispose of him. She must have been at least aware of it, perhaps more . . . Can you get any more details from her before . . . ?"

"I'll be talking to her again this evening. Can I reach you later . . . at this number?"

"Certainly, yes, of course. This changes things, as you can imagine."

"Give me an hour or two at the most. I'll get what I can." Uri broke the connection, shut off the water, and headed downstairs, his footwear changed.

Tala, as agreed, was waiting for him at the foot of the stairs, an amorous smile on her lips. As they headed out the door, she held on to his arm, denoting to anyone watching that she was in his charge, a requirement for her to be out on the street after dark. They had walked only a block in the direction of a small park before she began the conversation, still gripping his arm. "They are not going to attack the Los Angeles plant again. This time it will be another area entirely. I'm not yet sure exactly where. It may not even be on the West Coast."

Without breaking stride or otherwise indicating alarm, Uri replied, "How is it you know all this?"

"I have a contact on the other side . . . He is my real lover . . . we both want to be rid of the ayatollah's regime, to be friends with the West. It is best for all of us."

"Tell me who this is."

"I cannot, not yet. It is too dangerous for him."

"At least, then, *where* is he?" Uri was insistent.

"I cannot; not yet, at least." She left some hope that he might learn more at some point. But for now, she wouldn't budge; they walked on in relative silence after this. Only the cooing of the nesting doves in the trees could be heard in this relatively quiet neighborhood.

She suddenly relaxed her grip on his arm, saying, "We really should be getting back."

Uri was fine with that; he simply nodded and started back the way they had come. On arriving home, she was all smiles again as they greeted the family. Uri excused himself and headed upstairs to prepare for bed. In his room, he immediately called Tom, still at work. With the water running, he went over the remarkable conversation he had just had with Tala.

"Our information was that the agent was given up to the Iranians and . . . eliminated," Tom responded after just a slight pause. "We haven't heard from him in months. We knew he had an accomplice, did not identify him or her, for their sakes. But what she says may be true . . . we have to consider it, anyway. Have to wait for info from Lara, some confirmation. Don't want to tip our hand. For now, leave it at that until Tala comes up with more. Take the weekend to learn more about the location, try to relax . . . that's an order." Uri could hear the satisfaction in Tom's voice. He must feel they were making progress.

Chapter 21

Uri was installed in Iranian military headquarters, housed in the Castle, in the foothills of the Alborz mountains northeast of the city. General Alirezeh had arranged for a car to bring him and three or four others of his staff from downtown to his new offices here. As Heydar, Uri was facing his first real test as chief advisor to the general. He was given a small but well-outfitted office in the old stone structure left over from the seventeenth century.

His job was to translate American transmissions intercepted by Iranian agents at a location unknown to Uri; he guessed it was somewhere outside Iran where the locals had broken into the S-band the Americans were using. What the Iranians didn't know was that the fault in the S-band was deliberate, allowing them to "listen in." It had taken months for Tom's team to make certain the ruse had worked. But now, in addition to low-priority messages, Tom's team was sending missives hidden in a new code, so far unrecognized by the Iranians.

For the first two weeks, Uri submitted translations of the intercepts, using his knowledge of the American code that he had demonstrated for the Iranians, most particularly General Alirezeh. Tom briefed him daily as to what the messages were meant to convey. They were designed by Tom's team in New York to look like instructions for a team of American undercover agents hidden near the Turkish border, in preparation for some sort of strike against Iranian outposts in the mountains. In reality, they were merely a guise to confuse the Iranian military, especially Alirezeh and his "Black Ops" division.

* * *

Uri dutifully translated the intercepts in such a way that they appeared to be detailing a multipoint operation against Iranian research outposts around Esfahan. He communicated these daily to Alirezeh in his afternoon dispatches. To verify the accuracy of this information, Tom's team sent innocuous drones from high-flying aircraft into the area around Esfahan. These drones were immediately shot down by the Iranians, as Tom anticipated. But their contents were useless to the hapless Iranian military; even Uri seemed unable to find anything useful in them. However, these drones, in concert with the signals Uri translated, verified that something was indeed imminent.

Then one day, the general summoned Uri into his office with some important news. Alirezeh was trim for a man in his seventies, splendid in his tailored uniform. Just as many of the Iranian officers, he dyed his hair and moustache a shiny black in an attempt to present the image of a vigorous, younger man. His eyes were the most noteworthy of his features; they gleamed with an intensity that was almost matched by his predator-like nose. His stare was worthy of a great mountain eagle.

Uri had just arrived when the general presented him with some sobering news. The night before, the general told him tersely, a message from the Americans appeared, couched apparently in a new version of their code; markers indicated something very important and immediate. Uri was to put down everything else and strive to translate this dispatch.

Uri headed back to his office, knowing full well what it contained. Tom had alerted him just last night of this memorandum: it was the outline of the Iranians' plan for insertion of polonium-210 into the San Francisco waterworks! That is, it was the Americans' *countermeasures* to the plan they had reason to believe had been chosen by the Iranian strike team. It did not go into detail as to how or why the Americans had chosen this strategy to foil the attack, only that it was firm and operational. It was, as Uri knew, the plan that the other branch of his disinformation team had deliberately allowed to reach Alirezeh.

Uri took two hours to give the appearance of a difficult translation; it was a complex and detailed plan of counterattack. Seeming breathless and unnerved, Uri hustled back to the general holding his "translation" in shaking hands. Briefly, it stated that the Americans were convinced the Iranian attack on the water supply would be made on the Hetch Hetchy reservoir, well to the east of the city. The earlier information they had received suggesting the Americans were expecting an attack on the peninsular lakes was a ruse meant to encourage an Iranian attack on the Hetch Hetchy instead. The message even listed the actual lakes involved in the plan, with details of the terrain and access points!

Alirezeh seemed stunned, to say the least, as he read through Uri's translation. The expectation had been that the Americans would ready themselves for an attack on the Hetch Hetchy reservoir. Just this year, the US government was allowing pleasure boats onto the lake, access that had never before been granted. General Alirezeh silently read the report again. He permitted Uri to leave only after he carefully considered the full impact of this American transmission. *He was holding their top-secret plans to counter the expected Iranian attack!*

Uri left work feeling the euphoria of a man who has just sprung a monumental trap against his enemy. He was certain the Iranians would modify whatever plans they had made and zero in on the peninsula reservoirs. He headed home ready to telephone Tom with the good news.

Chapter 22

Uri delivered his news to a surprised and delighted Tom as soon as he arrived home that evening. "All right," Tom replied, "but we need to keep tabs on what they do from here on out. We can't just assume they will fall into our hands." The invigorated agent had an uneventful evening meal, then headed up to bed.

The next morning seemed no different as Uri had his breakfast, except that Tala was not present. Her "aunt" and "uncle" told him that she had been called away to some matter at the market but would be home in time for dinner. Uri then made his way up to the Castle in good spirits and on to his job. Nothing seemed at all changed as he translated more unremarkable messages from the Americans, mostly to do with supplies: food and clothing, but not arms.

It was near 10:00 a.m. when a uniformed sergeant tapped politely on his door. The general would like a word with him, he told Uri. But instead of delivering the message and leaving, the armed sergeant waited, apparently to escort Uri to the general's office. This seemed a bit unusual to Uri, but not alarming; he had witnessed more troubling incidents than this one. They moved as one along the corridor without arousing any curious glances from the other workers. They were used to armed men in the building.

But as they turned the corner and headed into Alirezeh's open door, everything changed dramatically. The door closed behind him, and Uri found himself confronted with five glowering Iranian officers and two enlisted men; the sergeant had quietly drawn his sidearm from its holster. Uri, who would ordinarily have identified the make and model of the automatic weapon, did not even glance at it. It was immediately obvious that he was under arrest. The hair on his neck rose, and his bowels loosened ever so slightly. This had come out of the blue; his mind churned as he struggled for an explanation.

"Well, Heydar, or whatever your name is," Alirezeh started in English, "how are you today? Or would you be more comfortable speaking Hebrew?" The officers, mostly colonels, Uri could see, laughed heartily.

"What on earth are you talking about?" Uri tried gamely in Farsi.

"Oh, good try, my friend, but you see, 'the jig is up,' as they say in the old American movies. I presume you are familiar with them."

Uri made a half-hearted try to reach his pocket, but two of the sergeants caught his hands before he could do so. They twisted both of his arms behind his back as an officer turned both of Uri's pants' pockets inside out. A small blue capsule dropped to the floor.

"Well, what do we have here?" Alirezeh said, chuckling. "Do you suffer from erectile dysfunction?" The others laughed appreciatively. "You won't have to worry about that anymore, I can assure you." He turned to his audience, ordering a sergeant to get Uri's briefcase from his office.

As the man left to get the briefcase, the general, clearly amused now, repeated his question to Uri. "Are you prepared to fill us in a bit about your true name and assignment, or do you need some persuasion?"

Uri had by now recognized what was going on; someone had turned on him, though he had no idea yet of who, or why it had come at this particular time.

He assumed the manner of someone falsely charged and took on an attitude of justified arrogance. "Look, General, I don't know what you have been told, nor by whom, but I assure you I am exactly who I said I was, and yes, that blue pill is, in fact, a libido enhancer, as you so correctly announced."

"Take it, then. I won't stop you from your apparent noontime pleasure," the general countered. Uri reached for the cyanide capsule but a little too eagerly. He would have been glad to get this over with right now. "Not so fast, my amorous asset of the enemy. You'll not get out of this that easily."

A quick frown of disappointment crossed Uri's face as he saw his easy death taken from him, the cyanide pill dropping into the general's pocket. At that moment, his briefcase appeared at the door in the hands of the sergeant. Uri was roughly thrust down into a chair as Alirezeh went through the contents of the briefcase. The room was deathly quiet as the general brought out items one by one. There were two folders of messages, coded transmissions in one and translations in the other. There was an address book that the general handed to an aide, then a Persian-made mobile phone that he pocketed himself. The search seemed concluded when suddenly Alirezeh pulled out, with a cry of triumph, another small mobile device hidden deep in an interior pocket.

"Well, now, what is this, my creative friend? Are you so embedded with eager females you need two mobiles to keep track?" The room exploded with mirth; it was clear the famous general was going to have some fun with this butterfly on a pin before feeding him to the fish.

"And you, 'Heydar,' will go along with our team to a place not nearly as comfortable as you are used to. Before they are through with you, you will wish you had complied with me right now."

"Here, Saad," he said to one of his officers, handing him the device. "See what your men can retrieve from this piece of American junk." The man took it and headed out the door. Uri at least had the pleasure of hearing the small explosion and cries of shock as the tiny cyanide pellet hidden in his phone hit its mark.

Chapter 23

General Alirezeh stared at his colonels as he strode back and forth in front of his desk, his riding crop smacking into his boot as he fumed at his men. It was a rather good imitation of Adolf Hitler in the closing days of World War II.

Just this morning, a woman had brought him some amazing and useful information. He stared at his officers as he raged: "The information we have on the Americans' defense is near useless! We now know our master translator is a counterfeit, in the pay of the enemy; our conclusions regarding their expectations of our attack points are of no value. 'Heydar' was just a clever impersonator, we now know, and the enemy is probably *aware* that we know. Therefore, they also know that we are aware that the 'plan of defense' they sent us is a *ruse*. So, they will assume we will scrap our scheme of attacking one of the pumping stations on the peninsula!"

He saw the confusion on the faces of his officers. "Never mind all that," he declared, smacking his whip against his boot even harder. "We will best them yet. They, the Americans, will conclude that we will, instead, attack the Hetch Hetchy reservoir. After all, it is even more tempting than the peninsula pumping stations. The decision of their politicians to open the reservoir to public pleasure boats will be an overwhelming enticement, they will reason, to pour in our poison from one or more of these little boats. Americans, as you know, have more money and time on their hands than they know what to do with. This Fourth of July will bring boaters by the hundreds to this, the largest freshwater lake within driving distance from San Francisco and the whole Bay Area."

The colonels marveled at the cleverness of their leader! He was beating the Americans at their own game. "While they may set up a secondary defense on the peninsula, they will have no idea, now that their gent has been neutralized, which particular pumping station to guard. We hall, as they say, 'catch them with their pants down.'"

The general paused at the sight of one of the colonels waving his hand. It was the youngest of the lot, Col. Sagib Moroneh. "Yes, Sagib, my friend, what is it?"

The slender, light-complexioned man, a hero of the Iraq War, asked in a most obsequious manner: "But won't the Americans be suspicious when they find no evidence at all of an incursion at the Hetch Hetchy reservoir on July Fourth?"

"Very good point, Sagib. Yes, we have considered that. So, we will have a small contingent of resourceful men there at the reservoir, with polonium, along with the means to scatter it into the water. It will be a suicide squad, of course, ready to spend eternity in Paradise for their sacrifice. They will no doubt be captured or killed by the Americans. But by then, they will find it is too late. Our bona fide team will have laced the peninsula with the bulk of the poison."

Chapter 24

Lara called Tom the next night. "None too soon," Tom said immediately, a dreadful foreboding in his voice. "He's been taken, I'm afraid." She sank limply down onto her bed. All sorts of images appeared to her, none of them good.

"What's happened, Tom?" she whispered. "Is he . . . ?"

"No, we don't think so," he replied, reading her mind. "They took him at work, we're pretty sure . . ."

"How did you . . . ?"

"The mobile phone, you know, the agency one? Like I told you, it's booby trapped. It must have been taken from him, and one of their techies used it, or tried to and . . ."

"It blew? You're sure it wasn't Uri being clumsy?"

"No, he knew better. It would only go off if someone with another handprint tried to use it, or open it. It's very new, not something they would be expecting . . . we got the signal just a while ago. Someone's got a cyanide present in their ear, eye, or hand. Uri failed to check in, so he's probably prisoner . . ."

"You don't think they—"

"Unlikely. If they found him, they know he's too big a prize to just discard . . . sorry, that's ill-put of me."

"Do you have any idea where . . . ?"

"Not yet, but soon, I'm sure," he said hopefully. "We have a plan in the works. It includes you."

"How . . . what do you mean?"

There was a brief pause as Tom decided what to tell her and how to detail her anticipated involvement. "He's been working with their military operations division the whole time you've been with their military intelligence. It seemed an ideal setup."

"Until he got caught," Lara added cynically.

"I admit it looks bad at the moment, but we have a lot on our side."

"Such as . . . ?"

"They know very little about him and so are not going to be hasty."

"You mean they won't kill him right away."

"That's right, actually. They'll figure they have more to gain by keeping him alive, and—"

"And torturing him until he can't take any more."

"Wait a minute! In the first place, killing him gets them nothing— and Uri's one tough guy. If they have this operation in the works, they're going to want to know what they're up against, and a dead agent is useless to them."

"But torture . . . oh my God, Tom, do you know what they're capable of?"

"Which means we have to act fast, use our advantage here—"

"What do you mean?"

"They don't have any idea about *you* . . . I mean, your identity. They have no suspicion that there is another asset inside their system, especially in military intel."

"Meaning?"

Tom was relieved to hear that she was still open to suggestions. "Meaning their military operations branch is obliged to bring the intel division into the game as soon as there is a breach of security. Our branch works the same way . . ."

"Wait a minute." Lara immediately began thinking of the possibilities Tom was suggesting. "You think they're going to ask intel to help interrogate . . . ?"

"I think it's highly likely. After all, they don't want to lose this gigantic opportunity. And they're very happy with your work so far, right?" There was a long pause as Lara considered this.

"Yes, I'll grant you that, but . . ."

"So, they have this huge operation underway, needing all the intel they can get, and here pops this opportunity—"

"But isn't that curiously convenient? Suspicious? Here comes this translator out of the blue—"

"Happens all the time. In a situation where they need all the intel they can get, why would they turn down something like you? There isn't the slightest hint of collusion between you and him . . . right?"

Lara thought hard about that. He was right; there wasn't any connection at all suggesting they were even acquainted. They arrived at two separate locations with totally different backgrounds and resumes. "So . . . what do we do?"

"I say give it a day or so. The two generals involved, Gharoub and Alirezeh, are actually good buddies; went to school together . . ."

Lara listened eagerly as Tom described her next dangerous assignment.

Chapter 25

It was less than a full day before Lara received the expected green light from General Gharoub. It actually came from her "friend," Major Asani. She should have expected it, seeing as he had been grooming her for the past week. He summoned her to his office the very next morning, smiling both in satisfaction and expectation. Something was indeed afoot.

"Dear Ms. Haddad," he began formally, but with high anticipation glowing in his voice, "an amazing thing has just occurred. Well, yesterday, actually. Our esteemed general has heard from our 'cousins' over in Operations."

She knew he was speaking of the military operations division. She sat up in her chair, full of excitement.

"It seems they have found a usurper in their midst, a spy for the Americans. And they now hope that we can extract the truth from this man. Of course, General Alirezeh, their commandant, has come immediately to us, knowing of your expertise in both Hebrew and English. This man, it appears likely, is either with Mossad or the CIA. You and I will get first crack at him."

Lara had to keep her eagerness under control. *This must be Uri!*

"He was reported by one of our female counterespionage agents." Asani must have seen Lara's reaction to the hint of a sexual liaison in his voice; the major picked it up at once. "Oh, I'm not suggesting any impropriety occurred on her part. We certainly don't allow that sort of behavior with our agents. We do give them certain latitude, but . . ."

Lara struggled to keep her composure. She hoped the major interpreted her discomfort as objection to a woman in the employ of the Iranian government using this means to extract information. "Of course, Major," she finally said.

"In any case, this man was found with the tools of his trade in his possession. Along with, I should add, a booby-trapped mobile phone that exploded as it was being examined. General Alirezeh is very distressed at the loss of one of his top men; he is eager to have this spy fully debriefed before being executed."

Lara twisted in her chair; she hoped her unease came across as a lack of pleasure at the idea of execution. She was, after all, supposed to be a desk agent, not a killer.

Major Asani was actually pleased by this show of femininity from his lovely officer. He continued to hope for more than formal interaction with her. "Unless you have a strong objection, we should make haste to the prison where this spy is being held. Our pending plan against the water plant requires us to take immediate action."

Lara just nodded her assent as the major rose, signifying they were to be on their way.

"If you will just bring your . . . ah, necessities, then, I'll drive us myself. The holding facility is, fortunately, just a few miles away."

Lara rose quickly, her head filled with the list of essentials she needed. She had already gone through a "rehearsal" in her mind, hoping for just this sort of opportunity. She had, for example, brought her "B" weapon in her bag. The *B* stood for *bamboo*. It was constructed of a single shaft of plastic that was similar to bamboo but stronger, some four inches long; it appeared to be a lipstick or other cosmetic in a shiny plastic container. It contained no metal, thus allowing it to pass through a metal detector. But once the cap was removed, a three-inch-long spike flipped into place, honed to a razor-sharp point. Used properly, it was capable of imparting sudden death. This had to be her only weapon . . .

She followed the major briskly to his sedan. On the short trip to the military holding facility, he briefed her on their mission. "The spy is being held at a secret jail just outside the city. There are no markings on the building, and there are only two entrances; one of these is an emergency exit only. This gives it the look of a low-security enclosure, not a high-security prison . . . to keep it from appearing a target for antigovernment ealots. We've found that the less-conspicuous enclosures are the least apt ɔ be attacked during any sort of demonstration."

He parked the sedan in a space reserved for high-ranking military, lacing a placard in the windscreen. With the major in the lead, they entered ie front door, guarded by a single sentry armed with an automatic rifle. He ecognized Major Asani at once, nodding discreetly to him. Lara, however, ad to sign in at the desk with a prim-looking female sergeant, armed with 9mm pistol. She looked back and forth between Asani and Lara ieaningfully, as though this were not the first time he had brought in female isitors. Although the major was allowed to keep his automatic pistol, Lara ad to have her bag inspected and then passed through a metal detector. To er great relief, there was no problem with her phone. Had it been otherwise, ie mission would have ended—badly.

"Do you need an escort, Major?" the sentry asked formally. Asani ıst shrugged and moved into the secure area; he had been here many times. ⹂ buzzer sounded as the two visitors entered a dark concrete corridor with single closed-circuit monitor and floodlight at the first bend in the hallway. ara could see ahead with the aid of the single light bulb, all the way to an xit about forty feet ahead. They passed quickly to the door leading out of ie tunnel and, presumably, to the holding cells.

The major rang the bell on the door, giving rise to a loud electronic elp. There was a buzz as the door opened to a well-lit room with three iilitary men seated at a desk. They jumped to attention as the visitors ntered.

"Major Asani, good to see you! We have been expecting you. And . . your, uh, associate?"

"This is my assistant, Ms. Haddad."

The soldiers eyed Lara with more than military interest.

"She will help interrogate your captive," Asani barked at the first ian, a corporal, gruffly.

"Of course, Major." The second man, a lieutenant, rapidly came to ttention. One did not question the famous major. The lieutenant motioned ɔr the corporal to open the single cell door. He leaped to the task, unlocking the door with a key on his belt as the third man, a sergeant, stood behind a desk. Lara took a second to look around the small facility. Sure enough, there to the left of the cell were the red handle and sign for the emergency exit. *Lucky these guys have taken our safety courses*, she thought.

Lara held her breath as the cell opened slowly, revealing a disheveled, unshaven Uri, his eyes blazing as he took in the scene. His face was badly bruised and his good eye blackened; it was clear he had been pummeled with a blunt object. "So, this is our American spy," Major Asani spat out derisively. "What do you have to say for yourself?"

Uri just stood there impassively.

"You have no statement?" the major challenged him. Uri said nothing but gave Lara a scornful grin, as if to say, "You Iranians require the aid of women, I see."

Asani told the lieutenant to prepare the interrogation room and turned on his heel, motioning Lara to follow him back into the tunnel "We'll be right back," he said to the guards. "I can see this is a tough guy: at least he thinks he is. I have some 'tools' back in the car." The tunnel door closed behind the two visitors as they started back down the gloomy concrete corridor.

Lara gave Asani a look of silent appreciation as they started back toward the entrance. She had taken the few moments in the interim to remove her weapon from her bag and secrete it in her left hand. "You certainly know how to handle these people!" she said as she lightly took the major's arm in her right hand, moving closer to him, allowing her body to graze ever-so-slightly against his. It was their first physical contact, and as she'd anticipated, that was all he needed. He reached around gruffly grasping her by the back of the neck, bringing his face down to hers.

This is it, Lara thought, *my one and only chance*. She brought her left hand around his neck, dropping her open bag at her feet. His hot tobacco-laden breath wafted onto her face as she pretended to yield to his advance, her lips open in response, her right hand around his waist, pressing into him. His mouth opened in anticipation; she could feel the hinge of his jaw dropping to allow him to thrust his tongue into her mouth.

And that was her signal. Her left hand, holding the deadly spike, drove it inward and down, directly into his now-exposed medulla oblongata, the nerve center for his heart and lungs. The spike did its job with remarkable swiftness; he gasped once, stiffened, then collapsed, gagging, onto the floor. Lara withdrew the spike and slipped it back into her bag. Simultaneously, she yelled for assistance from the soldiers.

"Help, someone, please! Something's happened to the major! Help!" She grabbed his keys, stuffing them into her bag. Finally, she removed his pistol and silencer from his holster, pushing them under her belt. Hopefully, the tunnel was dark enough for no one to notice.

There was the jangle of the alarm as the lieutenant and sergeant raced into the tunnel, pistols at the ready. Thankfully, they blocked open the door so they could easily return.

"Yes, miss, what is it? What's happened?" the lieutenant asked anxiously.

"I don't know. He just collapsed. Maybe a heart attack?" She appeared totally distraught.

"There's no blood," the sergeant reported, shining a flashlight on the body. "Must be something internal. Stroke, maybe?"

The lieutenant gazed at the motionless Asani as the sergeant turned the body over, searching for wounds but not knowing quite what to do. As the two soldiers looked at each other for ideas, Lara slipped out of the light from the overhead bulb and screwed the silencer onto the major's pistol. As the soldiers examined the body more carefully, two drops of blood suddenly oozed out of the wound on Asani's neck. Lara had no choice: she pumped a quick round into each of their faces as they turned to her. Without another sound, the two men dropped to the tunnel floor. She immediately picked up their pistols and stuffed them under her belt, keeping the major's silenced weapon at the ready.

Hearing the commotion, the corporal, who had stayed back at the prison enclosure, yelled into the gloom, "What's wrong? What happened?"

"Help, Corporal, please, we need help!" Lara headed back to the door, knowing he had a key, presumably the only one, to Uri's cell.

Seeing the silenced automatic in her hand, the confused young man backed into the enclosure. At her visual command, he unlatched his holster, dropping it on the floor as he moved away toward Uri's cell. Lara saw the key on his belt as she put the muzzle of her gun in front of his face. "Stay calm, Corporal, and you won't get hurt."

The young man swallowed hard as he stared at the enormous-looking weapon.

"Now open the cell door." He did as she ordered, never taking his eyes far from the silencer staring back at him.

A relieved Uri exited the cell, picked up the corporal's weapon and holster, and strapped them on himself. He hugged Lara for the briefest of seconds, saying unnecessarily, "We need to go!" and headed for the emergency exit. He banged it open with his arm, setting off a barrage of sirens that could be heard for miles, or so it seemed. Lara pointed to the major's sedan, and the strange-looking threesome headed straight for it, Lara leading the way and Uri controlling the frightened young corporal.

Uri directed the soldier to the backseat and strapped him in securely as Lara held him at gunpoint. He used some ropes Major Asani had conveniently left in the rear seat to use for the captured Uri. Once the soldier was immobilized, Lara got into the driver's seat and started the engine, using the GPS screen on the dashboard to head west, out of the city. Meanwhile, Uri, now next to her in the front passenger seat, probed the major's car radio, hoping that its signal would not set off an immediate alarm. He tuned into the emergency frequency of Tom's phone, using the nonsecure citizens band. He hoped Tom's staff would be able to generate a path to a helicopter rescue via an emergency pickup from the Caspian Sea. The remaining Iranian staff at the holding facility might not yet have had time to alert their army of Asani's assassination.

Uri found the correct frequency and, using their emergency code, radioed the coordinates of the city of Qazvin, 120 miles northwest of Tehran; the navy should be able to complete their rescue. If it were possible, they would hear a verification signal back within the hour. Meanwhile, Lara noted the GPS showed they were headed toward a major route south, toward the Persian Gulf; she turned onto it. That should get the Iranians headed in the wrong direction.

"The GPS—can you switch it off?" Lara asked the corporal. After a slight pause, she added, "Your life is at stake." The soldier nodded reluctantly as she pulled onto a small side road, protected by large trees and bushes. Uri released his bonds, and the young man gingerly got into the front seat, opening the glove compartment. As the two agents watched carefully, he unscrewed a globelike electronics package and handed it to Uri. The soldier nodded, in anticipation of his release.

"Not yet, Corporal, but soon," Uri said. The soldier grudgingly got into the back seat again.

They started off once more, still not noticing any police or army vehicles chasing them, nor hearing any sirens. Seeing a blank screen where the GPS display had been, Lara assumed they would now be invisible to the Iranian authorities. She turned quickly to Uri, who nodded subtly. As soon as she saw a likely spot, she exited again onto a small side road and drove west for about a mile, stopping at a barren area.

The corporal, fearing for his life, turned pale. "It's all right," Lara told him kindly. "We're letting you out here. You can walk back to the highway and get a ride to your base."

She returned his identification papers, then gave him about twenty dollars in Iranian currency. "Good luck to you," she said sincerely.

He looked back and forth between her and Uri, who just nodded. Still unsure of what was happening, he just sat there, uncertain what to do.

Finally, Lara asked him bluntly, "Why did you disarm the GPS when we asked you to?"

There was an awkward silence while he seemed to consider his reply. "The major and the others were going to kill him," he said, gesturing at Uri. "I heard them talking about it. What's more, they were talking about poisoning the drinking water in California somewhere. They were laughing about it." He paused. "You see, I have relatives in California . . . I never told anyone about them . . . but I couldn't stand by while they were being executed like that. Do you see?" He stared at Uri, presuming he, being the man, was in charge.

"May Allah be with you, Corporal. I trust you not to give us away. Roll around out there in the dirt as if you have been in a fight; say you escaped from us, that you have no idea where we're headed," Lara said.

The frightened soldier looked back and forth at his two captors, mumbled, "Thanks be to Allah," and dirtied himself as she had asked.

Lara turned the sedan around and returned to the highway. At the first opportunity, she crossed over and headed north toward a marker denoting the major four-lane to the northwest and Qazvin. A mile ahead was a cloverleaf junction, and she was able to smoothly make the transition. Should the corporal change his mind and report them, he would have no idea in which direction his captors had gone. She and Uri were aware that the last GPS signal the Iranians had from the major's sedan showed it heading south toward the Persian Gulf, a reasonable destination for the fugitives. With any luck, the agents would be at their emergency pickup point in less than two hours, within helicopter range of the Caspian. She noticed on the dash that Major Asani had conveniently kept the fuel tank near the full mark. They could survive on the sandwiches and water the deceased major had packed in the trunk.

Chapter 26

The two agents arrived at Qazvin just before dusk. Uri showed the effects of his imprisonments, though he didn't complain; he was too happy to be on the loose, and even better, with his loved one. As Uri rubbed his angry-looking bruises and shifted uncomfortably in the seat, Lara did all the driving. They compared notes on the details of the emergency pickup and headed to the small municipal airport on the north edge of town. It was hardly an airport at all, merely two airstrips perpendicular to each other with a weather vane and sock roughly indicating wind direction and speed. There was no control tower; there were strictly "visual flight rules only" here. This was to be expected if their rescue was to be secret.

They drove, as instructed, with Uri at the wheel, to the north end of the north-south runway and searched for the sign showing the campground. Sure enough, there was a battered, old sign amid remnants of oilseed plants. Oilseed was the main agricultural product in this semidesert area of Iran; it looked much like western Kansas. They parked the major's sedan in the shelter of crops taller than the car and walked in the direction shown by the sign. They were pleased to note that the yellow and brown dust had all but obliterated the insignias of the major's office from the doors, and the license plate was unreadable.

Tom's description of their surroundings, as they remembered, turned out to be quite apt. For the first time since they'd dropped off their captive, they spoke to each other freely. It had been nearly three hours, and the sun was settling toward the western horizon to their left. "It's almost empty prairie," Lara stated, looking around at the rolling hills to their left and right, with the steeper foothills of the mountains directly ahead.

Undulating waves of yellow oilseed seemed to send greetings, as if no other humans ever had walked among them.

They trudged on for another fifteen minutes before Uri pointed out the approaching sunset. "No chance of contact anymore today. It's well past fifteen hundred." He was referring to the time the observation drone was due to pass overhead, hopefully spotting them.

Suddenly, Lara glimpsed a nomad's hut in a small clearing; it nearly matched the color of the ripening oilseed. She noticed a scattering of similar huts, all but invisible against the tall stalks of crops. In the open flap of the first hut, a small, wizened old man sat, his face baked from years in this dry climate. "Welcome, my friends," he said in Farsi with a wide toothless grin, waiting for a response.

Noting that he directed his greeting solely to the man, Uri replied in Farsi, also with a friendly smile. "And you would be Omar, is it not so?"

"Indeed! My friend Tom has sent you here, am I not correct?"

The agents were startled but also pleased by the recognition. These were the first comforting words they had heard in a long time. "It is so, my friend. May we impose on you for a night or two?"

"Of course, my friends! Let me introduce my wife, Karin." He turned to an old woman even smaller than he, who was sitting just inside the tent. She too carried the imprint of the inhospitable climate on her sun blasted face. She smiled broadly at the visitors, exhibiting an irregular set of yellow teeth. The pair may have been a strange sight for the agents, but their greeting was clearly genuine. Lara and Uri bowed graciously to their new friends.

"May we serve you some hot tea and cakes? I understand you have had quite a journey." Once again, Omar directed his remarks to Uri.

That was as wonderful an offer as they could have imagined in this remote location. Tom had intimated that these nomads, who tended the crops during the growing season, were in the pay of the CIA, who maintained contact with them. They were fiercely opposed to the ayatollah and the rigid Muslim government. While Karin shuffled into the tent to see to the refreshments, Omar showed Uri the tent they were to occupy during heir short stay. It was discreetly separated from the remainder of the workers' housing area, much to Lara's relief.

"May we ask that you communicate our arrival to Tom?" Uri asked his host gently.

"It will be my pleasure," Omar said immediately. "It will be early morning there now, and he will be relieved to hear of your safe transit. Here, let me show you your temporary lodgings. You will have to excuse our primitive accommodations . . ." He gestured sympathetically at the community outhouse at the edge of the enclave. "It is, however, our mildest of seasons, so . . ."

Quickly moving on to more pleasant topics, he advised them that during their short stay, the cooks would be providing two hearty meals; also, clothing appropriate for the oilseed farm, as well as the weather, was on hand all courtesy of Tom Buckley and the US government.

The agents glanced into their temporary home and saw a comfortable-looking double bed next to a wooden table that held a pitcher of water, two clean cups, and a small metal mirror. There was, additionally, a chair and nightstand. Lara, with the hint of a smile, seemed to ask her mate, "What more could we have asked for?"

Their host nodded to the darkening sky, saying, "Night is approaching; let me show you the exact location for you to stand to identify yourselves come morning."

So, this was not a totally original arrangement for agent pickup, both visitors noted with relief. It must have worked before . . .

After a hearty meal, their host bid them good night and handed them a small flashlight, so they were not totally alone out here with the cicadas and nightingales. The occasional flurry of bats quit bothering them as they dropped the flap of their little shelter and fell into each other's arms on the down mattress.

Chapter 27

Morning dawned with increased activity in the little community outside the town of Qazvin. A central fire crackled to life as the workers readied for a day like all days, preparing to weed their crop with a tractor and other tools hidden from prying eyes by yellow netting. All must look enough like the ripening crops to keep them safe. Besides, these nomads must have been tending fields like these for decades, if not longer. How their compensation was provided, the agents never discovered.

At 9:30 a.m., Omar politely informed them that it was time to head for the observation point at the end of the runway. The agents were there in plenty of time, nervously eager to present themselves to the electronic eyes in the sky, hopefully friendly ones. As instructed, the agents removed their sunglasses. Uri was grateful for an old pair found in the major's glove compartment. With their eyes closed, they exposed their faces to the midmorning sun for twenty seconds at a time. The wind tousled their hair as the blistering sun baked them. The elevation was about two thousand feet here, so protection from its rays was minimal. They never did see or hear a drone, and of course, a satellite would be invisible. With only their trust in Tom and his troops to depend on, the agents headed back to the enclave at 10:30 a.m.; their only real duty, their reappearance at 15:00 for another try. After that, they could only wait and hope for a helicopter rescue at 10:00 a.m. the following day.

* * *

Exactly at 3:00 p.m. or as close as they could tell, the flash and roar of a US Apache broke through the calm of the high desert. There was a splash of yellow and brown as the giant bird settled onto the ground about ten feet from the excited agents. With a quick wave to their Persian hosts, the pair were gently helped by four crewmen into the waiting helicopter. The speedy aircraft had lifted off from its camouflaged ship not thirty minutes before, taking a circuitous path to the landing site.

"Strap in, sir, ma'am. We're jumpin' right off!" hollered the pilot, Cmdr. Scott "Buzz" Searles, over the intense noise of the eager machine, as if it were irritated to be on the ground even this long. They had already climbed on a path directly out of the sun and over a pass in the mountains. As they reached the appropriate altitude, Searles swiveled in his seat and greeted his new passengers with a toothy grin. "Bet you're plum glad to be leavin' this place," he yelled, as if from a semi at 70 mph. The three crewmen were used to the oversize Southern drawl; they smiled accommodatingly.

"You might say that," Uri answered, vastly understating his appreciation for the perfectly executed retrieval and maneuver. Within minutes, the blue Caspian Sea rose to meet them, the mountains already passing out of sight behind them. "About how fast are we going? Feels almost supersonic!"

The crewmen laughed at the overstatement. "Oh, nothin' close to that. Y'all want some gum? It he'ps a bit."

Uri refused with a wave of his hand, but Lara held out hers; her ears were screaming in pain. One of the crew obliged immediately. They all knew just a bit about their passengers but only the bare essentials of their mission in enemy territory. They were well aware of the dangerous situation they were in out here; the Iranians would not hesitate to bring them down if given half a chance. Lara glanced over her right shoulder at the young, tow-haired ensign manning the 30mm automatic rifle. It could fire more than thirty rounds a second. She knew there was a Hellfire missile launcher on board as well; she hoped neither would be exhibited today.

"How fast *are* we going, anyhow?" she yelled at the copilot, a smiling lieutenant. She couldn't read his name tag.

"Don't know exactly right now, but she can get up over two hundred knots flat-out, once we're on the straightaway," he yelled back with a grin. "We'll be on deck in less than twenty."

Lara looked out at the now-undisturbed sea. *Well, more like a lake, if you wanted to get technical*, she thought.

It was less than fifteen minutes later when Uri spotted the black dot near the horizon; it looked like a fishing trawler, perhaps two hundred feet long, covered with nets and cranes. As they descended, he could see the clear space aft of the tower, the helipad that would be their landing area. He also noticed a flag attached to the stern; he seemed to recall it as that of one of the satellites of the old Soviet Union, maybe Azerbaijan. He realized his heart rate was headed north of 150 bpm as the helicopter swung around to the west, preparing for landing.

It was not yet dawn as the ersatz trawler crept into the harbor at Baku, on the east coast of Azerbaijan. A waiting jeep drove them to a small military airport, where they said their farewells to Commander Searles and crew.

"I don't know where y'all are headed, but it sure does smell important," Buzz drawled from a bright salute as the jeep took Lara and Uri to a military aircraft, already revved-up and ready for them on the runway. They were handed their bags of essentials for their coming flight as they were escorted into the spacious, four-engine aircraft. A minimal crew greeted them with breakfast just as soon as they had taken off and reached altitude.

"Where we headed?" a still-sleepy Uri asked the crewman.

"Gee, sir, ma'am, I thought you knew," he stated deferentially to the two honorees. "There's a certain General Wainscroft waiting for you at Incirlik—the US Air Force Base—about five hundred miles west of here . . . that's in Turkey."

"Thank you, crewman . . . , yes, we are acquainted with the general and the base, actually. You have any idea what it's about?" Uri didn't really think he would get any details, but he was hoping . . .

"Oh no, sir, I'm afraid that's way above my pay grade," he replied. But we'll be there in about three hours, and he'll be waiting there for you both. I'll ditch these lights, and you can get some shut-eye."

Lara had already let her seat down as far as it would go; she was getting as much sleep as possible. It looked they were in for something special . . . and it was not a vacation.

Chapter 28

"Well, my friends, how nice to see you again . . . even though you look like you've been in a war zone!" The lean, fit three-star general with the gray buzz cut had hosted the pair on their last mission to Iran just a short year ago. That had turned out quite well, with the elimination of a major threat to the United States. Lara had the feeling, seeing the general there waiting for them, bright and early, that something big was up.

Wainscroft led them into his impressive offices on the main floor of the headquarters building and offered them chairs. "Well, it's bad, as I guess you figured. I wanted to give you a briefing before you get some well-earned rest. Quite simply, it's the US drinking water again—this time in San Francisco. The same bad guys, I'm afraid, and we're going to need your help—again.

From the word we're getting, it appears their General Gharoub of military intelligence has figured out we're on his tail. He got the fake messages that Uri sent to be translated." Looking directly at Lara, he continued, "The translations that you delivered to him—"

"I heard about that," she added quietly.

"At any rate," Wainscroft continued, "those details of the approaches to the reservoirs on the peninsula convinced him that they—the peninsular lakes and reservoirs—would be the easiest and best places for their troops to deliver the poison—"

"Wait a minute," Uri interrupted. "How did you find out . . . ?"

Wainscroft had just a touch of mirth on his face as he confided to his agents, "There is, in the office of their military intelligence, a certain Mrs. Khorasani, a trusted secretary. She can't translate the incoming dispatches from *our* agents, but she *can* read General Gharoub's outgoing nstructions and relay them to us. Has for years." Lara and Uri both reacted sharply to this bit of news. Wainscroft held up his hand to signify there was more coming. "But just after he made *that* decision, he gets word that *Uri* is not who he appears to be, but is, in fact, an American agent in disguise, so . . ."

"So that's why they came after me . . . but who tipped them off?"

"We haven't completely figured that one out, but he correctly concluded that their so-called intercepted messages were fakes, meant to send the Iranians into a trap. So, he changed their strategy and set his plans again on Hetch Hetchy, which they know is going to allow pleasure boats for the first time ever, on July Fourth. They'll set out a number of motorboats and sailboats onto the Hetch Hetchy reservoir, each with enough polonium to assure a major disaster when it reaches San Francisco in a few days—"

"And then?" Uri interrupted.

"Someone . . ." Wainscroft tipped his head to Lara. "An American agent apparently, got word of Uri's exposure and set up a daring raid on his prison; they assassinated his guards and escaped . . ."

Uri couldn't help grinning at his partner with admiration.

"So now, General Gharoub doesn't know what to believe, or do."

"And you got all this from the secretary . . . Mrs. Khorasani?"

"Right." Wainscroft sat back in his chair and waited for the agents' response.

Lara was apprehensive. "So how do we know what they're going to do?"

"We don't. But there's only a finite number of possibilities. And with Hetch Hetchy opening up on July Fourth, that's when we figure they'll hit. And to give them some more to chew on, we've let word out that the Harry Tracy Water Treatment Plant on the peninsula is down for maintenance. So, they might just figure we'll feel the Hetch Hetchy water is more secure"

The two agents looked at each other with a mixture of anticipation and apprehension. "Where exactly do we come in?" Uri said finally.

"You're our number-one asset team on the ground. You know the operation, the language, and the operatives in charge. You're our best at picking out what these guys are up to." He stared at both for a few seconds, then in a controlled voice said to them, "Look, you've had a rough few weeks. We know that. But you can make the difference between a disaster and a victory for our side. I think you know I'm telling you the facts of the matter. But, in the end, it's your decision. We have less than two weeks 'til the Fourth."

Lara thought for just a few seconds. "What's to stop them from hitting us somewhere else?"

"We thought of that, too. We have plans in the works for that . . . once this attack is made public. You know," he said to Lara, "we were able to track all your movements, courtesy of that tiny GPS in your phone. So, we know the locations of all the facilities your amorous major took you to . . ."

Lara smiled at Uri as if to say, "Don't worry, I'll tell you all the details."

"Our counterstrike will be quick, public, and devastating," the general continued. "Our Arab friends, as well as our allies, will be delighted."

Then the reality of the nearness of July Fourth hit them simultaneously. They stared at each other. They hadn't thought about the timing before the general's observation. But they knew they really had no choice.

Chapter 29

General Ali Gharoub, chief of military intelligence, and General Hossein Alirezeh, chief of military operations, faced an immediate and difficult quandary. They had assembled with their aides in the Castle to come up with a solution to the issue that had suddenly arisen: their whole organization had apparently been penetrated by spies sent by their archenemy, the United States.

The first break had come when a female Iranian double agent had reported to General Alirezeh that she had indisputable proof that one of his most valuable decoders, known to him as Heydar al-Nabi, was, in fact, the notorious Israeli-American spy Uri Levin. The double agent, known to the Americans only as Tala, had just recently been recruited into military operations. She had been working for the Americans as a hostess in Tehran; as such, she had proven her worth by exposing a valuable American spy with whom she had been friends. This American male agent, known to the both American and Iranian secret services as U37FGI, had been captured, tortured, and killed by the feared Iranian secret police, known worldwide as SAVAMA. Tala had taken over his code name and identity. She had learned through gaining the American agent's confidence how to communicate with American headquarters. What a coup that had been!

Tala had also gained Uri's confidence, and when she was sure of his treachery, she notified Alirezeh of Uri's true identity. It did not take long for his office to recognize that signals supposedly captured by Uri near the northeastern border of the country were, in fact, fakes sent by the Americans. Of special note were the supposed "soft" locations of water-pumping stations on the San Francisco Peninsula. These would be, if the information were valid, prime targets for the coming water-poisoning operation. Fortunately, Uri had been quickly apprehended and imprisoned on the basis of Tala's information.

General Gharoub was outraged by this breakdown in security at this level of his staff, the apex of military intelligence. He immediately had his team go back into the file of another new employee, Daria Haddad, and request dossiers from all of her supposed employers at Esfahan and other locations listed on her resume. The responses were not long in coming, especially when spurred by Gharoub's personal seal. Within twelve hours, it was obvious that "Daria" also was a complete and utter fraud. Checking her identity further, it became clear that not only was she an impostor who had wheedled her way into the highest ranks of Iranian military intelligence, but she was none other than the spouse of Uri Levin, whom they recently had in custody. It was she, of course, who schemed her way into releasing Levin from prison and escaping somewhere together.

Not since the treachery of Englishman Kim Philby and his cohorts in the 1950s and 1960s had an international spy scandal reached these heights, or so it seemed to the Iranian military command. They were certain to hear about it from their Russian colleagues, whose predecessors, the Soviets, had benefitted so greatly from Philby and his colleagues in the British nobility.

The newly elected Iranian president was, of course, furious when the information reached him. His rage reached a new peak when he then learned the American female double agent had been working directly in Gharoub's employ. He ordered the two generals to formulate a plan to assassinate the American spies and reorganize the water-poisoning plan.

Gharoub and Alirezeh quickly realized that the messages "Heydar" had supposedly intercepted, revealing "poorly protected water-pumping locations," were fraudulent, meant to mislead them. The Americans were attempting to lure them into a different strategy from the proposed strike on the peninsula to instead, the poisoning of the Hetch Hetchy reservoir. This alternative was made even more tempting by the news that this huge, open body of freshwater, the main source for the City of San Francisco and its environs, would be a prime target for Iranian operatives. The generals discussed this at length. It seemed the most reasonable target: several squads of agents sent into the poorly guarded reservoir just west of the famous Yosemite National Park could poison the water and never be discovered, let alone stopped. Even if they were captured, the polonium would already be irretrievably inserted into the lake, on its deadly mission.

It was only after a few minutes of self-congratulations that Gharoub recognized something that should have been immediately obvious to everyone: the spy Levin, upon escape, would let the Americans know that their offering of the peninsular pumping stations as "soft" targets had been revealed. The American leadership could not now presume that the Iranian attack would be made there; the attack would, instead, focus on the obvious alternative: Hetch Hetchy. This put a hitch in the Americans' plans—a fatal one. Even if there were any uncertainty in the Iranians' ultimate target, the American overall strategy was now critically flawed.

Alirezeh agreed with this reasoning in principle, but argued that a more prudent idea would be to hit one of the peninsular stations *not* specified by the Americans while also sending a few suicide squads as decoys into the Hetch Hetchy reservoir with enough poison to cause severe damage and confusion. Most, if not all, of these volunteers would be caught and eliminated, but they would find eternal pleasure in Paradise as their reward.

This was the plan that the generals finally agreed upon and sent on to the president as a prelude to their meeting. The teams of saboteurs, already in training, would get their final orders and be on their way to northern California within days.

* * *

It was late that evening when the two generals were called into the president's office. They stood as the president glared at them from his huge cushioned chair; it seemed more like a throne. They remained at attention, waiting for his reaction to the plan they had submitted. "At ease, gentlemen," he finally proclaimed, a thin smile crossing his narrow, heavily lined face. It was the face of a man who had seen both military combat and the political battles that had led to the demise of so many of his colleagues. "I have carefully read the plan you submitted. It is a good one, as far as it goes, but . . ." Gharoub and Alirezeh, who had both relaxed, stiffened, waiting for the rest of the news. "You have to consider my position. Both of you are responsible for the humiliating losses we have just suffered. We have not only taken these losses internally, within our own country, but in the Arab world as well. Two well-known American agents, working no doubt in concert with our Israeli enemy, have penetrated the highest ranks of our military and intelligence establishments."

Seeing their mortification, he continued, "Do you not realize that we have seen communiqués from our colleagues, the Russians and the Syrians?" Before either of the generals could reply, the now-livid president roared, "Not only that: Even our enemies, the Arabs, have heard of our catastrophe! It seems practically everyone in the world has learned of the humiliation we have suffered. Not to mention we also lost two of the Americans' most despicable secret agents from within our grasp, Uri Levin and his whore, Lara Edmond! We must alter our plans to make sure those two do not cause us any more disgrace than we have already suffered!"

Chapter 30

The president stalked around his grand office in the Castle, gnashing his teeth. In his short tenure at this level of government, he had never been so dishonored, and he took it very personally. How could he have trusted these men so explicitly? Ali Gharoub, that idiot general with his bleached teeth and dyed hair, who saw himself as a charmer! *How could the military council have opted to elevate him to the rank of general? Especially in the crucial department of military intelligence?* And his assistant, that goose Colonel Soroush, in his tailored uniform, so proud of his success with the ladies! *What could they have been thinking? Well,* he reminded himself, *they would make themselves useful now . . .*

Gharoub and Soroush entered the president's office gingerly; they had no real idea what was in store, but they knew it wasn't going to be any kind of honor. The debacle they had just permitted, the escape of two enemy agents, was the worst in the history of the young nation.

The president did not offer them chairs. This was going to be a dressing down; that much was certain. "All right, my friends," he began in a clearly cynical tone. "We have just experienced a monumental humiliation; there is no doubt about that. I can hear our Arab enemies laughing at us, along with the Americans." Both his victims colored visibly, but they knew something like this was coming from the volatile president. "The point is, now what is to be done?" He stared at them like they were insects under his microscope, waiting for the shellac.

"Well, I have for you a most critical assignment. One that, in one clean stroke, can reverse the tide of this battle. Here, briefly, is what I have in mind for you." The president watched closely for their reactions as he continued, pausing first for effect.

"The attack on the Hetch Hetchy reservoir, which was initially to be the prime segment of our plan, will now be just a diversion, as the generals recommended. So we need to make certain the other operation, the assault on the peninsular plants, is carried out without fail. We cannot afford another debacle like the one we have just suffered. The two infiltrators, the spies Uri Levin and Lara Edmond must be eliminated.

In addition, we must adequately prepare the second part of the plan, the attack on the peninsular pumping plants." The two officers looked at each other with what could only be called uncertainty: the plans had already been well set.

"We now," the president continued, "have good reason to believe that the plans for the, uh, disruption of the plants on the peninsula may have been compromised . . ." This was not exactly true, but he did not want these men, as incompetent as they had been, to waste their effort—and lives—on a fool's errand.

"Therefore," he continued in a bold voice, "we will alter our attack a bit and focus our main effort on the most vulnerable of the peninsula stations: the Pilarcitos Dam and Reservoir." His two officers twitched visibly at this major change in the strike plan. "The reason for this modification is twofold: First, we have reason to believe that this dam, and its pumping station, are considered to be, by the enemy, of lower value than the others. Second, and more important, is the fact that the Harry Tracy Water Treatment Plant that handles its water is not in working condition—our agents there have just lately informed us of the malfunction. So, with the other sources of water in jeopardy, the San Francisco Public Utilities Commission," he said derisively, "will be forced to use the Pilarcitos water supply, despite its flaws."

The president knew this was misleading, but he wanted these men to go into the fray fully believing their effort was crucial to the success of the plan and, just possibly, relieve them of some of the blame for the losses already suffered.

"What you will do is get the troops ready for the operation on the whole western flank of the peninsula . . . and use the most capable for a strike at the Pilarcitos station! The remainder of the team will attack the easternmost stations, those that are situated along the Crystal Springs and San Andreas reservoirs, as we had initially planned."

General Gharoub and Colonel Soroush reacted visibly at the order. An alteration of that magnitude in their carefully worked-out attack was highly risky; but, then, the enemy least expected risky plans. The Americans would never expect an assault so bold.

"We will inform the troops of this change in plans and have them await your arrival . . ." The two officers turned and looked at each other, incredulous at what they had just heard. Was the president actually sending them into battle? They had thought that their days of armed combat were over.

After enough time for the two men to absorb this news, the president continued. "General Alirezeh will be maintained here to act as liaison. I know this revised plan comes as a shock, but consider this: the future of our very nation is at stake. Even if we don't reach our ultimate goal, the enemy will be dealt a near-fatal blow; their leaders will lose all credibility among their citizens, and ours will gain mightily. Not only with our own people, but with all the oppressed people around the world! Think of all the billions, not only Muslims, but others who have been trampled by the Jew-run countries!"

The two officers were overwhelmed.

"And, my friends, who better to lead this daring effort than you two gentlemen, the finest military intelligence minds in the world!"

The general and his colonel reacted visibly to this compliment and this opportunity. They would be honored all over the Muslim world, by Arab and non-Arab alike. But if death were the consequence, nothing less than Paradise awaited them.

The president was gratified to see that his manipulation had worked. They were ready to take up the challenge. And if the assault failed . . . well, he had that figured out as well. He would inform the world that the horrific idea of poisoning America's water was the brainchild of the two rogue officers and not his government. The liberal media would eat this up like the hungry dogs they were. As Julius Caesar famously declared, "The die is cast."

Chapter 31

General Gharoub and Colonel Soroush met up in San Francisco at the rental car agency in the airport. They had flown in from New York via Paris. For the sake of security, they had taken separate flights from Tehran to Paris. It was in Paris-Charles de Gaulle Airport that they had laid out the detailed plan of attack. The CCTV would show the two men, now close-shaven and in business suits, apparently meeting for the first time in one of the airport bars. No notes were taken, and none were necessary. The four-hour layover in Paris was just enough time to structure the assault on the Pilarcitos Dam. They knew the troops in Oakland would have sufficient time to adjust to the change in strategy.

The would-be assassins had, in the past two months, found satisfactory housing in the newly formed and rapidly growing Shia community, situated along and around Telegraph Avenue near the overpass for State Route 24. The community welcomed the seemingly unconnected young men eagerly, especially when they proved financially able to live on their own in this foreign city. They appeared to go out every day looking for work, then would meet in a different location daily. Only one of the men would receive communication from Tehran, sharing it with the others. That was how they knew their new supervisors would be arriving, carrying their new orders.

Just the four team leaders met with Gharoub and Soroush in one of the Muslim community centers. There, they learned of the alteration in their plan of attack. They all marveled at the officers' mustache-free visages; without prior knowledge of these men, they would have been unrecognizable.

The general had assigned Soroush to tell the team leaders of the change in the peninsular assaults. But the colonel was more a desk officer than a field man; he was uncomfortable giving direct orders to men who had already put their lives on the line. So, Soroush was somewhat nervous telling these fighting men their plans had changed at the last minute. There would be no practice; they would attack the dam itself on the night of July 4.

The team leaders crouched over the card table as Soroush sketched out the geography at the dam. They accepted the new plans, albeit somewhat tentatively. But these superior officers were well known to all, at least by photos and reputation. They would have to trust them.

The officers then returned to their residences to meet up with their men to sketch out the individual plans of attack. The next item on the agenda was to make trial runs on their objectives. Each leader had to rent a vehicle for the attacks.

Two teams were to sabotage the pumping stations along the easternmost plants, those that lay nearest the freeway that runs along the west side of San Francisco Bay. One of these teams of four was led by thirty-five-year-old Turan, a veteran of skirmishes at the border with Iraq and Afghanistan. Then they simply had to wait until the proper time on the Fourth to cross the bridge over the peninsula and proceed to their locations. They would have to wait until near dusk to take action.

Chapter 32

Lara and Uri finally arrived at the Oakland, California, field office of Homeland Security after several days of traveling. The Fourth of July was less than a week away, and there was much to do if they were to successfully quash the Iranian plot. Tom Buckley was there to supervise the effort. Five agents from the local office, who hadn't met Lara and Uri previously, sat around the long marble table in the stark conference room. Two FBI agents from the Los Angeles office, Mary Robley and Bret Williams, were also there. Like Bret, Mary had worked with Lara and Uri on earlier campaigns.

Tom began by introducing everyone, then got right to business. "Let's first review the situation." The others sat in rapt attention, even though all were quite up-to-date. "First, I think everyone here knows the basics: we've got an unknown team of terrorists dedicated to poisoning the main water supply for the San Francisco Peninsula. They're armed with a deadly poison called polonium; you may remember that name from the episode down in Los Angeles. We're assured of all the help we need to suppress these individuals, from the feds as well as the state. But, for reasons of crowd and rumor management, we're keeping all news of the episode away from the general population. Also, the media have been warned, with extreme penalty at stake, not to make any speculations about the matter. Only the top brass at the local and state law enforcement agencies are even aware there is a 'matter' at all. We've got to avoid a panic, at all costs."

He looked sternly at each person in the room; no one said a word or even moved. They all knew what they were up against; the penalty of failure was catastrophic.

After leaving enough time for the serious nature of their business to settle in, Tom went on with the details. "As you all know, the threat is limited to two rather large geographical areas: the main water-pumping stations on the west side of the bay and the Hetch Hetchy reservoir. I can't go into the details of how we know this; let me just say that it is based on the best fieldwork available to us, and it has been gathered over substantial time and effort."

At this, several of those at the table glanced discreetly at Lara and Uri. The word was out, obviously.

"You are all aware that our force here is divided into two main squads: the federal agents will be assigned to Yosemite National Park and the reservoir, which is legally part of the park. The local and state effort will focus on the west side of the bay. As you all know, there are several pumping and treatment stations there. We're not certain as yet which are part of our enemy's plans."

That news provoked a murmur of uncertainty from the troops. *What were they getting into?*

One senior FBI agent raised his hand before Tom could continue. "Sorry, sir, but what about those treatment plants you mentioned? Won't they remove this polonium?"

"That's a good question, Steve," Tom responded instantly. "This is the same poison that they used to hit the Los Angeles plant last year. The Russians have also used it to kill a couple of political enemies. Anyway, the stuff is almost impossible to detect. And at the low concentrations needed to be deadly, you can forget the 'almost.' Worse, the treatment plants we have won't remove it from the water at those low levels, less than one part per billion."

Intense quiet blanketed the room. "Then, how do you get rid of it?" Steve asked reasonably.

"The simple answer is, you don't. You isolate the contaminated water and wait for the stuff to decay. I mean, the polonium decays on its own in a few months—"

"And all these treatment plants!" Steve was relentless. He simply couldn't believe scientists had no solution for the problem.

Tom just shook his head. "I know it seems incredible, but the stuff emits this deadly radiation, like a nuclear power plant. Like . . . Chernobyl." That remark sobered everyone instantly, allowing him to continue.

"The individuals in charge of each squad will be reporting into this field office only. Of course, someone here will be in touch with everyone at all times until the matter is resolved. We are reasonably certain the day of the planned attack is set for Friday, the Fourth of July. That, as you, know, is the official opening of the Hetch Hetchy to fishing and boating on the lake."

More sounds of frustration from the group at the table.

"Park officials have been told only that they need to stay alert for any unusual behavior, and report it to us at once. We will have the highway patrol standing by to control any situation that arises on the roads in and out of the park. They have watercraft, aircraft, and underwater rescue staff at their service, ready to cooperate, especially on that date. We'll meet again as the situation proceeds. That's all for now."

Before Lara and Uri left the room, Tom called them over to the side, where a large suitcase lay unopened. "I almost forgot my little presents for you." He opened the suitcase, revealing two handguns. He handed Lara one of the latest rapid-fire semiautomatic pistols manufactured by the Israeli arms manufacturer IWI. It was a lightweight 9mm Masada, made almost entirely of high-impact polymer. Uri's weapon was the latest in the Desert Eagle series known as the Baby Eagle III. It was a .44 Magnum pistol known for its high-pitched shriek, similar to that of an eagle pouncing on its prey. "We'll set aside a day for you two to catch up on some target practice."

Tom knew that despite his loss of an eye, Uri was still remarkably skilled with the Baby Eagle, able to hit the bull's-eye at twenty-five feet, 90 percent of the time. Lara was especially adept with automatic weapons, her dexterity making up for what she lacked in physical size. Tom enjoyed seeing the eager response of the pair; being outfitted with personal armed protection comforted them.

The rest of the team filed out to waiting vehicles. No written or printed matter left the room—this was all "learn and burn," and they knew it.

* * *

Lara and Uri spent the next few days in target practice and getting acquainted with both the reservoirs and the main pumping stations. These were situated along both sides of the peninsula. They went as tourists, not as federal agents. There was no point in arousing concern among the locals.

Then they made the long drive out to Hetch Hetchy, starting early in the morning. It took them more than four hours in light traffic to get to the west entrance to Yosemite, then another thirty minutes to the lake itself. As the lake came into view, about a thousand feet or more under the rim of mountains, they were astonished by its beauty. Buried downstream of the Tuolumne River was the famous O'Shaughnessy Dam, towering over its captive lake. The lake conformed to the long, deep, and narrow crevice in the mountain; its placid water shimmered like a giant blue sickle in the brilliant sunlight. A portion of the population loathed the dam, eager to see the geography restored to its natural beauty. But the demand for its pure drinking water was far too essential for that to happen anytime soon.

The long drive back to Oakland was consumed by the agents trying to decide on a strategy that would contain the possible attack on the Hetch Hetchy and also that on the peninsula reservoirs. The attack on the Hetch Hetchy was already assigned to the California Highway Patrol and the guards at the reservoir. Their task was to apprehend any visitors to that lake who appeared to be tampering with the water.

The peninsular reservoirs were a more complicated issue. Because the false report about the Harry Tracy Water Treatment Plant had been made available to the Iranians, the hope was that they, knowing the water from the western reservoirs would not be subject to adequate treatment, would arget those reservoirs for their main offensive. Furthermore, the bulk of the water in those lines originated from the lake behind the old Pilarcitos Dam, halfway up the peninsula. This is where Lara and Uri would establish their operation.

They brought Tom up to date on their thinking and he agreed, based on this information, to place the team that was most experienced with Iranian terrorists, the one led by Lara and Uri, in charge of defending the Pilarcitos Dam and Reservoir.

Time now became a crucial issue: there were just three days before July Fourth was upon them.

Chapter 33

With the holiday nearly at hand, Tom decided it was time to bring San Francisco Public Utilities Commission officials into the picture. The PUC must be informed of the upcoming activity to prevent any unfortunate interaction between the local and federal authorities. Tom was a firm believer in making direct personal contact rather than relying on telephone, email, or any other means. He contacted the Homeland office in Washington to set it up. Photocopies of Tom and his agents' picture IDs and brief resumes were sent by secure server to the utility commission's headquarters. Tom, Lara, and Uri made an appointment to meet with utility officials the following day at 9:00 a.m.

The three federal agents arrived in plenty of time, where they found the utility director had reserved a spot for them. They showed their identification to the sleepy-eyed attendant, who parked the car and showed them the way to the front door. The utilities commission offices were housed in an old granite building that appeared to have accommodated some other city or county organization. Temporary-looking signs covered older printed or engraved nameplates. The entire building had the odor of an old library or school. Its air-conditioning system struggled against the midsummer heat, which was sometimes oppressive, even in this ocean-cooled city. A male guard seated behind a card table had them sign in and show him their identification. He then directed them to Room 106, on the same floor.

They knocked on the glass window of the door proclaiming the office of Mr. H. R. Macdonald, chief of the San Francisco Public Utilities Commission. Hearing no reply, the three agents entered to see a large woman fanning herself against the uncommonly warm air. She was apparently the receptionist, Bertha Higgins, according to the nameplate on her desk. "Morning, what can I do you for?" she deliberately misstated.

Tom took the lead: "Hello, Ms. . . . uh, Higgins. We're from the Department of Homeland Security to see Mr. Macdonald." He was cordial but not effusive.

"Oh yes, let's see here." She looked at a paper desk calendar rather than a computer screen, although there was one on the right side of the desk. "OK, you're scheduled for nine. Can I see some identification, please?"

The agents pulled out their photo IDs and placed them on her desk. Ms. Higgins took a pair of large glasses from around her neck and perched them on her nose as she looked over the plastic cards, peering up occasionally, as if to compare the cards with the three people standing before her. After just a few moments, she looked the trio over again and said, "Go on in. He's expectin' ya."

Tom opened the door that led into a small office with a desktop computer on an old gray desk, similar to those seen in many federal facilities. Mr. Macdonald looked at them over steel-rimmed glasses and shook hands with Tom as the apparent commander of the little troop.

"Come on in and have a seat, guys; you, too, little lady," he said casually. He was a man somewhat the other side of sixty with a definite paunch. The bemused agents wondered if he had any idea why they were here.

They sat as ordered, and Tom began. "We're here, Mr. Macdonald, because of a threat—"

"Oh yeah, they told me about that. Please, call me Scottie." He smiled at them and sat back in his chair.

"All right, uh, Scottie," Tom continued uncomfortably. "We're from Homeland Security, as you know. I'm Tom Buckley—"

"Glad to make your acquaintance, Tom."

"And these are two of my field agents: Wakefield," he said, nodding at Lara, "and Elsworth." He gestured at Uri.

"Nice to meet ya." Macdonald replied without a glance. "So, how can we be of service to the federal government?"

"Well, Scott, it's about some threats to the—"

"Scottie, please. Everyone here calls me that, even my wife, rest in peace." He discreetly made the sign of the cross as Tom waited quietly.

During the brief pause, Lara took the time to peruse the room. An unlit cigar sat in an ashtray on an end table under the only window in the room. Directly above it, almost as a joke, a sign declared "No Smoking." The curtains were tobacco-stained from years of abuse. It was definitely not like any federal offices she had visited; the feds were unyielding in their adherence to any obvious infringements on the law.

"All right, uh, Scottie, it's about some threats we've received about the drinking water to the peninsula. We don't think there's anything to them, but . . ." Tom paused as the door opened quietly and a Hispanic-looking man in overalls crept in with a large, wheeled trash container. He sidled over to the wastebasket at the side of the room and emptied it into the larger one.

"Go on, Tom. Ruiz is all right," Macdonald said, laughing. "Aren't you, Ruiz?"

The janitor looked up, uncomprehending. "Señor?"

"It's all right, Ruiz, go ahead," Macdonald waved him on as his guests watched silently. "Been with us for years, good man." The agents, however, did not continue until the man left.

As the door closed behind the janitor, Tom continued, almost at a whisper: "Thing is, uh, Scottie, this might be serious." He wrote out the words *chemical poisoning* on a sheet of paper from his pocket and showed it to the chief.

Macdonald looked at the paper, then back at the agents and laughed. "Yeah, we get those threats all the time. Drunken kids, God bless 'em. Come up with all kinds of stuff. But don't you worry; we got it covered. You'd be amazed at the crap gets tossed in the water tanks—'scuse me, ma'am. But we got the latest in technology here: screens, settlin' tanks, aeration, chemical treatment, tricklin' filters. I mean, nothing gets through all that. Besides, we got chemical analysis downstream. We can spot anything at all, shut the lines down, clean it up."

He sat up and added, "Heavy metals, you know, lead, chrome, stuff like that . . . even AIDS germs! We got plenty of that here, you know." He sat back, satisfied. "You see, sunlight, oxygen, lime . . . all that takes care of just about anything you can imagine."

Tom waited a few seconds, then said somberly, "But we're talking about some vicious stuff here—*polonium.* You know, like what happened in Los Angeles?"

"Yeah, read about that. But this ain't LA, you know what I mean? Our guys are the best!" He oozed confidence.

Tom had about given up. "All we're asking is that your people be on the lookout for any strangers hanging out around any of the reservoirs or treatment plants. Give us a call if there's anything at all . . ." He wrote his name and cell phone number on a piece of paper and handed it to Macdonald, who looked at it briefly and placed it on the side of his desk, then stood. The meeting was over.

"Well, thanks for your time, uh, Scottie." Tom said to officially end the dialogue. The agents rose and quietly left the room. They said their goodbyes to Ms. Higgins and went out into the hall, scarcely looking at each other. It was a quiet walk from there back to their vehicle and a grim drive back to Oakland.

The janitor, Ruiz, carefully noted their departure. He had left Macdonald's offices with his trash can; then, unobserved, trash can and all, he'd used his master keys to open the unoccupied office next door. He listened carefully with his electronic stethoscope at the connecting door as Macdonald's conversation with the agents proceeded, then pulled out his cell phone and made his call. Vahid had been planted here three years ago for just this kind of situation. It was received with delight by his superiors in Tehran.

* * *

Once they were in the car, Tom looked knowingly at his two agents and said to them: "Don't worry about that guy, I've got this covered." Uri drove as Tom confirmed their afternoon appointment with Sheriff Sean Parker. The sheriff's office was in a modernized building near Van Ness Avenue and McAllister Street. Fortunately, Parker had reserved a spot for them in the visitors' area just outside. Though they hadn't met, the two men were familiar with each other's active-duty service in the US Marine Corps.

"Semper Fi," the two men greeted each other on meeting for the first time. They smiled, shook hands, and slapped each other on the back. All this as Lara and Uri waited patiently for Parker to issue them into his office. The four compatriots pulled up chairs around a bare metal table at the side of Parker's austere office; there were no adornments or other sorts of unnecessary furnishings. A plain gray government-style desk and chairs were planted at the windowless back wall, facing the door. A telephone and computer were the only objects to be seen. Bare fluorescent lighting flooded the room with a harsh glare while a low hum flared from a noise machine on the floor in the corner.

"We've been able to do a little background on the, uh, situation," Parker began without preamble. "Homeland in Washington gave us some basics." While Lara and Uri showed a modicum of surprise at this news, Tom just gave a slight shrug. His superiors could be trusted to give Parker what he needed to help him as much as possible.

"As I'm sure you already know," he stated, addressing each of the three agents, "the water system is rather old and complicated; it was put together over a long stretch of years with varying components and quality. Kind of grew like weeds. As long as things don't get dicey, it runs all right. But when you get a bunch of dedicated bad guys, like we're up against here, well, we could have real problems. And as I guess you've already found out, we're not going to get much help from the Water District." He threw his hands in the air in mild frustration. His three guests smiled in recognition; they had just witnessed what he was talking about.

"Anyway, as I understand it, you already have the Hetch Hetchy in hand, that is, a plan to counter their potential attack."

Tom just dipped his head in silent assent.

"But this old reservoir pumping-station assembly they've got here is a real bear to deal with; they could hit it almost anywhere. Now, I understand and appreciate the reasons you've chosen to figure they're going for the Pilarcitos Dam, and you're going to cover that one."

This time, Tom showed his agreement by merely raising his eyebrows. He could see what was coming: he was going to get some much-needed help.

"And I presume you have enough troops of your own to cover the pumping stations on the *west* side of the peninsula, those coming from Crystal Springs and San Andreas. What I can offer is some broad coverage of the *east* side, that is, the lines coming from Hetch Hetchy and the cross-bay tunnels."

This was good news. Parker and his deputies were intimately familiar with the local streets, as well as the water stations. Their assistance was welcome.

"So, we'll stay in touch through our secure police band. I understand you have the handsets."

"You know," Tom said, "I'm sure that we have to avoid any obvious presence around any of the water stations. People see that, and after what happened in LA, there will be panic galore."

"For sure." Parker was ready for this. "Only unmarked sedans and nonuniformed deputies the whole day and night. No one has been advised as to what might be going down, just to watch for suspicious behavior and report in. We have ten cars assigned solely for this operation."

"That sounds great!" Tom was pleased. "One more thing though . . ."

He saw Parker stiffen in anticipation.

"I don't know if you've been told. There is this badass poison they've got called polonium. It's probably in the form of a yellow powder, and it's the deadliest stuff you can imagine. So, be sure your troops wear double gloves, and even then, don't touch any plastic bags or bottles. It needs extra-special handling; it's worse than germs, viruses or nuclear waste."

Parker blanched at this news; he thought some chemical might be involved, but this sounded like science fiction. "I'll tell my people. They heard about Los Angeles, and . . ." Lara and Uri saw the abrupt change in his demeanor. What law enforcement officer wouldn't fear for his deputies in a situation like this?

They all shook hands; it was a somber group that said their farewells.

* * *

In an unusual coincidence later that same day, Tom received a call from his friend and colleague in the Washington, DC, forensics office of Homeland Security. Dr. Jerry Hubbard, head of the Chemistry Branch, told him of a remarkable development recently made at the Technion-Israel Institute of Technology in Haifa. A research group there had synthesized ion-exchange membranes; using them, they analyzed for specific trace contaminants in groundwater. Fearing a similar attack in Israel after the near-disaster in Los Angeles, they tested some of their new membranes to see if they might be specific for polonium. Luckily, they found one that was so sensitive, it could spot the deadly substance down to parts per trillion! Not only could they analyze the water, they could use large arrays of these membranes to purge the water of the lethal isotope. It might take months to clean up a domestic-size reservoir, but at least it was a viable option.

Tom was elated by this news and shared it with Lara and Uri. At least now, they weren't looking at a dead end.

But even more news came late that afternoon. Homeland in Washington had intercepted some chatter on Iranian satellite transmissions that indicated some highly important operation was due to take place in Northern California the evening of Friday, July Fourth. Tom immediately shared this vital information with Lara, Uri, and the rest of the Oakland teams, as well as Parker. The sheriff agreed with Tom that their forces must not spook the terrorists by showing up earlier than 5:00 p.m. at the presumed attack sites.

Lara contacted the six-person squad assigned to the western peninsula reservoirs, informing them that their Friday afternoon assembly point was to be the CHP headquarters just outside San Mateo. They would meet at the visitor parking lot at 5:00 p.m. Dusk fell on these summer nights at about 8:00 p.m.

Chapter 34

Four Iranian assault teams gathered at their residence for one last cup of strong Persian coffee just before dawn the morning of July 4. The day had begun with the ritual shaving of the jihadis' bodies, followed by the prayers for a successful entry into Paradise. They bid each other farewell with a hearty "Allahu Akbar" as Team One headed for the Hetch Hetchy dam.

One of the 2-man teams, towing a boat and trailer behind their rental van, paused as they entered a long waiting line at the entrance to the Hetch Hetchy parking lot. It had been a lengthy five-hour drive from Oakland, even with the sometimes-beautiful scenery. They had been told that delays were to be expected today, the first day that the reservoir had been open to the public. Boating and fishing were allowed this Fourth of July weekend, which led to locals and out-of-towners scrambling to hit these pristine waters.

Two lines of cars, trucks, and boat trailers snaked down from the highway to the shore of the deep-blue lake. Most towed motorboats, but a handful carried centerboard-type sailboats, handy for day sailing.

"Like entering a virgin, is it not, Ervin?" Zana, forty, the smiling Iranian driver, said to his passenger, giving the younger man a poke in the ribs. They both marveled at the crystal-clear waters ahead.

"I, uh, wouldn't, uh . . . know . . ." stammered the younger man, to Zana's obvious amusement.

"You will soon, my friend," Zana replied, slapping his cohort on the knee, and laughing. "Paradise will soon be ours, and you will feast yourself on beautiful young *houris.*"

The two men were a strange pair; the tall, scarred, and muscular Zana contrasted with the boyish Ervin. They hoped no one made the obvious assumption that they were a couple; they were nothing of the sort. They had been teamed up in the accelerated short course in terrorism at the hidden base near Esfahan, in central Iran. The elite plan to poison the drinking water of the wicked American city of San Francisco needed to be accelerated "due to unforeseen events," they had been told at the start of the seven-day course. They were part of ten two-man groupings who had been taught how to enter this huge manmade lake, poison it with a polonium-filled plastic bag, and then either escape to freedom or enter Paradise via an American-made white cyanide capsule. No one was to be captured, at any cost.

Their instructions were distinct: upon entering the reservoir, they were to proceed to any large, open area of water, pretend to be fishing, then surreptitiously dump the bag overboard. The plastic coating was designed to dissolve within twenty-four hours, releasing 100 grams of polonium chloride.

The teams had been split into two groups: those in rented motorboats were to find a spot near the undeveloped shoreline and pretend to fish; the others, in small sailboats, were to make their way across the lake and back. Both groups were to finish their work in about two hours, then return to Oakland, if possible, where air transport would be waiting. The boats and trailers were to be left along one of several two-lane country roads. They should all be finished well before dark on this long summer day. Either that, or martyrdom.

Finally, after another hour in the line, Zana and Ervin entered the gate and drove up to the guards, who looked at them suspiciously, no doubt about it. They were clothed appropriately, just as they had been taught. They had bleached-denim jeans and well-worn, long-sleeved shirts with football team logos stenciled on the front. Zana and Ervin had found some for sale locally with the name of a team that had departed recently for greener pastures. The terrorists were taken by the team's name: "Raiders." *How appropriate*, they thought. Perhaps the guards were just amused by the team name on their shirts; more likely, they realized, they were scrutinized for their dark complexions and Middle Eastern appearance. It had been nearly twenty years since the glorious 9/11 massacre on the east coast of this alien nation, but some of the older Americans still resented the presence of anyone who resembled those great heroes.

"Got yer fishin' licenses there, pals?" the curious guard said to them, gazing around the rental van, his peaked cap lifted to the back of his bald head. He walked around the van, checked out the boat and trailer, then returned to the driver's window where Zana produced his driver's license as well as his and his partner's nonresident fishing licenses. Seemingly satisfied, the guard gave Zana directions to the boat ramps and huge parking lot. All had been created in record time to satisfy the expected rush of boaters starting this weekend.

Zana thanked the guard, as he had been instructed at their hastily prepared training camp, and headed down to the waterfront. It was not yet nine o'clock in the morning, but there were already dozens of vehicles in the parking area, all with empty boat trailers. Other boaters waited, somewhat impatiently at the ramps, eager to be among the first to enter the pristine water.

* * *

Inside the guard shack, Andy, the chief, rubbed his chin as he questioned his assistant, a nineteen-year-old high-school dropout named Chip. "Notice anything unusual there?"

"Not from around here, I reckon," Chip replied easily.

"What was your first clue?" Andy drawled back in his best James Arness imitation. Old television Westerns like *Gunsmoke* were popular out here in ranch country.

"Well, they do have their licenses and what not . . ."

"But they don't look like no Raiders fans to me," Andy fired back to his nodding young assistant.

"Then where you think they got them shirts?"

"My guess is around the San Francisco airport in them tourist shops. No place in Oakland would dare have them around."

Chip sucked on a hard candy thoughtfully. "Yeah, I guess you're right there . . ."

"And who's going to fly all the way to that devil city just to rent a boat and trailer to fish way out here?"

Chip sucked even harder as he thought that one over. "Got a point here, Chief." He sat there for a few seconds before he jumped up and yelped, "You don't suppose they might have anything to do with that alert we got yesterday?" He was referring to the notice they'd received from the local FBI office about the possibility of strangers planning harm to the lake.

"Sure as my grandma don't have no teeth! We need to keep an eye on them." They watched as the two strangers headed down the new driveway to the parking lot and lake.

* * *

Zana drove carefully down the newly paved road to a large parking lot already home to two dozen or more empty trailers hooked up to a range of vehicles, all showing California license plates. He went straight to one of several ramps into the lake, all looking like they'd been freshly prepared. "Makes sense," he muttered.

"What's that, Boss?" Ervin used English, even out here.

"The boat ramps. They must have put them in just for us."

"Why would they do that? I don't underst—"

"You moron! That was a joke. Of course, they didn't put them in for us. They were just getting ready for this big weekend. First time for boats here."

"Oh yeah, I forgot." Ervin scratched his head and stared at the gleaming blue water, the sun already well above the horizon and blazing with heat. "Here comes somebody."

"Hi, there, guys. Need some help gettin' 'er in the water?" A fortyish man with a well-established beer belly ambled over from one of the trailers parked nearby.

"Well, yeah, that would be . . ." Ervin began before Zana kicked him in the leg.

"No, we're OK, really." Zana did his best with the colloquial English. "We just need to—"

The man laughed easily. "Not from around here, are ya? Well, that's fine. We live off the tourists." He laughed again. "Here, lemme give you a hand with that." He walked over to the trailer hitch and expertly unhooked the electrical connector, allowing Ervin to lower the trailer onto the pavement and take it toward the ramp. Not waiting for a reply from the obvious novice, the man hoisted the trailer and moved it easily to the waterline, backing the small motorboat into the water and handing Ervin the line from its bow. The water was amazingly calm and clear.

"Thanks, mister, uh, that will be fine. We can handle it now." Zana was eager to take over. No telling what this fellow might notice. They had to be careful.

"Sure, sure. You have a good time now, hear?" He smiled at them again and headed back to his vehicle.

"We appreciate the help. Thank you so much!" Zana called after him, walking the trailer back to the rear of their van and reattaching it. He left Ervin standing there with the boat as he parked the tandem in a nearby slot. He then waded into the shallow water, hopped in the open boat, and called out to Ervin—in English, of course—to throw him the rope or "line," as they had learned to call it, and join him. They had already stored all the supplies they needed for this outing onboard, so they were ready to depart.

The almost-new outboard motor fortunately sprang to life on Ervin's first pull, and Zana headed gratefully out into the open water. Ervin gazed in amazement. "You can see all the way to the bottom!" he yelled back to Zana. There were no other boats anywhere within earshot.

"That's right," Zana replied easily, now that they were well on their way. "It's an all-granite lake. Nothing to silt it up. The dam's just upstream. The lake's down here, out of the wind, so it stays nice and clean." He gazed around at the high hills reaching directly out of the water; then he slowed the boat to a crawl and looked over the side. He could indeed see the bottom n what he knew was close to 100 feet of transparent water. "I think we can do our fishing right here and get on with our job. No sense pushing our luck."

With the motor at idle, Zana pulled out their rods and tackle box. Even though there were no other boats within hundreds of yards in this huge lake, the two ersatz anglers made every attempt at appearing to be trout fishing. The virgin nature of this lake had made it an angler's dream.

* * *

'Hey, Chief, take a lookie here." Chip was watching the two strangers with the Raiders shirts, now well out in the lake. He had a pair of high-powered binoculars propped up on a stand.

"Whatcha got?"

"They're fishin' for trout out there usin' big old Northern lures!"

"What? Lemme see that." Andy gently took the binoculars and watched as the two foreign-looking men cast large multihooked plugs splashing into the still water. Chip was right; these men had no idea what they were doing. Some honking from the gate took his attention away from the strange scene out on the lake, forcing him back to their main business of herding the tourists in and out of the property. He'd call into headquarters as soon as the traffic eased up.

* * *

Zana looked at the time on the throwaway phone they had purchased near San Francisco. It was nearly noon, and they had to drive out of the park and back to the Bay Area hopefully before dark but after the late-afternoon traffic. Even on a holiday, that could pose a problem. He looked around for curious boaters, but saw none within hailing distance. "Time for the drop," he said quietly to Ervin, who nodded appreciatively.

Ervin reached under the transom and brought out a clear plastic container full of a bright yellow material. The plastic, they both knew, would dissolve within the next twenty-four hours, dispersing the hundred grams of deadly polonium in this, the main drinking water supply for the San Francisco Peninsula. This dose alone would cause a major health disaster; combined with the other jihadis out here, they would cause a calamity similar to that of a nuclear bomb. He reached over the gunwale and carefully placed the container into the still, deep water. Both men watched as the innocent-looking but lethal missile slowly made its way to the bottom, some hundred feet below. They looked at each other and grinned. The deed was done; it was time to head for home.

The two assassins had been happy to end their lives in Paradise. Now that their task was accomplished, they were happier to contemplate their safe escape as live heroes rather than dead martyrs. Zana started the motor and headed for the ramp, their sunglasses gleaming in the blazing midday sun.

They reached the ramp in fewer than fifteen minutes, pleased to see it empty of boats either launching or leaving. Zana brought the nose up onto the ramp, threw the bowline out to the waiting Ervin, and shut off the motor. There were a few people eating lunch on their trailers, but that was all. As practiced at the training camp, Ervin brought the trailer down into the water and the two men easily pulled the boat up onto it. Then they brought the loaded trailer into the space next to their van. Not a single person paid attention to them. They left their gear on the boat, as if they were leaving for just an hour or so to get something to eat or drink.

Zana drove the now-unhooked van slowly up to the exit gate, which opened obligingly. They were free to make their way up to the main road. There were no shouts of triumph; no sense drawing attention. But Zana punched his accomplice in the leg as they sensed freedom at hand.

* * *

"They're on their way! Better get here quick!" Andy was on the phone with the park's headquarters. They had been watching the suspicious pair ever since they appeared ready to leave the lake and were now desperate for the US Park Police to come and investigate. "Damn fools!" he yelled at his young deputy.

"What's wrong now, Chief?" Chip was worried. Andy never got this excited and angry.

"They say, 'Don't worry, they'll catch them. They'll never get out of the park.' Besides, they got other guys doin' something in one of the other lots, other side of the lake."

"Did you tell them about how they seemed to drop something in the water?"

"Yeah, of course I did! But they said they got other reports very similar; got to get to those first." The two men looked at each other impotently. Something was indeed going on; all they could do was sit and watch. After what seemed like an hour, a California Highway Patrol car pulled up to the gate, flashers on but no siren. No need to cause a panic; not yet.

Two uniformed CHP officers entered the booth and immediately started asking questions. "What was the license number on the vehicle? Which direction did they head out of the park? Where exactly were they on the lake when they dropped the object into the water?"

Andy could at least answer the last question with some accuracy; he had lined the boat up with two markers on the other shore and could estimate its distance from both. That would give the CHP a good starting point for a search. They quickly jumped on their walkies and relayed the information. Speedboats would be out there soon to see what they could find; the clear water might, in fact, yield something.

It was less than twenty minutes when a twenty-foot inboard cruiser showed up in the lake, slowing down as it reached the vicinity of Andy's guess as to the location. One of the officers in the booth guided them, conferring with Andy at the same time. When the patrol boat appeared to Andy to be in the approximate spot of the "drop," the CHP officer radioed the pilot of the boat. It stopped, and the pilot waved to the booth, indicating they were about to start the search. Three scuba divers slid into the water. The men in the guard booth watched intently, all with binoculars. Caution flags appeared as each diver disappeared from view.

Fifteen agonizing minutes passed before one of the divers broke the surface, displaying a net with a plastic container in it. With the binoculars, the onlookers could see it contained a bright yellow substance. While Andy and Chip looked at each other, puzzled, the CHP officers were on their walkies: "They got it; it's what we were afraid of. Over and out." Their faces were more than grim; they were terrified, fully terrified.

"You guys have to keep this quiet. We can't cause a panic. " one officer warned the two park employees in no uncertain terms. Poison had been dropped into the lake. Fortunately, conditions were perfect for its discovery; the granite lake made for excellent visibility, especially with the bright overhead sunlight. The yellow material had shown up like a diamond in newly washed mud, even at a depth of one hundred feet.

Once the three divers had been retrieved, the CHP speedboat raced to the ramp exclusive to park headquarters, near the dam. The Park patrolmen told Andy and Chip what was to happen next: The suspicious material would be taken to the FBI lab in Oakland by helicopter, analyzed, and the results given to Homeland Security.

The two men looked as solemn and scared as the CHP officers. They knew now what they had just witnessed: an attack on their drinking water, no doubt by the mullahs in control of the Islamic Republic of Iran. It was just like the recent event in Los Angeles. Andy looked at the glass of water he had just drawn from the tap and poured it down the drain. Only bottled water from now on.

* * *

Zana drove easily, now relieved of the stress of the boat and trailer. He exited the lake area onto the main road leading out of the Park, headed for Highway 120, west toward Oakland. Without the trailer, they were inconspicuous among the other vacationers headed in both directions. They could also take the hills and curves at normal speed. "Home free!" Zana grinned at Ervin, who was now relaxing a bit as well. "Call in and see if they can get us reservations out of Oakland."

Ervin did as ordered; almost at once, he started speaking with someone in English at the other end. There was a pause, then Ervin looked up at Zana, saying, "They're going to call back in five minutes or less. We're to keep off the phone until then."

Zana just nodded; things were going well. Paradise would have to wait awhile. He smiled as he thought of the hero's welcome they were about to . . .

His reverie came to a sudden stop as he saw the flashing red lights in his rearview mirror. Then the sirens shrieked; the game was over. He looked over at his young protégé with a somber expression and motioned to the glove box. Ervin knew what that meant; he reached in and grabbed the little bottle containing the white capsules. Giving one to Zana, he swallowed the other and tapped his superior on the shoulder.

"Allahu Akbar!" they yelled in unison as Zana swallowed the death pill, pulling the van across the two-lane road, onto the shoulder, then . . .

The two assassins never felt a thing as the van left the road, plummeting eighty feet into the granite boulders at the bottom of the hill, bursting into flames. Their deed was done.

* * *

The crackle of the radio on the CHP officer's shirt brought the rest of the men in the guard booth upright. The officer left the speaker on so the others could hear. "Unit 55, we have an 11-80 here on Highway 120, twenty miles east of the park entrance. Closure on the escapees. They have terminated chase. Ambulance called. No apparent survivors. Over and out."

The radio went silent. Then the park employees' walkies came to life: "Suspects in the lake case have been apprehended; no survivors. Two males DOA. Further details soon. Over and out."

The CHP officers tipped their caps at the two gate attendants and headed to their vehicle. Their job here was done; they just had to wait for the lab results on the yellow substance and further instructions.

Chapter 35

Lara and Uri pulled up at the CHP headquarters in San Mateo at 3:00 p.m. o meet one last time with their team. They dispersed the men, except for ɔne energetic youngster named Ivan, to aid the sheriff at the Crystal Springs and San Andreas reservoirs a few miles away. With Lara at the wheel, they ɔok a circuitous route up to the Pilarcitos Dam, not encountering any other vehicles or personnel. They were glad to have the security of their off-road SUVs on these treacherous dirt paths. With them they carried a minimum ɔf rations, clothing, and equipment, including their new personal weapons.

News came at 6:00 p.m. from the Oakland office of Homeland Security: the occupants of two motorboats and two sailboats at Hetch Hetchy had been apprehended after each exhibited suspicious behavior that day. One motorboat had stalled in a deep part of the narrow lake. The occupants failed to surrender, the boat was hauled ashore, and the men were arrested. The FBI and Homeland Security officers were continuing their interrogation. The other motorboat had drawn suspicion from officers on shore after noticing that the "boaters" seemed totally inept at rigging and handling their fishing gear. The two occupants had been able to reach shore and escape; both of these men died during the ensuing police chase.

The sailboats had both capsized, the occupants unable to maneuver their craft in the light air. The sailors had apparently taken their own lives by ingesting unknown substances. Autopsies were ongoing.

Scuba divers recovered three clear plastic containers from the lake near to where the boats had been operating. The containers each held a bright-yellow substance. Fortunately, all had caught on relatively shallow underwater cliffs; the lake itself was over one thousand feet deep at some spots. The captured material was taken to the FBI lab in Oakland for analysis. Divers were still out in the lake, searching for the one apparently missing container.

With this news, the chances for an attack on the Pilarcitos Dam seemed to increase dramatically. The Iranians were bound to have put in place a multipronged effort. The teams of defenders were updated and put on high alert.

Later that evening, a report came in announcing that the divers had indeed found the remaining container of yellow substance not far from one of the boat ramps.

Chapter 36

The three men in gray coveralls glanced at each other in the darkness of the Fourth of July evening. The penetrating misty-wet fog blew in from the west with increasing bite as the last rays of daylight disappeared in the west. Visibility was less than thirty yards; the walking trail above the dam was devoid of the usual casual hikers along the Pilarcitos Reservoir during daylight hours, no doubt because of the inclement weather.

The logo on their gray rental jeep parked alongside the path matched that on each of their coveralls. It showed a picture of a tall dam with the acronym *MPWD* stitched below it in bright white letters. The county personnel were familiar with the Mid-Peninsula Water District, whose province it was to maintain and protect this integral part of the crucial San Francisco area's water supply.

Most of the water for the peninsula, the men knew, came from the Hetch Hetchy dam far to the east, across the bay in the Sierra Nevada mountain range. The team of attackers had received word just hours ago that the Iranian attack on the Hetch Hetchy had failed miserably. Thus, the burden was placed firmly on them to poison the water.

The City of San Francisco and its environs also depended, they knew, on the local rain and groundwater, much of it originating in San Mateo County to the south. Years of low rainfall and the resultant droughts had caused bitter "water wars" that pitted farmers, environmentalists, and residents against each other in the city and suburbs of more than five million people.

This particular reservoir had been created well over one hundred years ago on this hill 1,400 feet above sea level, mainly so that gravity could provide most of the energy to carry water to the city.

The terrorist team above the old earth-fill dam felt the full responsibility of the effort to poison the water. They put their faith entirely on the skill and experience of the military men in command of their mission. General Gharoub and Colonel Soroush absorbed the news of the failure at Hetch Hetchy with the feeling of heavy weights placed around their necks. The mission's whole success now depended on two officers only lightly experienced in battle and a small group of young men away from home for the first time.

The three men in gray appeared from cover above the large, semicircular dam. Saman, their team leader, was stocky and muscular. They had made a practice run to the reservoir the night before to assure their jeep could handle the dirt trails. Each man carried a backpack that held, in addition to their digging and water-testing gear, a 100-gram water-soluble container of polonium chloride powder. On their persons, they carried automatic pistols in the unlikely event they should be apprehended. Each also carried additional fifty gram "contingency" containers of polonium chloride. Should they be in jeopardy of capture, they were to throw these into whatever body of water was close at hand.

The terrorists began checking the valves and meters on the downhill side of the trail, pretending to be measuring the water temperature, salinity, and pH, as well as trace contaminant levels. From this point north, the water flowed directly into the municipal water supply. In case they were seen, the men appeared to be busily taking water samples from ports, labeling the bottles, then placing them in their packs. Only when they were certain of safety would they climb to the top of the dam and drop their deadly flasks into the reservoirs.

Saman's name tag read *James* on his breast pocket. He turned up his collar against the cold, damp wind. Though impossible to see in the dim light and heavy clothing, he had a dark complexion and a frightening appearance. He was a convicted killer, pardoned by the government of Iran in order to participate in this highly dangerous mission. His underlings, Kamran and Seyed, were also convicted felons, but in order to participate in this assignment, each had been allowed to keep his right hand rather than have it publicly amputated. This was the standard penalty for stealing food. Both were substantially younger than Saman and less experienced, but they were prepared to become martyrs for this strike against the West.

Kamran's uniform bore the name *Bill* on his pocket; Seyed's was labeled *Pete*. All three men had been released from Evin Prison, one of the most infamous and notorious prisons in the world. Beatings, torture, mock executions, rape, and brutal interrogations were everyday routine in that nightmarish place. For four decades, the anguished cries of prisoners had been swallowed up by the drab walls of the low-slung lockup in Tehran. To each, death would be a better fate. But all were hoping for pardons upon completion of their task.

The teams had flown into San Francisco International Airport through Los Angeles on false passports after an accelerated course on terrorism in Iran. They carried with them an immensely fatal dose of polonium chloride powder, enough to slaughter the entire population of the "City by the Bay." While they were aware of the near-miss their predecessors had experienced in Los Angeles just a few months prior to this attempt, all were convinced of the advances that had been made for this attack. In any case, the worst possible scenario was martyrdom in the service to the glory of Islam and everlasting pleasure in Paradise.

The dark-colored van being used by Gharoub and Soroush was well hidden under some large ficus trees out of view from the three men in overalls. Because Pilarcitos was deemed the most critical of the peninsular sites, the two officers had been ordered by the president to personally supervise the effort. They were situated now well across the trail and out of sight from the footpath over the dam. The officers sat crouched uncomfortably in the back, watching for intruders while listening for news on their communication device. So far, the convicts appeared to be performing their duties just as practiced.

The only news they had received from Tehran was that of an apparent failure of the raid on Hetch Hetchy.

The most significant change in their strategy was to insert the poison into the water supply downstream of the last sampling point. With the Tracy

Water Treatment Plant disabled, as they had been told, there would be no delay between the time they dumped the polonium into the flowing stream and its delivery to the unsuspecting Jews and other Satan worshipers.

Suddenly, a slender figure emerged from the bushes alongside the trail from the dam. The two Iranian officers crouched even lower behind their seats as the person approached. The intruder was clad in military camouflage, carrying a radio and an automatic weapon. On a hand signal from his general, Colonel Soroush emerged from the far side of the van, flipped on a high-intensity Maglite, and quietly ordered the person in English to stop, disarm, and drop to the ground.

* * *

Lara, caught unaware in the beam of the Maglite, did as ordered, silently cursing herself for checking out this hidden area without cover. *How could she have been so careless?* Her clumsy attempt at reaching for her radio did not go unnoticed. But she was stunned to recognize the voice, even in his highly accented English. *Colonel Soroush! How in the world?* As she dropped her Masada pistol, the light hit her full in the face. Her only consolation was the fact that she had sent a last-second text message to Uri telling him where she was headed.

"It's the American spy!" Soroush declared in Farsi, just loud enough for Gharoub to hear through his open window. "But with blue eyes; come see!" They examined the prisoner with some amusement. She still wore the disfiguring facial inserts and dyed hair, so she was instantly recognizable to the Iranians, even though the brown contact lenses were missing. But her clear blue eyes flashed in the beam of the Maglite.

"Come here, you Jew bitch," Gharoub ordered in English, grabbing her by the hair, dragging her to the van. To him, this was almost as important a development as poisoning the water. How they would make her pay!

* * *

Uri saw the message light blink on his short-range radio and saw that it was from Lara; he read it instantly. When she didn't send another message moments later, he assumed something, or someone, had stopped her. He grabbed Ivan and carefully headed for the top of the dam. From there, they could see a powerful beam of light dancing around on the ground near the ficus trees on the other side of the footpath. They heard the sounds of a struggle, then recognized the outline of a vehicle at the edge of the wooded area.

With a hand signal, Uri ordered Ivan to take the footpath around the trees while Uri came up from below. Uri's heart was fully in his mouth as he recognized Lara's camouflaged figure in the pale moonlight. She was in the grasp of a large man who held her arms and upper body. Another smaller man was reaching for her feet. But Uri could see that Lara was not about to let herself be taken so easily.

In a well-practiced maneuver, Uri whistled shrilly. It was the call of a small bird common to the tree-lined suburbs of Tel Aviv; Lara knew at once who it was and what it meant. She seemed to relax for just a moment, apparently yielding to the man reaching for her feet, Colonel Soroush. As General Gharoub, holding her upper torso, tried to get a better grip around her shoulders, she kicked out with her left foot, aiming at the smaller man's unguarded groin. With her right foot supporting her weight, she simultaneously twisted in Gharoub's grip, swinging her right elbow directly into his nose. There was a satisfying sound of cartilage and bone breaking as both men yelped in pain.

Soroush grasped for his pistol just as Ivan burst into the open. Gharoub reached into the van, bleeding heavily from his face. But he was clearly battle-trained; he started the engine, then took a blind shot at the spot where he had last seen Lara fighting with Soroush. Uri, watching from twenty yards away, could not fire safely, for fear of hitting Lara or Ivan. He had to wait to see what actions his companions could take.

As Ivan grappled with Soroush, the rear wheels of the van spun wildly in the mix of dirt and fertilizer at the base of the tree. Soroush struck van a grazing blow across the back of his head with his pistol, apparently not wanting to give away his location by a gunshot. Ivan, stunned, was unable to stop his assailant from flinging himself into the back of the van, which sped away through the trees.

Uri dashed out into the small clearing, reaching his wife and Ivan. Both were exhausted from their struggles but relieved to see Uri. He and Lara hugged each other eagerly, Uri checking her for any serious wounds. "Not here, you fool," she whispered loudly to him.

"Always with the jokes," Uri replied with a Yiddish accent. "I think maybe you're converting."

She punched him lightly in the ribs; she was all right. "Where do you think those two are headed?"

He was more worried at the moment about saboteurs at the dam than the officers.

Ivan offered a reasonable guess. "There are those sampling ports we read about at the other end of the dam. They're nearly at water level, so it would be easy to drop something in."

That seemed like a good place to start. Lara radioed Tom and briefly went over the events so far. He agreed that they should try the south end of the dam; he also said he would contact the sheriff and apprise him of the action at Pilarcitos.

With Ivan at the wheel, the three checked out the sampling ports. The maneuver took a bit of time, as they had to first drive down to the main road, then up again on the far side of the dam. Just as they reached the fencing around the sampling ports, they saw two men in maintenance uniforms clamber into a gray Jeep with the logo of the water district on its doors, heading the other way. If they tried to turn around and pursue them and they were indeed county workers, they might lose track of the criminals. On the other hand, if these men were part of the gang, this might be their best shot at them.

* * *

The terrorist team at Crystal Springs under the leadership of Turan and the team at San Andreas under twenty-five-year-old Marduk got word from their liaison in Oakland that security had been breached. By listening in on hidden police bands, they had learned of the fight at Pilarcitos. If that team had been discovered, the others were in danger of imminent capture. The teams were ordered to halt operation and make their way to safety . . . or termination. Both teams aborted operations and clambered into their vehicles. They would have to take evasive action to avoid the authorities. Otherwise, it was cyanide and Paradise.

Chapter 37

At 7:00 p.m. on July 4, San Francisco Sheriff Sean Parker received word that two of his patrol cars had detected fresh tire prints near Pilarcitos Dam late that afternoon. They showed the distinct marks of an off-road vehicle. He immediately left word for Tom Buckley at the Oakland office of Homeland Security. Then he contacted the water district office. Had any maintenance vehicles been sent to that dam in the past twenty-four hours? The somewhat uninterested receptionist told him that she would have to ask the chief, who had already left for the day.

Gritting his teeth, Sean tried to stay calm. "Please reach him as soon as possible; it's urgent," he said as pleasantly as possible.

"Yes, it always is," she replied, breaking the connection.

Tom called less than five minutes later. Sean told him about the tire prints. "Yes, this could be it," Tom said after the briefest of pauses. "They could have been scouting the territory last night. Where exactly were they?"

"On the dirt trail near the dam, coming from the road below."

"We need to get some units over there, and to the other reservoirs, too, as soon as you can free them; but only unmarked cars, no sirens, OK? We don't want a panic."

* * *

The news broke over the high-alert police and federal radio bands simultaneously: intruders had been detected at one of the municipal reservoirs, and there was reason to believe that similar attacks were ongoing at one or more of the other district lakes. Without waiting for Tom, Sheriff Parker leaped into action. He put out a bulletin to his deputies and made sure the highway patrol did likewise. All available units were ordered to upper and lower Crystal Springs, as well as the San Andreas lakes, searching for suspicious vehicles or activity.

* * *

Saman and his small gang of terrorists at Pilarcitos heard the commotion at the far end of the dam and came to an immediate, chilling conclusion: they had been discovered. They knew that their leaders, Gharoub and Soroush, were hidden under the ficus trees in that area, yet had sent no alarm. That could mean only that they had been taken by surprise. Saman signaled to his men: Kamran and Seyed grabbed their tools along with their bottles of polonium powder and leaped into their Jeep. Saman then made a quick decision to climb toward the top of the dam and toss in his container of poison. Scrambling back down, he got in the Jeep, and the three conspirators headed downhill toward Interstate 280, meaning to escape. Saman got on the radio and tried to warn their compatriots at the other two reservoirs of the setback. If the enemy were to find the polonium they carried ... At that thought, the three men all tossed their remaining containers out the window, into the brush.

Saman reached Turan, the veteran leader at the Crystal Springs reservoir, and quickly confirmed the bad news; the authorities had apparently discovered the general and colonel. Turan agreed this called for at least a delay in their plans; they must abort and try to reach their headquarters in Oakland.

Saman then got hold of the team at San Andreas Lake; those men were also aware of the situation. They agreed their best option was to flee and try again another day. It was disheartening but necessary.

* * *

Tom and Sean, rushing toward the reservoirs in separate cars, had by this time been apprised of the ongoing events. Two police helicopters were dispatched to aid in the ongoing chase but were soon grounded by the now-dense fog. Police warned the news agencies to stay away from the area completely until further notice; there was to be no word of the situation to the general public.

Saman and his crew careened down the hill from the 1,400-foot Pilarcitos Dam, continuing east in the direction of Interstate 280 and safety

* * *

Uri and Lara, along with the injured Ivan, headed across the dam toward the northern end of the reservoir, reasoning that the sheriff's forces would likely intercept the men in coveralls heading more directly to the interstate There were only the two trails down the hill. Uri drove silently, using only his parking lights to see through the mist. Suddenly, as they turned through a sharp hairpin on the steep dirt trail, they saw below them a pair of bright headlights through the fog. It had to be the men from the dam! Uri kept a safe distance behind the unmoving vehicle, certain his dim parking lights were not visible. As they came around another sharp turn, they saw not the jeep carrying the workers from the dam but the dark van that had carried Soroush and Gharoub! It appeared to be undamaged, the doors flung open Lara knew what they had to do; she sent brief text messages to Tom and the sheriff, giving them each their position.

"Stay here and stay armed!" Uri whispered to Ivan, who was crouched in the backseat. "You have your sidearm?"

Ivan raised his automatic rifle in response, barely visible in the fog shrouded moonlight. Uri just nodded silently and gestured to Lara to emerge from the passenger side and head to the downhill side of the apparently disabled van. With any luck, the two Iranian officers had been injured or even . . . he didn't even bother thinking about the other possibility.

Uri, watching his wife vanish below the open vehicle, crept silently past on the other side. He had with him his Baby Eagle III, a six-inch knife and a small Maglite. He could see nothing beyond the van stopped ahead of them, straddling the middle of the road. He approached it from the brush below, then chanced to flash his light into the front seats. There was Soroush flung against the dash, blood covering his face.

Lara signaled from the other side, but with her Maglite off.

"Are you injured?" Uri asked the silent colonel. There was no response, no movement at all. "Where is your general?" Nothing.

Just then, a shriek came from their own vehicle, above them on the road. It was Ivan. Then Lara heard the unmistakable voice of Gharoub in Farsi: "If you want to save your miserable colleague, step out onto the road, both of you!" he ordered.

"All right, here we are!" Uri yelled back, also in Farsi, stepping onto the road.

"I see only you, you Jew bastard, Levin. Where is your whore?"

Uri paused for a moment before responding; no sense reacting to the man's deliberate insult. "She is coming up on your downhill side. We will let you go if you leave our man alone, I promise."

Lara, meanwhile, had taken the opportunity to open the door to the injured colonel, stuffed her handkerchief into his bloody mouth, disarmed him, and tied his hands to the wheel with his belt, taking care to remove the keys from the ignition. He seemed unconscious.

"Are you all right, Ivan?" Uri yelled to his colleague. There was no reply as Uri made his way toward the uphill side of his car.

"Stay right where you are," came the voice of General Gharoub in English from behind a small oak to Uri's right. "And get your bitch out here, or I'll kill you right now." He held a light on the inert form of Ivan in the rear seat, then fired a nearly earsplitting shot from his AK-47 directly over Uri's head, snapping off a large branch. "Now, where is she? We have some unfinished busin—"

His last word hung in the air as his head exploded. A high-velocity round from Lara's Masada finished his sentence for him.

Lara holstered her pistol as Uri rushed over to check on Ivan. He was lying on the rear seat, trussed up and gagged, but otherwise not further injured. At that same moment, they heard the van on the road ahead of them roar to life, wheels spinning as it hurtled downhill. The two agents looked at each other; Soroush must have had a spare key. While Lara tended to Ivan, Uri signaled Sheriff Parker. His men could capture the colonel more easily. They had to determine their next move.

Chapter 38

Col. Bijan Soroush, bruised and bleeding but alert, drove down the relatively straight road from the east side of the Pilarcitos Reservoir toward Interstate 280. That would give him the option of heading north toward San Francisco or south toward State Route 92. From that intersection, he could head either west toward the Pacific Ocean, a hilly, little used route, or east across the San Mateo–Hayward Bridge to the East Bay.

After some thought, he decided on the latter alternative. Once he crossed San Francisco Bay, he could make his way to freedom a number of ways, but he needed to proceed north to Oakland. The team members, those who survived, would meet at the community center to check in and get further instructions. They were still on their mission of jihad. But from the meager reports he had received over the radio, it was not looking good.

The Hetch Hetchy team had failed miserably, of course. Soroush had learned that earlier. Of the three teams on the peninsula, their highest hopes lay with that headed by the experienced Saman and his two adventurous colleagues, Kamran and Seyed. They had been underway with their operation on the other side of the Pilarcitos Dam when the female American spy had discovered him and that lout, Gharoub.

The last report he had received from that team was that they felt they had been discovered and were making a "strategic withdrawal." But, they added, at least one container of poison had been thrown into the lake behind the dam. That was the only good news of the entire day so far. One bottleful of poison would throw the City of San Francisco into an unimaginable panic, one similar to word of a nuclear attack!

On the downside, the other two teams assigned to the San Andreas and Crystal Springs reservoirs were unaccounted for. Still, if the Pilarcitos team had been successful, the mission could be considered a victory.

If Saman's team made it safely off the dam and out of the reservoir area, they would head back to Oakland or, even better, take their own lives without divulging any information. With that inspiration, Soroush continued downhill toward the highway.

It was only five more minutes on the now-paved trail until he saw the access road to I-280. He blended into the southbound traffic and headed, somewhat relieved, toward San Mateo and escape on the highway east, across the Bay.

* * *

Marduk and his team of relatively inexperienced warriors quickly gave up their operation at the news of the unraveling of the mission and fled along the San Andreas trail, heading east to the nearby freeway. "Quickly, everyone!" he yelled to his two charges. "Get rid of all the poison. Throw it out into the bushes." They did as they were told as Marduk drove madly for the access road onto the freeway. They cruised through an underpass that led them to the northbound lanes of I-280 at a suburb called Millbrae, relieved at their narrow escape.

As they hurtled along, eager to find a rapid-transit station, they were oblivious to the helicopter that had spotted them, the police thinking they were out-of-control auto thieves. Upon checking in with the sheriff's office, the officers learned there was a good chance the vehicle contained the foreign agents they had been warned about. The helicopter spotlight highlighted the four-wheel-drive vehicle, and two sheriff's office units hit their sirens in pursuit, one circling around from the southbound side of the freeway.

Marduk, petrified with fear, exited at the ramp to San Bruno. He knew there was a rapid-transit station there. But as he drove around the station looking for a place to leave their vehicle, he and the others were horrified to see an astonishing number of patrol cars, red lights flashing and sirens blaring. There was no doubt in Marduk's mind as it went into "Paradise mode." He jammed his foot down on the accelerator and aimed

he car, tires squealing, into the huge concrete abutment at the far end of the
ot. Later estimates placed its speed at impact at 70 mph.

* * *

Turan was well practiced in night raids from his years of working with the
Hezbollah terrorists in northern Israel. He had, in fact, trained dozens of
recruits in the skills needed to make their way down from southern Lebanon
into the Galilee. There, he had shown them how to silently slit the throats
of unsuspecting Israeli farmers and schoolchildren.

His team on the San Francisco Peninsula had, just last night, scouted
the way from the freeway to the access road, called Cañada Road, just below
the Upper Crystal Springs Reservoir.

Now, as they approached their objective on foot from Cañada Road,
he realized he had misjudged all the difficulties involved. The bank was
steeper than it had looked from the access road; worse, it was more
treacherous than it seemed the night before, slippery from the dense fog.
Finally, there was a strong chain-link fence guarding the lake from curious
trespassers.

Turan made a quick "battlefield decision" to alter their plan and
attempt to reach the bank of the lake from the uphill side. Chances were that
the long western edge of the lake would be more accessible, especially with
their hefty off-road vehicle. They climbed in and headed for the southern
end of the reservoir just as the news came in of the failure at Pilarcitos and
the likely pursuit by the state and federal authorities. Considering the time
needed to get back to the highway, Turan made another impromptu decision
and headed for the access road and safety. Just as they were about to enter
the roadway, he noticed a large, beat-up metal trash barrel under a tree.
These Americans are indeed fastidious, he thought.

"Quickly, get out and dump all your poison in that barrel." As he
handed his two recruits his own stash of polonium, he added, "Make sure to
stuff it all down at the very bottom. Cover it with as much food and other
garbage as you find in there." He knew that Americans were as fond of

eating fast food as they were loath to handle its greasy, rancid remains. The poison would stay in the barrel until a trash truck came to collect it. If his team should have the misfortune to be caught with no chance of suicide there would at least be no evidence of their deadly mission. And with no chance of completing their mission, Paradise could wait for another opportunity.

Turan and his men made their way back onto the freeway, then north to Highway 92, east toward Oakland, just as they had the previous night. Long sighs of disappointment, mixed with a bit of relief, issued from the failed jihadis as they headed back to the community center and an uncertain future.

Chapter 39

Sheriff Sean Parker was maintaining radio contact with Tom Buckley, even as he drove along the highway toward the reservoirs. He shared each bit of news as it came in from the highway and helicopter units.

There was no doubt that the terrorist attack was in full swing. What was also clear was that Tom's troops had foiled the attack on the Pilarcitos Reservoir, although the fate of the jihadis was as yet unknown. Also uncertain was the status of the poison. Had any reached the water? Fortunately, they did have access to the new test for water-borne polonium. Tom had shared with him the classified information from the chemists. They called it an ion-exchange-membrane device. It consisted of a material held in place on an inert matrix, or membrane.

Any polonium stuck on the membrane then showed up on a radiation detector. It was touted to be accurate to the parts-per-billion level or better. The lab's research effort began right after the Los Angeles scare. *And just in time*, thought Sean.

Other news dealt with the fate of the jihadis at the San Andreas and Upper Crystal Springs reservoirs:

Sean heard that the team at San Andreas attempted to escape but had committed suicide at the San Bruno BART station, driving into a concrete pillar in the parking lot. So far, no polonium was detected at the scene, but the investigation was continuing. The immolated remains of the jihadis were undergoing DNA testing, which was so far inconclusive.

The good news was that the water in both lakes had so far showed no polonium content. Searches were ongoing at both these locations, and at Pilarcitos, for any suspicious containers.

The jihadis at Crystal Springs had been spotted by the California Highway Patrol helicopters. They were seen leaving the reservoir, heading east across the San Mateo–Hayward Bridge. Authorities followed at a safe distance by air and highway units in the hopes they would lead the officers to a meeting place in the East Bay.

Sean reasoned that the jihadis were headed for the Oakland community center. Though troubled by the failure to find any of the poison, he took two deputies and drove directly to the center, sirens loudly blaring to make their way through the evening holiday traffic. When they reached their destination, the building appeared unoccupied. There were no vehicles in the lot and the large double doors were shut.

Soroush and what remained of his troops were hidden in the large meeting room of the community center; their van was parked inside, out of sight from the street. The sheriff and his deputies burst into the center through the main entrance, guns drawn, but were surprised by the sight of the SUV. As they examined it, the terrorists emerged from behind them bludgeoned one of the surprised deputies and took Sean prisoner at gunpoint. Overwhelmed, the other deputy dropped his pistol and raised his hands. Soroush, anticipating more police, had one of his men drag the unconscious deputy to the center of the room, forcing Sean and his remaining officer to the same location.

At that point, Lara, Uri, and Ivan, who had been hiding in the adjacent building, rushed into the center. They had seen Sean and his men enter the building and were coming to assist in the anticipated arrests. Instead, a triumphant Colonel Soroush appeared from the shadows, waving an AK-47. He ordered the trio to drop their weapons just as another patrol car noisily pulled up outside. While Soroush's men herded the federal team toward the center of the room, the arriving police officers raced in through the open door, pistols drawn. Soroush used a megaphone to warn them that the sheriff and the others would be killed if the jihadis were not permitted to escape in their SUV. Four other jihadis appeared, all carrying automatic weapons.

Soroush ordered the newly-arrived CHP officers to drop their pistols. When five seconds passed without any response, one of the jihadis, on a hand signal from Soroush, shot another deputy in the knee; he dropped to the ground, screaming in pain. "Get in that vehicle," Soroush ordered the Americans in a commanding voice; he was finished fooling around.

"Take me instead," Uri offered. Soroush, surprised by this surrender, didn't see Lara slip around the back of the car and crouch behind a hot-water tank. With everyone watching him, Uri surrendered, noisily dropping his pistol with a flourish. The jihadis seemed transfixed by the Baby Eagle III lying on the wooden floor; none of them had ever seen anything like this strange new weapon.

This bizarre break in the action allowed Lara to move closer in the dim light. She came out of the shadows behind Soroush, her weapon drawn.

"Tell your men to drop their guns!" Lara commanded in fluent Farsi, jabbing her pistol in Soroush's back. "You have ten seconds or your life ends!"

The mortified colonel just stood there transfixed. The jihadis all looked to Turan, the second-in-charge, who was well-acquainted with the stories about Lara; she was a fearless killer, they all knew. *That she-devil will not hesitate to kill our beloved colonel, Turan reasoned. Without our leader our team will be like a rudderless ship in a terrible storm; we will be slaughtered like sheep. We must remain alive for another opportunity to reach glorious martyrdom and Paradise.* He dropped his AK-47. The remaining jihadis, overwhelmed by Turan's surrender, glumly dropped their firearms, even as Soroush spun around, glaring at them furiously.

Meanwhile, Ivan silently eased closer and floored the nearest jihadi with the butt of his automatic rifle. He then stepped into the light, taking command along with Lara. At that moment the silence in the room was broken by the thunder of powerful police megaphones, blaring from outside.

To put an end to the confrontation before the highway patrol officers stepped into a gun battle, Uri stepped hard on the instep of the confused jihadi next to him, simultaneously twisting the man's arm behind his back. The overwhelmed young terrorist screamed out in pain and dropped the weapon he was holding; it was Uri's Baby Eagle. Uri picked it up and threatened Soroush once more with a determined command: "Tell your men to drop their guns now, or you all die!"

"Aghaz-na-see-sheem!" roared Soroush in reply, knowing that the two American agents were quite familiar with the obscene phrase. It translated roughly to: "I'll use your mouth as a toilet!" The jihadis seemed heartened by this demonstration of courage by their colonel.

Ivan used the opportunity to kick an AK-47 away from the nearest jihadi; the youngster cursed himself loudly for his negligence. Ivan, still in a great deal of pain, grimaced as he picked up the weapon, using it to prod its former owner with a reminder of what was in store at the slightest provocation.

Another jihadi, seemingly emboldened by their apparent numerical advantage, struck the sheriff across the face. Ivan, in reply, fired a short burst of 7.62 mm slugs just over the man's head, the rounds ricocheting wildly off the concrete walls. The terrified youngster dropped to his knees, his rifle thrown aside, his hands in the air. Just then, more patrol cars arrived outside, their sirens screaming loudly. Flashing red lights illuminated the room through the row of windows at the top of the far wall, lending a vision of Dante's "Inferno" to the horrific scene. To a man, the terror team dropped their weapons in surrender.

Within seconds, the newly arrived police and Homeland Security agents, with Tom leading, stormed in and ended the fight. But not before the humbled Soroush ended his own life with a dose of cyanide.

The terrorist attack was finished.

Chapter 40

As the combined forces of federal and state officers arrested the disheartened and disappointed Iranians, Tom asked Lara and Uri to come with him to the Oakland offices of Homeland Security. They drove the short distance in less than five minutes, vivid memories of the action-filled night reverberating in their heads. It had been the most exhausting and unnerving night in their immediate memories.

"Take a couple of seats there in the front row," Tom said with a forced casualness. A large high-definition television screen was mounted on the wall of the small theater. Filling in the room behind them were most of the nonessential personnel awaiting the anticipated show. Drone strikes at unannounced targets were on the menu, according to Tom's brief introduction.

The presentation began with grainy images that were somewhat familiar to Lara. Uri was not acquainted with the facilities Lara had visited as a guest of Iranian military intelligence. These first views were taken from a high-flying aircraft above the Alborz mountains north of Tehran. The brown cloud of smog was distinctly visible just below the aircraft. As the supersonic plane dropped into the highly populated area, a smaller projectile dropped into view. The mother ship regained altitude, though its cameras continued to follow the path of the smaller craft. As the larger plane picked up speed, heading back for the safety of the Caspian Sea to the north, two vapor trails appeared in the sky directly beneath it. Only moments later, two antimissile rockets spewed out of the mother ship, erasing the attackers in bursts of smoke and debris. Shouts of glee erupted from the audience as the screen filled with the remnants of the Iranian defensive shields.

The screen now abruptly changed, showing another offensive missile dropping into Tehran airspace, but this time no pursuers appeared. Far below, signs of explosions appeared as distant cloudbursts near ground level. These brought on more excited cries from the gallery.

The scene now shifted to an apparent onboard vista as one of the Hellfire missiles from the first US plane tracked its own death spiral out of the sky above the outskirts of Tehran. Lara recognized some of the scenery as that of the northwest suburbs, even as the missile streaked by at high speed. She watched, spellbound, as it bore in. Then, suddenly, the camera slowed as the missile neared the ground. Lara was then able to identify some of the structures in the thinly populated area she'd visited on her first trip with Major Asani. The trees vanished as the missile leveled off in flight heading straight into what was clearly a parking lot. She was able to even distinguish individual government vehicles at this speed.

The digital image on the screen stopped abruptly as a voice came over the speakers.

"What you're about to see is not pretty, but remember, we're down to very low speed here. A warning was issued two hours before impact to all personnel in this, the polonium-packaging facility. We were hoping to avoid any civilian or even military casualties."

There was complete quiet in the viewing room as the screen once again displayed the images from the missile. The entrance to the building recognizable to Lara, vanished from the screen just before all evidence of the concrete structure disappeared in a flurry of smoke, dust, and flame. She hoped the warning given to the Iranian personnel had been taken seriously. The transmission ended abruptly; this time, however, there was nothing but anxious, guarded silence from the audience.

Lara, as no doubt all in the room, knew that the few hundred grams of deadly polonium would be scattered throughout the unpopulated area around the now-obliterated facility. But the short half-life of the isotope would present a danger to the residents for about a year or so; it was not the same as a nuclear power plant meltdown. She felt certain the Iranian government would claim that only a lab accident had occurred; residents would be told to avoid the immediate area until cleanup could contain the wreckage.

Another video display began after just a short pause, during which Tom informed his audience that what they were about to see was an even more deadly display. There was complete silence as the screen showed an even-higher altitude flight over northern Iran. This time, there was no sign of enemy defense missiles. Lara had no doubt of what she was about to see. Her knowledge of the vicinity told her they were viewing the area well northeast of the city of Tehran, far into the unpopulated foothills of the mountains. She remembered clearly her second tour with the major, this time to the polonium-production facility at the illegal heavy-water nuclear reactor. The world would do well without it.

Still, Lara's heart was in her throat as the killer drone was released, high-altitude cameras following it down through the clouds, into the forest below. A soundless mushroom-shaped cloud appeared, rising into the air well below the mother ship; then the view shifted to that coming directly from the deadly missile itself. Lara recognized the building; she knew she would. All the fencing and the guard stations were visible, apparently unoccupied. *Thank you for that.* She was even able to see the radiation-hazard warning signs at the slowed camera speed; then nothing but static. Visions of Hiroshima and Nagasaki flashed through her mind, even though she realized that no nuclear-fission reaction was possible from the destruction of a heavy-water reactor. She could only hope the Iranians had been judicious enough to get all personnel out of the building after the warnings, just as at the destruction of their packaging plant earlier that day.

The presentation concluded, and the room lights came on to a silent, stunned audience. It was a few minutes before the select group slowly and silently left the room.

Chapter 41

Tom escorted Lara and Uri to his temporary office in the Oakland headquarters. He was exhilarated by the excellent outcome of the night's activity. The scene at the community center had been sorted out by then, with the surviving jihadis arrested. The others had been taken to a nearby hospital; Soroush was sent to the morgue. Tom sat the agents down in a pair of comfortable chairs; he had something else to tell them.

"I thought you'd like to know . . ." Tom began with a big smile on his face. Both agents, despite their weariness, showed their full attention. "The president—ours, that is—sent all the satellite and drone data from the attack you just saw to our international partners . . . and other countries as well. We wanted to be sure that all nations recognized that the Iranian preparations constituted an act of war. Preparing for a large-scale chemical attack on civilians is certainly that; and the US preemptive measures were totally justified." He paused for just a second to let that sink in. "The international response has been damn-near unanimous. The heads of state from all major countries viewed our attacks from their own satellites and were hoping to hear from us as to what led to them."

"Please go on!" Lara was practically jumping out of her chair.

"Well, first of all, Iran already filed an official complaint to the United Nations, claiming an act of war had been perpetrated by *us*. That' to be discussed at an emergency meeting of the UN next week. The Iranian were furious at the delay." Tom waved his hand in a gesture of dismissal. "That's not going anywhere; our allies have seen and understood everything we sent them. France, Germany, and the UK are totally convinced our attack was justified. Iran had to allow the UN 'discovery team' access to the areas Elemental analysis of the remains of the two facilities we destroyed show just what you would expect from destruction of a heavy-water reactor uranium, bismuth, and polonium, for starters. Then there's the fact that there is no sign of a nuclear-fission event—none of the elements that are produced by a nuclear missile or bomb. So, there was no nuclear assault by our side; all the radioactive material in that debris was from the Iranian reactor itself." Tom watched the agents' faces: they were spellbound.

"Within an hour, we heard from both the Israeli and Saudi governments approving our actions as well. That was to be expected; still, it's nice to get the official word." Tom paused to see what Lara and Uri might have to say, but they were waiting for the rest of the story. "Belgium and the Scandinavian countries were very guarded in their responses, not casting blame on either side but not happy, either. You know, of course, that those countries have large numbers of Shia-Muslim refugees."

Lara and Uri remained silent at the unstated inference.

"Then there's Russia: we were most worried about them." Another long pause, then: "The guys at the Kremlin only said they were waiting to fully analyze their own satellite data. Which means they've got nothing to refute our arguments; they're solid, and the Russkies know it."

The tension in the room dissolved with a shaking of hands all around. Genuine smiles appeared on the agents' faces for the first time that evening.

After a minute or so, Uri had a question.

"One thing I still don't understand, Tom." Uri had a seriously quizzical look about him. "How did the Iranians connect me with the fake signals?"

"That's right, you don't know about that yet. It was your hostess. 'Tala' is the name she went by."

Uri looked at Lara, who shrugged her shoulders. Uri had not mentioned anything about a liaison with a woman, and she hadn't asked.

"Tala was a double agent, it turns out, actually working for the Iranians."

"Hard to believe. She had me fooled." Uri was dumbfounded. Lara glanced his way, seemingly indifferent, but relieved. "So, how did you find . . . ?"

"One of our own deep-cover people, Gharoub's secretary, known as Mrs. Khorasani. I'm pretty sure you met her."

The woman was known to both agents; General Wainscroft had also told them about her in his briefing on their transport to Oakland. So, it was the two women, so innocent-seeming, working for opposite sides. . .

"Tell us, then; what happened to them?" Uri asked.

"Your hostess, Tala, was responsible for the elimination of one of our top field agents in Tehran; she told you about him. How she took over for him as Agent U37FGI."

Uri nodded; she had indeed.

"It was she who had him . . ." Tom didn't need to elaborate.

"And what has happened to Tala, may I ask?"

"Mrs. Khorasani took care of that." Tom again didn't go into details.

"What's happened with the poison? Any word?" Lara changed the subject after a moment. She hoped Mrs. Khorasani was safe.

"All good, I'm happy to say." Tom looked relieved. "First, our guys found all the polonium, we believe. Of course, we'll still be checking the water, but at any rate . . ." He held up his hand to indicate he would get into details. "We discovered a bottle of the powder caught in the rocks just below the top of the Pilarcitos Dam. Looks like when the bad guys got surprised, they quit climbing and one of them just tossed his poison over the dam, thinking the bottle would make it into the reservoir. They're constructed of a polymer material that dissolves in a few hours; the polonium then would . . . well, you get the picture."

"But how do you know you got it all?" Lara implored him.

"That's more good news. That new detector we got . . . it works just as advertised. When we tested five gallons of clean water with just a dusting of the powder in it, the indicator lit up like crazy. Even with the water diluted down another *thousand* times, the membrane caught the polonium and immediately detected it." Lara and Uri visibly relaxed at this news, waiting expectantly for more.

"We found four more containers, all intact, in the bushes along the access road from the San Andreas reservoir to the freeway. Again, the water n the lake showed negative on the poison. Of course, we're holding off on etting water from the reservoirs into the municipal system until we get complete verification from the federal labs, but . . ."

"You seem so sure of this newfangled membrane-detector gadget . ." Lara wasn't convinced.

"Well, we did get a positive at Crystal Springs, but not in the lake tself. There was a garbage barrel where the road meets the highway. Our guys figured they might as well test it; turns out all the rain we had this eason just about filled the barrel—"

"And the water in it tested positive!" Lara yelped.

"You guessed it: big-time positive. That terrorist team must have ossed their stash into the barrel while they were hightailing it out of there."

Uri was keeping track. "So, you figure that's all of it?"

"Seems like it for now. We've started live-animal testing on the akes already . . ."

Lara shrieked. "Live animals!"

Tom immediately calmed her fears. "Carp from the lakes. And the water from Hetch Hetchy is also testing negative, so I think we've got everything covered; at least, that's the way it's looking. The water district as enough other sources to keep from going dry while the testing's going on, but—"

"Wow, that is great news, Chief!" Lara blurted out.

Uri laughed, shaking his head in disbelief. "I think it's time for us to get some sleep," he said to Tom, who was in agreement.

"We've got you two a great room in a prime bayside hotel. We can inish things up tomorrow."

The two agents took a rental car from Buckley's office and, with Uri driving, made their way down the freeway that ran alongside the bay. They ound their rather plush-looking hotel on a rise far enough off the busy road o be reasonably quiet. Before Uri could dash into the hotel lobby with their imple luggage, Lara grabbed his arm and led him to a promontory directly on the still water. Without saying a word, they stood there, marveling at the iew. Across the bay, the lights of San Francisco, with its famous bridges, twinkled magically at them through the fog. A million or so people from all over the globe were there, safe and secure; all but a few of them were unaware of the monumental human disaster that had been averted that very evening.

Lara, without a word, took her husband's hand. He smiled and squeezed hers in reply; they headed for the hotel and a good night's sleep.

END

Acknowledgments

The author wishes to thank the offices of the US Department of Homeland Security, led by Chad Wolf, Secretary. The men and women who serve there have been a tremendous asset to the free world in ways that cannot be divulged. It is sufficient to note how unsuccessful our enemies have been ever since the unspeakable horror of 9/11. Every citizen is indebted to them.

The Israel Defense Forces, led by Lieutenant General Aviv Kochavi, are essential in keeping their vicious enemies at bay. Most notably, the elements of Mossad and Shin Bet, have been tireless in their efforts in keeping their nation, as well as the United States, nearly totally free from organized terror.

The individuals in both these organizations must, of course, remain anonymous, but their work is, and always has been, indispensable in the never-ending fight against the forces of inexpressible evil.

On a personal note, the author is grateful for his sweetheart, Gisel, once again, for all her help and encouragement. The process of creating an interesting, credible story from the germ of an idea is long and difficult, as all authors know. Without her, it would have been all but impossible.

I'd also like to thank my editors for their efforts on my behalf.

Printed in Great Britain
by Amazon

84101474R00150